MOSES IN THE PROMISED LAND

MOSES

IN THE PROMISED LAND

R. Howard Bloch

Peregrine Smith Books
Salt Lake City

First edition
90 89 88 5 4 3 2 1

Published by Gibbs Smith, Publisher, P.O. Box 667, Layton, Utah 84041

This is a work of fiction. The resemblance of any character to any person living, dead, or living alternatively is purely coincidental.

Design by Smith & Clarkson

Cover art by Ron Bell

Printed and bound in the U.S.A.

Library of Congress Cataloging-in-Publication Data

Bloch, R. Howard
Moses in the promised land.

I. Title.
PS3552.L554M6 1988 813'.54 87-32709
ISBN 0-87905-216-3

■ For Ellen, Alvin, and Leo

■ Who's going to save me from all these vegetarians?

GÜNTER GRASS

For the only way one can speak of nothing is to speak of it as though it were something, just as the only way one can speak of God is to speak of him as though he were a man, which to be sure he was, in a sense, for a time, and as the only way one can speak of man, even our anthropologists have realized that, is to speak of him as though he were a termite.

SAMUEL BECKETT

1

UNDERGROUND MAN

■ In the hour between work and a reception at the home of his former therapist, Moses Reed, thirty-six, black, expert in the management of wood-infesting pests, stopped at the corner of Pine and Page. He entered the Daedalus Pub and placed a quarter in the video game between the condom dispenser and the public heart monitor. The screen began to flash and clear. Little belches of light gave way to excited sound, inaudibly high notes that tickled the ear, low ones that caught the groin, riffs of repeated ticks like knitting needles drawn quickly across a washboard. Oval, one-eyed, gobbling dots moved in all directions through the maze of ladders and tunnels.

Reed felt at home in the electrified world of tight holes and hidden passages. The bleeps and blurts of ingesting flickers, the sea of pursuing jaws eager to suck up the stickmen he controlled with two red buttons, helped to ease the transition between the world of termites and his fellow man. Reed's fingers moved so quickly that it looked as if he were playing a piano trill.

A missile came out of nowhere. In firing back Reed twisted one shoulder, his legs already crossed. He bit his lip and stopped breathing until the racing projectile, bigger and bigger, shattered into pieces and disappeared. A narrow escape, and then the game was over.

The exterminator's bouts of electronic superstition assumed prophetic proportions. The score recorded on the digital display stood as a talisman, an omen as true as any of the Tarots on the Avenue. A good go-round meant references and jobs, not just the little patchings and painting of dry rot around the bathtub or sink, but whole cellars eaten by beetles and bugs, maybe even fumigation. A bad series cast a spell. It held the prospect of car trouble, low estimates, a close call under shaky jacks, or no work at all. That afternoon's reading was uncertain overall.

Reed strode to the counter and sat down. He watched Alfred Wharfield pour white wine from a screw-top jug, skillfully twisting the bottle so as not to lose a single drop. The glug-glug-glug recalled the gurglings of gutters and drains. His attention shifted to the transparent blocks which, aquariumlike, ringed a large plate glass window through which he could see the awakening lights of Beacon.

"The usual?" The ruddy faced barman with the full beard startled Reed. Without waiting for a response, he reached under the counter and in a single motion Wharfield lifted a glass and pointed the mouth of the jug at the exterminator.

"How's the underground man?"

"All right, I guess, could be worse. I've moved to one that's pretty gone. Termites everywhere, even in the attic. We'll go the route."

"That's great for you. How about the owner?"

"You know the man never sees it that way. But folks usually end up agreeing with what I say."

"What's that?"

"That a house's a living organism just waiting to be reclaimed by nature." This was perhaps the longest sentence Reed had pronounced in weeks. "If you don't take care, that's just what happens. Nature takes its own back. It's all part of the ecosystem."

"Christ, man, you sound like some goofy guru or like Blessings and her tidepool rhumba." Wharfield swiveled one hip and began to laugh. The rhythmic heaving of the big red beard revealed several missing teeth. Those that remained were yellow. As his belly joined the rhythm, his T-shirt reading *Save the Whales* lifted slightly below a spouting behemoth to expose a patch of hairy tissue closing about the navel. "So who's the lucky owner?" Wharfield asked. But before Reed could answer a suited man at the end of the bar motioned toward a pair of empty glasses.

"Okay, okay, I'll be right there. What was it?" the barman shouted.

"Cab Sauv," the young urban professional grumbled, "and well chilled."

"Two Cabernet Sauvignons right away."

The crowd thickened at the Daedalus as the filtered winter sky marked the end of a day in a land whose seasons were more a matter of subtle changes of light than the violence of snow and ice. Wharfield knew practically everyone who came through the double swinging doors: the workmen who wired, plumbed, and painted the homes of Beacon, sailors missing fingers, the old people whose voices were raspy from years of too much smoke and drink, the woman in a brightly colored jumpsuit whom he had seen leaving with members of both sexes, the secretaries with their showy engagement rings and tinted hair, the graying airplane mechanic, the loners who sat and stared, the witty university professors in their turtlenecks and tweeds anxious to impress each other with the salt-of-the-earth atmosphere to which the Daedalus Pub, unlike the fern bars just over the hill, might lay claim.

Though the swelling of drinkers meant that they risked being overheard, Reed knew that the fear of indiscretion provided an edge of excitement that nourished their unlikely friendship. He loved the secrecy, and the others counted on it. Hadn't Elson, who, after all, had a Ph.D and taught literature at Bountiful State, explained that the opposition's urge to be open about their carryings-on would cause them one day to slip? "They're no better than petty criminals," he could remember Elson saying, "and like criminals, they possess an unconscious wish to be caught. Sooner or later they'll get careless and start to flaunt what they cannot fully control." Reed smiled to himself as he recalled too how Leon Zimmer, struggling to rise from the depths of a badly sprung sofa that smelled of weak infant urine, began to squawk, "Cut the shit, Professor. They're jerk-offs, pure and simple. They've got us by the balls, and all you can do is philosophize." Reed wondered what Blessings would say if she could have heard Zimmer then.

Wharfield returned to Reed. Leaning over the mahogany, he whispered, "Come on. Who is it this time?"

"You remember Larry Newton? Lives with Pam Sidel? The Capital Exchange?"

"Don't say. Man, you are moving right along. Pretty soon you'll have made the circle."

"And I'll be home free. Leon says this one could be it. Just the same, it gives me the cold willies. Feels like they're closing in. You know they're on to Blessings."

"Forget that woman. You know better than anyone that her elevator doesn't go to the top floor. I can't imagine what it was like being married to her. Never mind. The place couldn't be better. Do you need any more stuff?"

"Like I say, this has got to be it."

"Coming right up."

Reed could not tell if these words were meant for him or for the gesticulating woman with blond teased hair, white powder makeup, and eye shadow so dark and wide that it made her look like a raccoon. Wharfield lifted a section of the countertop just below a small framed photo of James Joyce in Trieste. He headed toward the walk-in cooler, returning in a matter of seconds with a crumpled paper bag which he placed on the bar in front of Reed.

"These should hold you for a while," Wharfield said. "I just jerked them out of the box so there might be some loud stuff on both sides. We wouldn't want Larry and Pam to start dancing now, would we?" He refilled Reed's glass. "Say, where's the underground man off to tonight?"

"You won't believe this. Remember that shrink Blessings and I were seeing before we split? Luftman. He invited both of us to some kind of winter solstice party up at his place which I hear is really something. We're supposed to bring Ocean, too."

"Yeah, those shrinks do live in style off other people's trouble. I bet you'd like to get a look at Luftman's foundation. You probably bought a piece of it."

"You're right. I would like to see his house. Blessings saw it once. She came home all upset from one of her Primal Scream Seminars. Went to see Luftman, and what do you think he did? Took her home for a drink."

"Jesus, if drink therapy is in now, I'm gonna get analyzed. I thought people went to psychiatrists to stop. Hold on, I'll catch you in a sec." Wharfield darted toward the row taps of sticking up like fancy batons in a Shriners' parade. Pulling simultaneously on the porcelain handles marked Red Rock Ale and Black Rock Stout, he filled two chilled mugs, waiting patiently as successive waves of deflating foam gave way to the bubbly amber liquid. He set them down in front of a pair of house painters so covered with tiny flecks of paint that they appeared to be wrapped in gauze.

"So," Wharfield picked up with Reed where they had left off, "you mean to tell me that the money you make fixing other people's houses you pay to this guy to talk about his house, and you haven't even seen it. And now that you're no longer paying, he invites you to dinner?"

"Something like that. Like I say, Blessings was there once. She kept talking about Luftman's this and Luftman's that. Then I started to dream about it—immense, all wood, undergrade, leaks all over, and rotting, filled with mold." Reed, in fact, had more than dreamed about Shawn Luftman's house. They spent three sessions discussing the hostility latent in wishing one's therapist's house to crumble. Reed could still remember being impressed by Luftman's lecture about houses in order and houses out of order. One day he had even asked the amiable therapist if the money he was paying for therapy might not be better spent on fixing up his own dreary apartment. Luftman launched into a lengthy explanation of the difference between psychic and physical space. The subject never came up again.

The minutes passed and the noise of the Happy Hour grew, but Reed hardly noticed Wharfield's ever-swifter orbits between the wall of bottles behind the counter, the disarray of tables at the far end, and the sink of graying soapy water. It was at the end of one such circuit that Wharfield apologized for his inattention with the offer of another round.

"No thanks. I'm late as it is. Catch you next week." The bug man and the barman shook hands, thumbs entwined, palms squarely grasping. They went their separate ways.

As Reed drove his aging pickup across Beacon he reached into the bag that Wharfield had given him. His hand located automatically, like that of a blind man goosing the floor, the rectangular box so dusty and beaten that no one would have taken it for a cassette player. Fumbling as he had done so often in the darkness of low-slung cellars, he inserted a cartridge in the flap at the box's center and counted with finger and thumb. *Stop/Eject, Rewind, Fast Forward, Play.* And there it was—the Commodores, whose voices he had loved when in high school, now grown older with him and mourning the dead among their number. "Marvin, he was a friend of mine. And he could sing a song, his heart in every line. Marvin sang of the joy and pain. He opened up our minds; and I can still hear him say, 'Gonna be a long night, gonna be alright, on the nightshift.' You found another home, I know you're not alone, on the nightshift . . ."

The apartment in which Reed lived without ever raising the shades resembled nothing so much as a cave. The unsewn drapes suspended by nails across two northern windows, the stacks of records, books, and dishes piled on wooden crates, looked, to the eye adjusting to the change from sunlight to cavernous darkness, like the stalactites and stalagmites of some prehistoric dwelling. Odd pieces of string and tape hung out of drawers and floated from the top of the mounds of accumulated debris. Even in the dimness it was clear that the walls had not been painted in a long time. The few pictures that hung there—a faded poster of a bridge in the fog, a picture of John Lennon in a World War I helmet, the caricatural sketch of a young child at the zoo—were too small for the cleaner squares around them. The dresser top was a jumble of minimal drugs, deodorant, nose drops, mouthwash, a large bottle of generic aspirin, hemorrhoidal ointment, dental floss, and Noxema cream. Among the jars and tubes stood an old display case with rows of dried butterflies on pins. Their wings had turned to dust at the bottom. Several old photographs were stuck in the dresser's rear mirror. One showed an older black couple, nicely dressed. The man was sitting in a padded velvet armchair with lace doilies on each arm and on the headrest. The woman, in a gaberdine suit with a handkerchief protruding from her bosom, stood at his side. To their left, an old television set, one of the very first models with a round screen, sat on a table next to a layer of magazines spread like a fan.

Reed undressed quickly, pressing the message button of the telephone recorder as he leaned down to undo his shoes. He waited and heard only scratchy silence punctuated by clicks. The sounds were repeated, not once but three times. People had been calling and hanging up without a word. There were more of these lately and almost no calls about jobs. In earlier days Reed would have been anxious about paying the rent and child support. But lately he had had steady work, passing from rotting house to rotting house by word of mouth, or personal reference, as his mother would have said. Still, the anonymous callers gave him the shivers, made him wonder if someone were watching. The old feelings of being followed were returning, and he vowed that if he could find the right moment he would ask Luftman about seeing him again. "They're like a rabbit running across my grave," he thought, stepping into the shower.

Shawn Luftman's house was beyond Reed's wildest dreams, and God knows he knew from the ground up what seemed like half the houses in town. He had crawled under large houses and tiny boxes, designer houses and ready-mades, under architectural wonders and those that had been assembled by a machine. He had spent time in the bowels of old and new, split-level and multistoried houses, houses that seemed to express some whim of their inhabitants and those completely lacking in character. He once had worked among the levelers and jacks of a house that sprawled five stories down a hill, one room to a floor, which reminded him of a train that had leaped its tracks on a mountain turn. He had replaced the underpinnings of a pink stucco geodesic dome with an entrance like an igloo, and fumigated the home of a businessman, which had no windows except in the attic where, it later turned out, the man had run a highly profitable pyramid scheme in Japanese whiskey futures. Reed had never been paid.

Nothing Reed had ever seen before came close to matching the compound of his former analyst. It was surely the embodiment of some deep madness. The garden appeared endless and the buildings too numerous to take in at a single glance—the toolshed, barn, playhouse, barbecue hut, enclosed pool and cabana, guest quarters, dog, cat, and bird houses, not to mention the children's treehouse snuggled in the branches of a well-trimmed oak. A bank of bulbs lit the yard beyond the house and the outbuildings. Everything seemed bigger and brighter than day.

Reed walked slowly as if in a trance the hundred or so feet through manicured azaleas and camelias to the porch where he could see people talking. He felt as though he had been transported into some distant landscape of the mind, yea, his own therapist's mind. Wharfield was right—the marital difficulties he and Blessings had experienced before their divorce almost three years ago had paid for some little piece of the paradise at his feet. And he wondered if he should look at the base of trees or on the back of scattered lawn furniture for a little plaque of recognition: "This chair was made possible through the generous payments for service rendered to the former Mr. and Mrs. Moses Reed."

Approaching the porch he could overhear a group of middle-aged women in designer jeans arguing with the passion once reserved for their marriages, now happily entrusted to Luftman's care, about which of Beacon's numerous bakeries made the best croissants. One of the little clan spoke for the Wild Flour, while another disagreed, vehemently claiming that the Bread Basket could not be surpassed. "Your'e both nutritionally incorrect," a third interrupted with the heat of a brick oven. "I would rather eat white bread than put one of their rolls in my mouth. The only croissant worth eating is at the Whole Grain Access. They cost a little more, but they've got twice the food value of the rest."

"They taste like soybean powder to me," the first woman objected.

"No, really, if you spread a little organic marmelade on top, you can get so used to the taste, you wouldn't think of eating anything else."

Reed remembered seeing the new awning go up just around the corner, but rarely got home in time to shop anywhere but the local supermarket. Besides, he thought, the wide girth and sallow complexion of the Whole Grain's defender should be enough to keep anyone from going near the place. The women had moved on to the subject of trail mix by the time he passed through the door.

Reed recognized no one among the hundred or so guests sprawled throughout an endless chain of wood-paneled rooms. He hoped he would spot Ocean, but even his ex-wife would have been a welcome presence as he looked for a familiar face among the various tables of hors d'oeuvres and knicknacks, the extravagant collection of modern sculpture and primitive art, the chatter of elegant men and women whose own apparent ease only made the exterminator feel more alone.

He had spoken with no one at all until, having been handed a drink by one of the college students serving white wine, Reed found himself standing next to a tall woman with hoop earrings and a braid on top of her head. As the server filled her glass she turned toward him and asked, "Are you a friend of Shawn's?"

"No, I mean yes. We've known each other for a couple of years. Actually, I did a little work on his house," Reed lied, "a little remodeling. And I guess we've kinda remained in touch ever since. How about you?"

"Oh, I've known Shawn for years. We studied together at the New Institute for Psychic Research. Yes, we've been through a lot together, and it's never very easy, you know."

"What's not easy?" Reed asked.

"The life process, realizing our potential, integrating the self."

"Oh," Reed pursued, "are you a therapist too?"

"I used to be. Now I'm into writing and lecturing and find less and less time for patients. I can reach so many more people this way."

Reed had no idea he was talking to Kate Yamato-Gelber, Jungian analyst and cofounder of the Psychiatrists for Equal Pay for Equal Work Task Force. Dr. Yamato-Gelber, he soon learned, had just published her first book, *Tao and the Silent Treatment,* which, she confided, had caused quite a stir.

Not realizing how anxious the creator of the Silent Treatment was to speak, Reed asked Kate Yamato-Gelber what she meant by integrating the self.

"The self is what we experience inwardly when we feel a relationship to the eternal that connects everything outside of us to us. It's a form of meaningful synchronicity through which we glimpse the underlying Tao. The Chinese have a saying, 'When the pupil is ready, the teacher will come.' This describes the connection between the human psyche and external events, which is basic to non-Western thought."

Reed was bewildered. Luckily, Kate didn't seem to care that he was no longer listening. She kept looking out of the corner of her eye, over his shoulder, perhaps, he thought, even right through him. Suddenly her eyes hit on something that made her jump. Reed turned around to see that it was a woman in a sari who had for a long time been hidden by one of Luftman's larger-than-life African statues.

"Excuse me," Kate said politely, "I must greet an old friend who has just returned from India." And without even so much as a warm look, Dr. Yamato-Gelber darted toward the woman who, with equal haste, left the man to whom she was talking. They embraced so hard and long that their feet kept leaving the floor alternately like some giant gyroscopic amusement park ride.

"Holly, you look great, I mean really fantastic. How long has it been? No, don't tell me, I remember. It was at my Good Grief Seminar." Holly nodded. "Tell me, how was it? When did you get back?"

"About a month ago, though we're still looking for a place to live. You don't know of anything do you, Kate?"

Dr. Yamato-Gelber shook her head. "Tell me about it."

"Well, it was really, no, I mean *really,* fabulous. You know I studied with the most serene man I've ever met. He's gone about as far as anyone can in the field. I just hope I can hold on to one-tenth of it so that I can teach some of the people here."

The field to which Holly Redding referred was that of firewalking combined with certain techniques of hatha yoga and anal retention. The serene man with whom Holly had studied was Bubba Kahlil, whom his detractors accused of being a failed disciple of the Spiritual Master Da Free John and who had discovered at some point in his own training an almost superhuman capacity to control his sphincter muscle, a power which he referred to modestly as his "divine gift." The man was able to take into his bowels fully a quart of liquid and to hold it for periods that would have made lesser mortals violently incontinent.

"It's so, so energy efficient," Holly said. "Once he has taken in the water, he walks over the hot embers and releases. What you get is the world's most natural steam. It's like a sauna that just does wonders for the respiration. Have you seen my posters? Everyone's talking about them. They're all over town."

"No, I'm afraid . . ."

Holly drew from a large madras sack a sheaf of little blue sheets. "Here," she said extending them, "maybe you could place these at your talks. Go ahead," she urged, "read it." Kate glanced grudgingly at the boldface type: *Firewalking, the First Step to Overcoming Fear.* She looked up.

"No, I mean the whole thing," Holly insisted, "go on, dare to read and relax." Dr. Yamato-Gelber, captive of her own sensitivity to others, continued. "During this four-hour session, everyone participating will be taught how to walk barefoot on hot coals without burning their feet. Methods for overcoming fear will also be taught, whether it is fear of walking on hot coals, job interviews, death, sexuality, nuclear war, or whatever limits your life." At the top of the page was a picture of Holly, arms outstretched like the healing Christ, gown blowing behind, ecstasy upon her suntanned face glowing with self-possession, eyeballs tipped away from the burning coals, skyward.

"Isn't it fantastic?" Holly asked. Kate nodded weakly.

"Listen, Kate, you and I just must have lunch soon. I'd like to discuss some of the particular problems women have in firewalking, and I think your goddess material could be very helpful."

"I'd love to." And as the therapist and the firewalker thumbed through their datebooks, Shawn Luftman, dressed in pleated golfer's pants, a bright dashiki, and tinted glasses, stood on a large Polynesian drum clapping his hands.

"Please, please, could everybody listen for just a minute," he repeated, until the noisy crowd, which had been dispersed throughout the Luftman mansion, gathered around their host. "Okay, now, we're running a little behind schedule, the ceremony is supposed to begin at sundown, an hour ago. But of course the rule here is the same as I encourage my patients, nonthreatening flexibility. It is our duty to be flexible at all times. Nonetheless, I'd like to ask you to get another drink and whatever you want to eat, and then let's regroup. My wife, Celeste, would like to say a few words about the importance of the seasons. We will light the fire, and there will be prizes for all the children. Help yourself, and we will meet in the living room in a few minutes."

It was then that Reed spotted Ocean just a few feet away in the milling company. He had made an earlier tour looking for his son and, not seeing him, assumed that his ex-wife was still in the middle of some scattered mission of mercy. She would no doubt arrive after everyone had gone. But Reed was pleased, and relieved, to see the slight child whom Blessings, at Luftman's command, had yanked from under a desk in the study. Picking him up, he asked, "How's my man?" The boy looked away and squirmed.

"Oh, come on now, don't do like that," Reed said.

Still there was no response. Though Reed could not accept his son's lack of recognition, he had learned to live with it and even had made his peace with such gestures of rejection. "After all," Luftman had assured him, "it's not just you. The boy has withdrawn from the world as a way of assimilating separation. He'll come back." Ocean Reed had not yet come back, however. And his father, unable to contain the writhing seven-year-old, let him down to search again for the shelter of Luftman's massive roll-top desk.

The crowd of holiday revelers again settled to a hush the minute Celeste Luftman took her place, buttocks fitted against the curve of the baby grand piano.

"I would like to explain why we are here tonight," the petite brunette in a billowy linen toga and matching turban announced. "I hope that no one is embarrassed by a personal confession on such a special occasion. For a long time Shawn and I thought we could live without religion. Our lives, consumed by the little tasks we perform every day, filled with all we could desire of the material world, seemed complete. But we were wrong. Something was lacking, and that something was not exactly religion. No, we live in an enlightened age beyond religious superstition. What was lacking, we discovered during a couples retreat in the groves of Canaan, was tradition. This is why Shawn and I gather our friends and loved ones every year when the sun is farthest from the earth, about to start coming closer, to celebrate ourselves and affirm the immortality of our souls, which never die but pass into other bodies after death. Let's all join hands in a circle and light a fire on this the longest night of the year. Summer, would you strike the match and kindle the winter solstice light?"

The Luftmans' daughter, after several attempts to ignite apparently damp newspaper, set the room aglow as mother and father chanted a few incomprehensible syllables in a language they said was ancient Celtic. To their left Shawn's parents—dressed from head to toe in purplish muslin—sat like druids, bewilderment written all over their aged faces. The twenty or so children sprawled on the floor were mesmerized.

Luftman's daughter had hardly finished putting out the match, and her parents certainly had not stopped singing, when an obese woman in a designer tent dress jumped from her seat. The wide black flapping panels made her look like a condor about to swoop down upon hapless prey.

"Listen, nobody move. That goes for you especially, Marshall." She looked menacingly at her own son who was the only one not frozen in place. "Now that we have heard about the importance of religion, or whatever they call it, tradition, I'd just like to remind everyone that whenever we are privileged enough to have light, someone toils to make it happen. Someone suffers, whether it's the people who cut the wood or printed the newspaper. The fire we have just lit is also a sign of oppression, and a symbol that the fight for social justice continues wherever there is a working class."

The condor woman proposed holding a discussion. She flapped her arms above the children as if to fan them into some kind of reaction. Yet the captive young bolted in the direction of the Luftman family entertainment center, until Luftman, sensing that things had gone awry, again took his place, clapping, and beating with his feet on the drum.

"Okay, now that we've had our little ceremony, and made an important political statement as well, the fun part begins. Let's gather the children again. There will be presents for all." The condor woman retreated, and no sooner had the therapist pronounced the word "presents" than the children began to file back like ants leaving the colony, having heard of some sweet treasure trove. They swarmed excitedly around the baskets of goodies in the front hall.

Reed could not help wondering how so many presents fit into the condor woman's lesson that nothing in this life comes easy. But his curiosity was dulled by a second, then a third, glass of wine and by the undeniable festive folly that dwelled in his former therapist's house. Almost as soon as Kate Yamato-Gelber left him for Holly, he had spoken with Tank Mountainfire, a huge woman with shaved head except for an axle of purple spiked hair and a leather suit covered with zippers. Tank, who looked like a sumo wrestler in army boots, explained that she owned the Bloodroot Café, a feminist vegetarian restaurant which was combating sexism by serving only the freshest vegetables and fruits.

"I'm afraid I don't understand," Reed said. "How do vegetables fit in?"

"Meat eating is a masculine thing. But we have found a nonaggressive, holistic, nourishing way of dealing with sexual inequality. We're starting at the root of the problem by starting at the top."

"How's that?" Reed asked.

"We're changing the way people think by changing what they eat. I myself am the creator of several of our most effective dishes. I just know you would love them." Reed almost gagged as she began to describe her special point of pride, a tofu prune butter layer cake topped with shaved carob. The woman reached into her bag and handed Reed a card. "You know you really ought to come by for lunch sometime."

"I'm afraid that would be hard for me," he said, "I work. Maybe I could make it for dinner, though."

Tank looked disappointed. "Oh, I'm afraid we're only open for lunch. Wait, we do serve late brunches on the weekend." Reed was as relieved at the convenience of the excuse for not visiting the Bloodroot as she was embarrassed at the scantness of her hours.

Reed was approached by a former speech therapist who now made his living interpreting in sign language musical performances for the deaf.

"You cannot imagine," the man assured Reed, "the excitement of transmitting with your hands songs that are actually about hands."

"Could you please explain," Reed said, in what he felt was becoming a leitmotif of the evening.

"Well, you know, like 'He's Got the Whole World in His Hands,' 'Hand me Down my Dancing Shoes,' 'Holding on to God.' They're my favorites." The man, slightly tipsy and making Reed promise not to tell a soul, confided that he was working on a series of oral interpretations of mime shows for the blind. "If you tell, I'll kill you." Reed was startled. "I mean I would just die, I would," he whined with the conviction of a drowning earthworm.

Reed managed an uncomfortable escape from the speech therapist by saying he needed to relay an important recipe to a woman who ran a progressive restaurant. Stepping backward, he found himself almost next to Blessings. People were beginning to leave, and he realized he could no longer put off speaking to her.

"You have no idea what they're doing," she began. "The people trying to buy the Blackstone are exactly the same as the ones putting up the money for the Chief. They're going to get away with it too. Brad Thayer's got connections to Truscott, and Leon thinks even to the Mafia. And you won't believe this. He's a cousin of Waters, who's been selling animals on the black market to the university labs. They grew up together in New York, and they're still getting money out of state. Never mind, he's got friends in big business."

Reed had grown used to the conversations that seemed to begin in the middle of a thought that had been years in coming. He had learned not to become overly frustrated or angry. Luftman had given him what seemed like good advice. So, trying to displace Blessings's frenetic connections and wild mood swings by the simplest, most pressing topic at hand, he said simply, "About your note. I'm not sure whether it's such a good idea for me to take Ocean home with me. I've got to prepare a job early in the morning, and it's gonna be tight getting him back to Dred Scott. I thought we had agreed . . ."

"We had," she was quick to confirm, "but I've got a really important meeting right after this. It's kind of an accident that I just found out about and was lucky enough to get invited to. Can't you be a little flexible for once?"

This last line irritated Reed, who felt he was too often the one to take up the slack of Blessings's hopelessly disjointed existence. Hadn't Luftman explained that giving in to her irresponsibility only compounded the problem? Yet it was hard where the child was concerned. They argued for several minutes. Then Reed had an idea that shocked him at first. Since they were at the home of a family counselor, why not take the matter directly to him? At the time of their marital difficulties Luftman had encouraged them to bring disputes into the office. Why not bring them into the home?

Blessings at first objected that Luftman was on his side.

"Nonsense," Reed replied, "didn't he invite both of us tonight? Besides, you're the one asking to bend the rules."

Blessings conceded. "Okay, okay, you win. You always do. Let me find Ocean and tell him we'll be a few minutes more. I'll be right back." She disappeared.

Luftman was made visibly nervous by the dispute between Blessings and Reed, yet he seemed eager to help, and the three of them settled comfortably in the Luftman bedroom which, Reed reflected, was larger than any house in which he had ever lived.

"Listen," Luftman began in a somewhat paternal tone, "we don't have a lot of time, so let me ask what seems to be the trouble?" The generous therapist relished the moment of intimacy. Hearing about old problems was like seeing an old friend again after a long absence. The fact that the marriage had been dissolved was merely an episode in their relationship. And, as Blessings feared, he sided with Reed, citing Article Sixty-five of the state psychological charter: "Couples should honor for a period of at least, but not exceeding, three days, emergencies notwithstanding, any contractual arrangements made by either party for the care of minor children in order to give both parties the chance to plan their lives."

"This is an emergency," Blessings protested.

"Could you be a little more specific," Luftman asked.

"There's a meeting, it's already started, I'm going to be late as it is."

"What kind of meeting?" the patient therapist insisted.

"The Grassroots Alliance."

"The what?" Luftman asked.

"You wouldn't know anything about it. It's a progressive neighborhood alternative fighting the mess in City Hall. If you have time, I can explain the connection to what's going on all over the globe. But I can see we don't, so I won't. Anyway, there's some important new information, which means I really have to be there."

Luftman had no idea what Blessings was talking about and realized that drawing her out might take hours. He was anxious to get back to the departing guests. "Listen," he said, "I know how much the meeting means to you, but Ocean comes first. We've got to remember that if Reed is not able to meet his commitment tomorrow morning, he will not be able to be a good parent."

"I knew it," she said sharply, "this is another one of your male power trips, and it all gets dumped on me."

By this time Luftman was fidgeting. "You two will have to resolve this one yourselves," he protested, "so I will just leave you here." Before they could object he was out the door.

Reed could not help thinking how strange it was to find himself alone with his ex-wife in his therapist's bedroom, and he wondered what Luftman's life must be like. The room was filled with modern art. "This stuff gives me the creeps. Can the naked man on the exploding bicycle be Luftman? Can the lobster lady on the beach be his wife? This has got to be the twisted funkiness of white folks. And how about all the electronic gear? The big-screen VCR. Is that what makes marriage work?" He was tempted to look in drawers perhaps to catch a glimpse of Luftman's pajamas or to see if he read pornographic magazines. Blessings reminded him, however, that it was getting late and that he should say goodbye to Ocean.

"I'm going now. What time can I expect you in the morning?"

"I should be through by noon and get him back for dinner," he replied. The two descended Luftman's staircase and parted on the patio.

By the time Reed left Luftman's his head was swimming. He had not eaten dinner and had had a little too much to drink. But his giddiness was also caused by his glimpse of the world he had imagined so often in his dreams and which seemed, in reality, so dreamlike. After all, he had grown up on the fringes of a ghetto in the Midwest, his parents had worked themselves to the bone so that he and his sisters could finish high school and attend a local teachers college. He knew he had disappointed them by taking up a manual trade, and again by marrying Blessings. It was not so much that Blessings was white, but that she was full—as his mother said—of so many "funny ways."

Luftman had worked hard to eliminate Reed's own sense of failure. He had explained session after session that Beacon was different. It was a new land, the beginning of a new era in which anyone who felt unhappy could make the kind of meaningful decision that true personal freedom required. The kindly therapist had even waxed poetic once when, looking into Reed's eyes with tears in his own, he assured the bug man that it was here that the promise of happiness guaranteed by the Constitution would become a reality. "The beauty of Beacon," he confided, "is that the time and place has come where lifestyle is open to all."

Reed found himself sitting in the front seat of his truck when he remembered his decision to ask Luftman about seeing him again. He thought about returning. Instead, he began to ask the kind of questions Luftman had taught him to pose, like why he had forgotten. The evening, he decided, had been just what he needed. It drew his attention away from troubles of another kind. He had walked through a fantasy land and let himself go a little for the first time since his divorce. "I should really make more of an effort to meet people. It doesn't have to be on such a grand scale. Maybe I could get Shawn to introduce me to some more of his friends." He tried to imagine what it would be like to eat lunch with Kate Yamato-Gelber at the Bloodroot Café.

Reed turned the ignition. A red light flashed on the dashboard which long ago had become so scratched and faded that he no longer knew what its clouded signals meant. He reached underneath and juggled a clump of wires. The light went out. The motor turned over.

Reed put the truck in gear and started down Campanella Street. It was when he tried to slow for the stop sign at Campanella and Moore that he first realized something was wrong. By then it was too late. Frantically pumping the brakes, he slid through the intersection which was also the crest of the steepest hill in town. Suddenly he was sailing down the other side. Try as he might, twisting the wheel, leaning practically out the door, he could not stop. Reed yanked the emergency brake. Nothing. He stepped on the left pedal, shifted back into first, then released the clutch. Reed's head jerked back as the car slowed all at once, skidded one hundred and eighty degrees, and began to roll down the sharp incline at the same speed as before. Half conscious of what was happening, he tried steering backward in the darkness through the rear view mirror that came to rest on the back of his neck when, completely out of control and at a speed of over seventy miles per hour, the old pickup truck hit an immense eucalyptus tree and burst into flames.

2

BLESSINGS

■ Many of the guests still leaving Luftman's could hear the sirens racing up Campanella Street. Some even saw from a distance the attempt to extinguish the burning fuel mixed, as only the firemen could tell, with the faint smell of eucalyptus oil. None, however, guessed that there was any connection between the pleasant celebration of winter solstice in the Beacon hills and the accident which by now had attracted a crowd.

Blessings, who had preceded Reed down the same steep incline, did not learn of it until the next morning when Sergeant Brainard of the Beacon police knocked on the door of her altered cottage.

"I'm awfully sorry, Ma'am," he began, "but I have some bad news. Perhaps it would be better if we stepped inside." They retreated into the small room whose disorder, beyond any remedy short of moving, Blessings managed successfully to hide from all but a handful of friends. The sound of Saturday morning cartoons could be heard from the bedroom. "You are related to Moses Reed, aren't you?" he asked.

"Uh, yes, I was. We're divorced, I mean we were married. I can tell you exactly what went wrong."

"That won't be necessary, Ma'am. I'm afraid he's had a bad accident."

"There must be some kind of mistake. I saw him last night."

"It was last night, Mrs., uh, Reed."

"Winter, I took my own name back," Blessings said proudly. "If we were to remarry, I wouldn't change it again."

"I'm sorry, Mrs. Winter. But according to our record, he struck a tree in the 2200 block of Campanella Street at approximately 9:15 P.M. He was dead on arrival at Sisters Hospital. There are some details that should be taken care of, if I might ask for a moment at this difficult time."

"Please, sit down," she urged. "Could you repeat again what happened?"

"From what we could tell, Mr. Reed was coming down the hill, lost control of the vehicle he was driving, a 1971 Ford light truck, and skidded under clear weather and road conditions. The truck did catch on fire, but I think it safe to assume that your husband, uh, your ex-husband, died upon impact. I am afraid too that there is one further complication—the presence of alcohol in Mr. Reed's blood."

"It's true that we were at a party where drinks were served, but Moses never drank anything but wine. Besides, I spoke to him right before leaving. He certainly wasn't drunk or anything like that."

"I'm afraid it's a case of driving under the influence, ma'am."

"Under the influence?" Blessings recoiled. "Do you realize how much we are all under their influence? I mean you don't even realize how conservative the developers are until you start to look at their connections. Then you start to see how everything they're doing influences our lives."

"Pardon me, ma'am, but perhaps we could move on to some of the paperwork."

"I know it may be hard to take all this in right now, but I could show you . . ."

"Please," Sergeant Brainard insisted, "we've got to take care of a few details. Then I'll get out of your way. Regulations, you understand. Now, are you Mr. Reed's nearest of kin?"

"I guess, I mean I used to be. There is our son."

"How old is he?"

"Seven."

"Let's see, minor child," the sergeant repeated out loud as he wrote. "Home for the weekend?" he asked. Blessings nodded.

"He has a sister. And his mother is still alive," Blessings blurted, "but I can't believe this. Are you sure you've got the right person?"

"Absolutely sure, ma'am, I'm sorry. Could you give me Mr. Reed's sister's and mother's address."

"I must have his sister's buried somewhere. I could find it if you give me a sec. His mother lives over on Washington Street. We brought her out here from Ohio after his father died."

"It would be useful to have the specific address," said the sergeant. "If it's not too much trouble."

Blessings found the addresses—Reed's sister's in a drawer in the kitchen, and his mother's in the telephone book—and Sergeant Brainard noted them in his loose-leaf steno pad.

"Now there is the matter of personal effects. Did your husband . . ."

"Ex."

"I'm sorry, ex-husband. Do you know if he made a will? Did he have a safe-deposit box? Does he have a lawyer?"

If Blessings had not been so shocked, she would have laughed. "A safe-deposit box, you must be kidding. That's for the hill people. We could hardly scrape enough money together to pay the rent."

Blessings's voice, increasingly shrill, drew Ocean away from the loud television set. As he peered around the door frame Sergeant Brainard caught a look at Blessings's bedroom which was even more disheveled than the room in which they sat. The bed seemed merely a raised island in a sea of domestic debris.

"Come here child," said Blessings, "there's some real bad news. Daddy's been hurt in a car accident."

Ocean said nothing, but moved timidly toward his mother, burying his head in her arms. This seemed like the proper moment for Sergeant Brainard to withdraw. Offering Blessings his card, he urged her to call if he could be of help.

After the sergeant had left, Blessings rubbed Ocean's head and said, "The truth is your daddy's more than hurt. We may never see him alive again, at least not in that old body of his."

"When will we see him?" the boy asked.

"Not until we discover who he will be reincarnated as. And that could take a long, long time."

Blessings came to Beacon in 1973, having completed a double major in ecology and earth sciences. The not inconsiderable sum her father had left, and that she had inherited upon turning twenty-one, enabled her to explore a number of options for the future. She had, for example, almost immediately upon arrival, taken a course in midwifery that turned out to be disappointing, even, she confessed, somewhat sterile. Not only did the instructor, a domineering woman whose midwife agency, Partners in Parturition, have a virtual monopoly over home births in Beacon, but she demanded from those who wanted to join her a level of scientific mastery that Blessings found excessive. She did, however, learn a good deal about anatomy, which, together with her background in ecology, later led to a small business that ultimately flourished.

Blessings, in an attempt, as she phrased it, "to replace her gynecological with ecological friends," joined the Sierra Club. And, in the course of one of their field trips entitled "Tidepools and the Ecosystem of Saltwater," she gathered a number of shells, a sea urchin, and the first bit of sponge that, within a matter of months, she was to market under the name of Moonflow, the first completely organic sanitary napkin. The label carried an invitation "to participate naturally and fully in a woman's organic time of the month."

The sponges, distributed through local headshops, initially did not sell as she had hoped. But the actual product cost her next to nothing—gas for the trip to the seashore, a few cents for cellophane. She was still selling small quantities when the toxic shock syndrome scare swept the nation, instilling the fear of death into women using commercially produced tampons. Literally thousands, and no longer just a few ecologically aware earth mothers, scampered for Moonflow Natural Menstrual Sponges. She could hardly keep up with the demand. Blessings had, if truth be known, already lost interest in the business by the time it succeeded. Thus, when one of the large manufacturers of sanitary napkins offered to buy her out on the condition that she retire the trademark, Blessings used the money to purchase the cottage in which she lived.

It was during another Sierra Club seminar, "Rodents, Ants, Termites, our Underground Friends," that she met Moses Reed, who impressed her immediately with what she sensed to be a preternatural knowledge of the subject. He asked her out, and they began dating. Their courtship consisted primarily of trips to the tidepools of the coastal basin and return with the bed of his pickup truck filled with still dripping salty sponges. They were married in a redwood grove in Canaan County, on horseback, at the foot of a natural geyser. The actual ceremony, pronounced by a Bishop in the Universal Life Church, consisted of an oath promising a lifetime of love, nourishment, meaningful communication, and mutual growth. The wedding party feasted on all manner of organic hors d'oeuvres, and those who felt sufficiently nonthreatened by the warmth of the occasion disrobed and took mud baths. Blessings and Moses, as each would later admit to Shawn Luftman, had grown, though not mutually. Instead, Moses Reed went deeper into his subterannean life, feeling at home only when he was under other people's houses. The more he retreated, as the perceptive therapist observed, the more Blessings took upon her own shoulders the burdens of the wider world.

At about the time that Sergeant Brainard was at Blessings's, Jack Trenton, technical consultant to one of Beacon's burgeoning computer firms, phoned Alfred Wharfield who, having worked until 2 A.M. at the Daedalus, was still fast asleep.

"Sorry to wake you," he yelled into the phone. "I just opened the *Tribunal* and Reed's dead."

"Is this some kind of goofy joke?" the barman asked, still half asleep. By the time he had brushed his teeth and dressed, Trenton was in the Wharfield kitchen.

"It's hard to believe," Wharfield said, wiping water off his face. "He was in the bar only yesterday evening. Said something about a party at his ex-shrink's house. Luftman. You checked the address?"

"Already looked," Trenton replied. "Home phone's unlisted."

Wharfield poured boiling water into a dirty handcrafted mug and spooned honey from a large tin whose crystallized drips had fastened it to the table. "Something funny going on here," he said.

"What is it, dear?" Margot Wharfield, who had just marshalled their three children at the door, asked. "Be gone with you, now," she urged the older boys. "You'll be late for your Tai Kwan Do."

"Nothing really," Wharfield replied. "Jack's here and says some guy who comes into the bar got killed."

"If you will, there are at least two things wrong," Trenton continued, lowering his voice. "But there's no time for analysis. We've got to get to the tapes before anybody else does."

"You said it. What say we take a little trip right now?" Leaving the half-full mug, Wharfield reached for a faded denim jacket with a button reading *One Nuclear Bomb Can Ruin Your Whole Day* on one lapel and *When Guns Are Outlawed Only Outlaws Will Have Guns* on the other.

Wharfield and Trenton didn't have to get near Reed's building to realize the futility of going any farther. A police officer stood in the doorway, right under the lintel on whose peeling paint one could still read Traymor Arms. Across the actual entrance someone had stretched a thin yellow plastic ribbon announcing, upside down, *Police Line, Do Not Cross.*

"What now?" Trenton asked.

"I hate to say it, but there's only one way in, and there's no preventing it getting blabbed all over town."

Had Wharfield and Trenton arrived at Blessings's a half hour earlier, they would have encountered Sergeant Brainard bearing the bad news. Instead, they passed him as he headed back toward the Traymor in an unmarked car.

"Listen," Wharfield said, standing in Blessings's doorway, "we know how upset you must be, and that's why we wanted to come over as soon as we heard. On the way over Jack and I were talking, and we made a little decision. You know how fond Reed was of music. I used to give him some of the tapes from the bar. We'd like to put some of his favorite songs together as a tribute, and we kinda thought we might play it at, well, the funeral service. The trouble is, we'd need to borrow tapes I've given him, and that means getting them from his things. We thought maybe you could help."

"I really haven't given much thought to the funeral," Blessings said. "As you can imagine, we're in a state of shock. I'm not even sure his mother knows. Let me think about it and give you a call."

"We'd kinda like to get started as soon as possible," Wharfield insisted. Blessings promised to call back before evening.

Blessings began to busy herself with the burial arrangements. She particularly dreaded the visit to the funeral parlor. She had participated once in an organized protest against the American way of death and, more recently, on Gravediggers' Solidarity Day, had marched with Local 38 in support of their long and bitter strike. "It's a bad time to die;" she thought, "you have to cross the picket line to get buried." She would inquire about who would actually be digging the ground for Reed to lie in, and, if necessary, she wondered if Wharfield and Trenton might help out. "But no," she caught herself, "we'd be scabs."

The interview with the funeral director, a Mr. Mulligan, at first went smoother than she expected. He showed her a number of expensive caskets, and she asked to see something simpler. The thin man with a mustache, who reminded her of her own dead father, pulled out a pine casket with a large gaping knothole right where Reed's face presumably would be.

"That one will do," Blessings exclaimed, supposing that Mr. Mulligan must surely think her heartless or cheap. He, of course, had no way of knowing that, by choosing the box with the least hardwood and brass, she felt she was helping the termite man to rejoin as quickly as possible the familiar world of underground pests.

When they moved to the small office to discuss the actual burial, things took another course.

"Does Mr. Reed have a family burial plot?" he inquired somewhat officiously.

"I beg your pardon."

"I wanted to know simply where burial would take place."

"I hadn't thought of that. We're so young, you know. Do you mean what cemetery?"

Mr. Mulligan nodded.

"What do you suggest?" Blessings asked.

Mulligan was expert at sizing up the grieving client. He knew, dressed as she was in the floppy down parka that kept losing its feathers, it would be useless to suggest any of the high-priced plots he sold so easily to the families of despondent young professionals.

"I know how difficult such decisions are, but might I suggest an alternative burial site, one where Mr. Reed would be laid to rest with some of the most politically correct people in Beacon Land. If we act quickly, I think I can get you into Mao Tse Tung Memorial Park."

The idea intrigued Blessings, who remembered vaguely hearing of such a place at the time it was renamed. "What will all this cost?" she asked.

"I can only make a rough estimate right now." He turned his swivel chair toward a personal computer on the shelf and began to punch keys. "Let's see. The coffin you selected is six hundred dollars. Our services, that includes embalming and use of the chapel, is eight hundred fifty dollars, the hearse is a hundred and fifty for a ride that far. And I think I can get you into Mao Tse Tung for a little under twenty-five hundred if we act quickly. Perpetual care would, of course, be extra. Let me see, would you by any chance be interested in purchasing at the same time a plot for yourself so that you might one day lie next to Mr. Reed? Mao Tse Tung has a special this month on doubles."

"We're divorced."

"I'm sorry, I didn't realize." Mulligan kept pressing keys as Blessings tried to calculate mentally.

"That would come to something in the range of four thousand dollars exclusive of flowers."

Blessings gasped. "Four thousand, why that's outrageous! I'm sorry," she continued more calmly, "I must be very upset, but that's more than I had dreamed. Is there any alternative? I mean, how about cremation?"

"Yes, of course, we could arrange cremation for considerably less—something, say, in the range of five hundred for our services." He turned again toward the computer. "You would not require a casket or embalming in that case, and the hearse ride would be shorter. That comes to approximately twelve hundred dollars."

"That's still more than I had planned on," Blessings persisted. "Perhaps I should investigate other possibilities."

"Oh my God," she muttered out loud on the way home, "twelve hundred dollars is more than I spend on myself in a year, and I'm alive. It's more than I paid for my car. These corporate death dealers are such rip-off artists." And, without so much as removing her jacket once she was in the door, Blessings again seized the Yellow Pages. She fell first upon *Entertainment Bureaus,* one of which specialized in fantasygrams. "Singing and Stripping Telegrams," the ad promised under the picture of three overweight women dressed respectively in leather, rubber, and fur. She quickly turned the page, only to encounter *Escort Services—Straight and Gay, Oriental and Caucasian.* The mildly erotic poses repulsed her. "Pornography, what fucking pornography." As she flipped through the thick volume, her eye caught *Eviction Services* before coming to rest under *Funeral Directors,* upon the half-page spread of The Necrobiotic Society of Northern Beacon Land. Its very first phrase appealed to all she had been feeling. "If you reject the traditional view that death has to be expensive and unecological, then you should inquire about our unique plan. We are dedicated to serve with dignity, sincerity, and support, all ethnic and sexual affiliations. Our competent staff, fully trained in the sensitivity arts, provides services including consultation, document processing, cremation, scattering on land, sea, or any place worldwide, morbidity intervention. Rental casket available. No job too small or delicate for Necrobiotics to handle. Layaway plan. Visa and Mastercard accepted."

Within a matter of minutes Blessings had arranged for her ex-husband to be cremated and his ashes remitted to her for under five hundred dollars. She felt a small sense of triumph and no little relief at having handled the whole affair without losing her temper or shouting at anyone. She was brushing her teeth for the first time that morning when the phone rang.

"Mrs. Reed," a nasal voice began.

"My last name is Winter."

"I'm terribly sorry. I was also pained, very pained to hear about Moses. My name is Axel Cooper. I hope I'm not intruding, but a friend of Moses's told me the awful news and gave me your number. You see, I am head of a firm called Lifeline. We perform a unique service that for the first time ever makes immortality a reality." Before Blessings could tell Axel Cooper she had made other arrangements, he began touting the advantages of having oneself frozen as soon as possible after death.

"Life extension through cryogenic suspension means in simple terms that we now possess the means to preserve the body until a cure is found for whatever may have caused a temporary interruption in life."

"Is this some kind of phone prank?" she interrupted.

"No, nothing is more serious than the idea that when we die we may be dead forever."

"Then," Blessings began to get excited, "if you knew anything about my ex-husband's death, you should know he died of internal injuries and broken bones and that his body was burned. I've arranged to have him cremated naturally without any of your intrusive, electronic freezer bullshit."

"Well, you don't have to get nasty no matter how much stress you're under. I was only trying to help with a life-giving alternative that many right-thinking people are considering these days. But go ahead finish off the job with cremation . . ."

Blessings hung up, and within an hour of having left Mr. Mulligan, she was headed with Ocean in the direction of Reed's mother.

Ovella Capps had learned of her son's death from a neighbor. She received the news with the same mixture of sad faith and detachment that had helped her to survive first the loss of Reed's father, then of the unfortunate Mr. Capps, a gutter man who fell from his ladder before their first anniversary, and now the failure of her own health.

There was no weeping in the short time the two women sat together in the half-light of the small house on Washington Street.

"Trouble always comes in a bunch, don't it," the older woman consoled her ex-daughter-in-law.

Blessings was anxious to reveal the plans she had made for the funeral. "I know that Reed wouldn't have wanted anyone to get ripped off by any of the big corporate places. I was already at one this morning. So I've arranged something quieter without all the constituent consumption. I think you will like this place, Mama." She reverted to the old term of affection which had disappeared with the marriage.

"Is it a church?" the older woman asked.

"Not exactly, but friends of Reed have volunteered to put together some of his favorite music, and I am sure there'll be church songs." Actually, Blessings had forgotten all about Wharfield and Trenton's visit. The half-truth jogged her memory. Now that she was obliged to make it come true, she could feel panic like a band tightening around her head out of which the rest of her body seemed to want to wriggle.

"Do you think you could watch Ocean for a bit?" she asked. "I've still got a couple of things to settle."

"Whatever you think is best," Ovella said. She moved her wheelchair to be nearer Ocean who had retreated under the kitchen table where he was picking the edges of an increasingly bare linoleum floor. As Blessings left, she could hear Ovella Capps humming out loud, and she imagined her swaying back and forth in her wheelchair as she so often had seen her in a rocker in the happier days when she and Moses were together and Ocean was just a baby.

The birth of Ocean Reed was something of a media event.

Blessings, upon discovering that she was pregnant, joined the most natural of the natural childbirth classes. This meant driving in excess of fifty miles for the weekly sessions of meditation and transitional breathing. It was worth the commute, however, for Rainbow Henderson, who had been in Blessings's midwifery course, in the intervening years had perfected certain techniques of uterine rolfing adapted to the needs of women sufficiently integrated spiritually in their third trimester of pregnancy. "It's not for everyone," she explained in the preliminary screening session, "but it's a highly effective form of deep body tissue work for those who are ready for the ultimate birth experience."

One night after a particularly strenuous class, as the rest of the pregnant couples were gathering their pillows and mats, Rainbow tactfully asked if the Winter-Reeds would be willing to participate in a photo essay on "supernatural childbirth." She promised others that in return for allowing themselves to be photographed in the process of actually becoming parents they would receive the home delivery of a child free of charge plus ten free copies of the book delivered to their home. Reed was at first skeptical. Oh, he knew that it was perfectly acceptable, and even for a while almost obligatory, for proud parents to show slides of the recent event to friends. He had been to one such evening and could still remember feeling embarrassed at the sight of his host's pudendum enlarged, a child's head emerging, on a screen after dinner. He preferred the parents who at least had the discretion to restrict their enthusiasm for the birth experience to photographs in a wallet. But even that made him uneasy, and Rainbow, as sensitive as she was to the modesty of others, picked up on his hesitation.

"Don't be shy," she urged, "what could be more important than sharing such an important event with others? For centuries birth has been hidden, kept secret. Now, we have the means to go public and let the whole world know about our private miracle."

"What about all the equipment," Reed asked. "won't it get in the way?"

"No problem, like really no problem," Rainbow assured him. "There's good and bad technology, and this is the good. I mean allowing more people to share something natural is a good use of all those little machines." She giggled and hugged Blessings, who convinced Reed to allow Rainbow's boyfriend Lenny to come to the birth with his camera, lights, and a team of support personnel to record what henceforth the ebullient midwife kept calling "our little birthing drama."

When the moment came, the midwife and her crew arrived in a converted delivery truck with an enormous rainbow painted on both sides and a plexiglass bubble on top. They carried into the house a handwoven birthing smock, which resembled a hairshirt, several strands of Indian jewelry, and a pair of sweat socks that had been rubbed with a combination of emetics and herbs.

As the labor pains increased, Blessings puffed. Two women, experts in natural hair design, plaited her hair, and pinned it in a braid. Several of the male extras who had arrived unexpectedly in the delivery van created a birth arbor. Waving branches above their heads, they hummed tantric chants. Moses lay naked next to his laboring wife. To this day, if you pick up the *Beacon Book of Birth,* you will see a series of pictures of the entry of Ocean Spray Winter-Reed into this world between two grayish sweat socks, on a bed of newspapers spread on the kitchen floor.

Things were never easy in the early years of parenting. Trouble came almost immediately, in fact, over disposal of the placenta. To the surprise of both parents, Rainbow asked Lenny to fetch the wok from the van.

"What for?" Blessings asked.

"I'm not sure whether I mentioned it or not," the midwife replied, "but it is customary to eat the placenta as kind of a communal meal. It'll help us all come together. Some people prefer baking, but I've got the most fantastic recipe for stir-fried . . ."

"Stop right there," Reed interrupted, "not here you're not . . ." But before he could finish Rainbow replied, "I think that decisions at a time like this are best handled by the health professionals in charge. What do you think, Blessings?" The tired new mother, torn between the desire to please both midwife and husband, acquiesced. Reed never forgave her.

Like most of the young couples in Beacon, the Reeds were stretched thin between the demands of their respective jobs, the attempt to maintain or even just to keep up a house, and, at the same time, to contribute to a variety of socially conscious causes.

In the beginning they would take Ocean along on the trips to the seashore. Blessings could sort sponges and package Moonflow while the baby napped. She would carry him on her back while making light deliveries, that is, until the proprietors of headshops began to comment upon the presence of a child in the adults only environment of paraphernalia and incense. One day one of the managers, an emaciated man with a long pigtail, round dark glasses, and little studded earrings all up and down both earlobes, confided, "Kids don't mix with the trade."

"What trade?" Blessings asked.

"The head trade," the man lisped through capped teeth, "come on, I mean like you know what I mean."

Blessings was somewhat surprised and on another occasion might have let it pass. But she used this unprovoked act of aggression as an excuse to transform her experience of child raising into a full-time occupation. The offer to sell came just about then, and she was able to use the capital derived from Moonflow Natural Menstrual Sponges to open Nature's Child Day Care Center.

From that time on she was able to keep Ocean by her side in an atmosphere, as she promised the parents of prospective enrollees, of nonhostility and eco-respect. After a while, however, she also tired of caring for small children, and by the time Ocean was himself ready for preschool, she closed Nature's Child and opened a part-time plant watering and maintenance service run out of her home.

One enthusiasm so replaced the other that in the ensuing months she began to neglect even her own child, who withdrew increasingly from the world. The child's behavior, Luftman noted, was merely the symptom of the beginning of the end of the marriage.

At the first phone booth Blessings called Wharfield, who had been waiting with Trenton ever since that morning. "I wanted you to know that we'd be holding the service on Tuesday," she said. "We're counting on you for the music. And, oh, I don't know whether I should say this, and I know some people might think it's not politically correct, but could you include, oh, what the hell, something religious? It's for his mother more than anyone else."

"You've got it," Wharfield replied, "but there's still the matter of Reed's records and tapes. You see, only he had some of the songs that would be most fitting for a memorial service. What we wondered is if you have a key to his place."

"No, I don't."

"Do you know how we could get in?"

"Not really. I mean, I used to know someone living in the building. Maybe Moses left a key with him."

"What about the key he had on him?"

"I don't know. The policeman who came this morning . . . can I call you back in a sec?" And before Wharfield could respond Blessings hung up. She fished in her pocketbook for Sergeant Brainard's card.

The efficient officer informed her that personal effects like keys are not normally remitted until it has been determined to whom they should go. "Mr. Reed does have a mother," Brainard reminded her.

"But she's in a wheelchair," Blessings protested.

"I'm sorry, Mrs. Winter, but there are regulations, and I cannot give you anything until our work is complete."

Blessings did not call Wharfield back right away.

Where anyone else might have appreciated or at least been indifferent to a friend's generous offer to contribute to a dead ex-husband's memorial service, and would have respected the protocol of the police, she had been put on guard. Wharfield's arrival that morning on the heels of Sergeant Brainard, along with something she sensed but could not quite define in Brainard's voice just now, aroused her suspicions. "The men are up to something," she thought. "One wants me to get him in, the other wants to keep me out." Blessings decided to drive by Reed's place to see if she might learn some clue from a neighbor as to what was going on.

Blessings did not need to enter the Traymor or even to talk to anyone. As she rounded the corner of Dolittle and Breed, the mere sight of the yellow ribbon confirmed all her doubts. She drove by quickly in order not to be detected by policemen who, in fact, would have been unable to distinguish her car from any other of the army of weather-beaten, faded, yellow Volkswagens of Beacon Land. Had she continued home she might have heard Wharfield's repeated attempts to reach her.

Instead, she drove directly up the hill, careful to avoid the block of Campanella Street where Reed had died. In front of Luftman's, she tried to retrace in the daylight his steps in the dark. So much had happened since last night that it was hard to remember where exactly they had parted company and in which direction he had walked. She had read somewhere in a detective novel that the memory of witnesses could be stimulated by recreating the circumstances of a crime. So, standing in front of the gate at 530 Campanella, she recalled that Reed had parked on the uphill side and began to walk to her right.

"That's it," she said out loud. "I remember that fire hydrant by one of Luftman's fancy yuppie cars." She had not walked fifty feet when something caught her eye which made her jolt. A large oily stain, one edge of which sparkled with fine and apparently fresh metal filings, glistened on the pavement right in the spot where she was now certain Reed had parked. She reached to the ground and, first touching the grainy mixture and then rubbing it between two dirty fingers, she ran to her own car. Breathless and suddenly afraid that the same thing would happen to her that happened to Reed, she drove home, carefully grasping the wheel with one hand and holding up the palm of the other to preserve the unctuous evidence.

Blessings picked up the phone as soon as she was inside the door. She could not decide whether she should call Wharfield or Sergeant Brainard first. Dialing Wharfield, who was at the very same instant trying to reach her, she took the busy signal as a signal to call the police.

"Look," she began as soon as she recognized Brainard's voice, "I know there's something funny going on here, and I want to know what it is."

"Now calm down, Mrs. Winter," the officer replied, "just tell me what the problem is, and we'll do all we can to help."

"Well, first I drove by my husband's, I mean my ex-husband's apartment, and there's police."

"Routine," he interrupted.

"Then," she continued, "I drove up to where he parked last night, and there's a suspicious stain on the ground."

"What kind of stain?"

"I'm not sure exactly what it is, but it's oily stuff. I could come right over and show you on my fingers."

"I don't mean to contradict you, but the streets are covered with all kinds of stains."

"This one is different, there are metal filings in it, exactly where he parked."

"Mrs. Winter, the Beacon hills are full of teenagers who work on their cars in the street and leak oil all over the place. It could be almost anything. I'm not exactly sure what you're saying. Are you suggesting there's wrongdoing here? Do you think someone wanted to harm your Mr. Reed? You know these are serious charges."

"I know, I know. No, Moses was a really peaceful person. Like me, he was afraid of the world, even his own shadow. He wouldn't harm a fly." She caught herself. "Oh, I'm sorry, I didn't mean that. I mean I don't think he had any enemies." She became flustered. "I'm not sure what I mean right now. But something is wrong, and I intend to find out what it is."

"Please calm yourself," Sergeant Brainard repeated, "and don't hesitate to call me personally if you note anything unusual."

"I already did," Blessings protested, wiping her dirty finger on a paper towel.

"I mean anything more than a little oil in the street."

Blessings felt foolish. She knew that many people considered her crazy and that to push any farther at present meant to lose ground. Besides, it was always possible that Brainard knew nothing and that the others were to blame.

Blessings phoned Wharfield, who was eating a large spoonful of honey on a fried egg. "Look," she assaulted him, "I can tell when one of your male power games is coming down on me, and I'd like to get the straight story."

"What story?" the barman asked.

"First I drive by Reed's and there's a police line, so I go up to Luftman's and there's the oil stain, then Brainard tries to make me believe it's teenagers fixing their car. Now what gives?"

"Wait a minute, hold on, just slow down. What's this about an oil stain?"

"So you knew about the police line?"

"Yes," Wharfield admitted, "I saw it on the way to your house."

"I knew it, I knew it. Why didn't you say something then?"

"I didn't want to upset you. But what gives with the oil stain?"

"I don't know whether to trust you or not. Anyway, I was at a party at Luftman's with Moses last night. I saw him right before leaving, so I retraced his steps and found this little puddle of oil with metal shavings in it right where he parked. I've got it on paper."

"Are you sure it's where he was?"

"Yes. No. I think so. Look, I'm not sure of anything except someone's leading me around in circles, and I won't stand for it."

"Okay, okay," Wharfield backed off. "Let's say something is wrong. Have you told anybody else?"

"I called the police."

"You what?"

"I tried your number, and it was busy."

"Shit," she could hear Wharfield say.

"So I called Sergeant Brainard, the one who came by this morning to tell me about Reed. You'd better tell me what's going on."

"Well," Wharfield advanced cautiously, "I'm not exactly sure anything's going on, but I'd like to take a look myself."

"Oh, no, no you don't. You can't fool me like that. You tell me what's up or I don't show you a thing."

Wharfield glanced at Trenton, who was seated across the table and signaling that it was time to change tactics. "All right, we're not sure, but Reed could have been the victim of foul play."

"What kind of foul play?" she asked, not expecting an answer, but rather feeling that the mere mention of the word was sufficient. Wharfield was silent.

"Listen," Blessings said, "if there's any suspicion of foul play, I'm going to phone the police right back. Sergeant Brainard offered . . ."

"I wouldn't do that if I were you, or at least I would wait a while," Wharfield interrupted.

"Why not? You had better make this a good one or I'm calling this minute."

"Well, I don't know anything concrete. All I know is that Reed has been working recently on houses of people tightly connected to City Hall, and it's possible . . ."

"I knew it," she interrupted him in turn. "It's the Chief, isn't it? Maybe the developers are in on it too. That proves it. They have their own FBI. Maybe even a CIA. I think one of them's been following me around."

Wharfield knew that sooner or later Blessings would relate the whole conversation to her own secret world of corporate paranoia, and he was relieved at the diversion. "Look," he gathered his thoughts, "I'm not sure who knows what, but we can't trust anyone, not even the police. So why don't you and I go up there together tomorrow morning early." He looked at Trenton for approval. "About seven o'clock. I'll pick you up."

Blessings hesitated. "Okay, I'll be here. Got to run now, bye." She hung up.

Blessings and Wharfield were careful to park around the corner from Luftman's. Wharfield had borrowed Trenton's Labrador retriever, and, as the two of them moved slowly down Campanella Street, stopping often in front of bushes and tires, they appeared to be neighbors out for an early morning walk. It was not until they had reached the spot where the condor woman's BMW had been parked that Blessings's suspicions, aroused the preceding morning by the mysterious stain, were confirmed. The sparkling oil spot was gone.

"That's it," she gasped.

"That's what?" Wharfield asked.

"That's where it was, and now it's gone." She circled the spot staring at the ground.

"Are you sure? Are you absolutely sure?" Wharfield pressed. He too looked down at the mosaic of stains which, on the dirty pavement, irretrievably held the secret of almost every car that had ever parked on that particular spot.

In order not to draw attention they continued moving another hundred feet beyond Luftman's, then retraced their steps, lingering once more over the absent stain.

"I knew it," Blessings blurted, shaking. "Someone was fooling around with Moses, and now they're fooling around with me. What am I saying? It could be you."

Wharfield was hurt but not surprised. "Let's go through this once again, who did you tell about the stain?"

"You and Sergeant Brainard were the only ones, I swear."

"Look," Wharfield advised, "I wouldn't tell anyone else."

"Hey, wait a minute, there's a crime here, and you want me to hush it up. How do I know you're not in on it?"

"You'll just have to trust me," Wharfield protested, "you have to trust someone."

"Why should I? You know more than you're telling. You're as bad as the rest of them with your power trips, treating women like inferiors. We've been through all this in the movement."

"Through what?"

"You know what I mean, where the women fetch coffee and the men get to give speeches. For all I know you could be in with Truscott and the Chief, you could be working for the Board. When it comes right down to it, you've been to so many different meetings nobody can tell which side you're on." Wharfield knew that when Blessings got going she was like a car spinning its wheels on ice. It was better, he thought, just to let her continue. To deny any of it would only convince her she's right.

After dropping Blessings off, Wharfield drove to Trenton's. Without looking up, the awkwardly tall computer expert hunched over a screen asked, "Well?"

"Well, nothing," Wharfield replied, "there was nothing there."

"If you will," Trenton spoke ponderously with the same grave tone each time, "the question is whether there was ever anything there in the first place."

"That goofy woman's so suspicious now that we'll never get near Reed's stuff. She won't go for the funeral music one either."

"You asked her again?"

"Same story. No key."

In the days between Reed's death and the funeral, Blessings phoned just about everyone she knew. Even those with whom she had lost touch were bombarded by a conversation of which she never tired. The call to Barbara Wolfe, president of the Beacon Ladies League, was typical.

"Hi, it's Blessings," she began, "I know I haven't talked to you in a while, and I'll try to be brief. I know you think I'm crazy, but someone's killed my husband."

"I'm terribly sorry," the matronly Mrs. Wolfe replied, "I thought you were divorced."

"I forgot, I mean my ex."

"That must be quite a blow. How did it happen?"

"Well, the police say it was drunken driving, but I think they're in on it too." Blessings had told the story so many times she no longer knew what she had told to whom.

"In on what?" Barbara Wolfe inquired.

"We found proof that someone had tampered with his truck right before it all happened, but when I went back to look it was gone."

"What was gone?"

"The oil stain, with the metal filings."

"I see." The curious president of the league made a genuine effort to understand. "Where did all this happen?"

"Up on Campanella Street. You see we were at a winter solstice party at our couples therapist's. You should see his estate."

"I thought you said you were divorced."

"I am. I mean, we are. Were. But this guy, Luftman, invited his patients, I mean ex-patients. Moses had a glass or two of wine, nothing more. I know he wasn't drunk because I saw him right before the end. We had an argument about the Grassroots Alliance."

"I'm afraid I'm lost," Barbara Wolfe protested. In fact, the more Blessings talked, the less she was convinced Blessings had ever been married, that her ex-husband was dead, or that, right before dying, he had visited his former therapist. Finally she politely withdrew from the conversation, claiming to have to pick up her teenage son at his Native American solar cooking class.

So the calls went. Ellie Pearl, the lawyer who had handled Blessings's divorce, appeared to be deeply shocked.

"I know you must feel guilty," Blessings assured her, "but you shouldn't feel responsible just because you referred us to Shawn. Nobody could have predicted Reed would die leaving his house." Ellie Pearl immediately sensed a return of the old paranoid fantasies, but was hesitant at a moment like this to recommend more psychological counseling. To the question of whether she would use her lawyerly skill to investigate the death of the man she had once been hired to sue, she was decidedly cool. She did, however, promise to meet with Blessings the following day.

Ellie Pearl was sitting on the bench facing the statue of Ho Chi Minh. She had just arrived and was mixing a fruit and granola topping into a large cup of frozen yogurt. Blessings came running from the other side of the square, dodging the people who had come out of surrounding offices to lunch in the weak winter sun.

"Hi, listen," she gasped, "I'm glad I caught you. You haven't started to eat, have you?"

"No, what do you mean? I thought we were going to eat a bite together."

"We were. I mean we still are. But I'm glad I caught you before you took a bite out of that cup. Do you realize it's made out of styrofoam, and the chemicals they put in it can really screw you up inside? It's worse than eating fast food."

"I'm not about to eat the cup," the lawyer said.

"It doesn't matter. Little bits of styrofoam can break off into whatever you're eating, and I've heard the stuff can lodge in your system and cause all kinds of trouble later. It's exactly like eating asbestos. You remember? They didn't discover until twenty years later it caused lung disease."

"What do you suggest I do? I'm starving and don't have time to go get another lunch and talk, which I was looking forward to."

"Well, try not to stir things up, and eat from the middle of the cup. That way you won't get too polluted. Next time ask for another kind of container, or, the best idea is to bring your own and let them fill it. You shouldn't be eating that yogurt anyway, you know. It's commercial stuff, filled with sugar. Besides, it comes out of a machine and nobody . . ."

"Tell me how you've been bearing up these last few days," Ellie interrupted. "I realize we haven't seen much of each other lately. We never get a chance to communicate except at moments of crisis, I mean really communicate." The two women used to talk often, sometimes intimately, at the time of the divorce. Ellie, in fact, had taken care of much more than mere legal matters. She would be the first to admit that since Blessings's breakup had occurred at the time of her own marital difficulties she took an unusually personal, some would even say proprietary, interest in the client who, though for professional reasons she could say nothing, was seeing the same marriage counselor as herself. Ellie had become a confidant, and, as she had told Sid, her future ex-husband, almost a surrogate mother to Blessings. In return, Blessings, as head of Nature's Child Day Care Center, had cared for Ellie's children.

"Well, things are crazy like always. I know you don't believe it, but the more I think about what's been going on, the more convinced I am that someone wanted to do away with Moses." Blessings recounted once again how she had gone by Reed's apartment under guard, how she had first found the oil stain and then lost it, how either Wharfield or the police, or maybe both, were keeping some dark secret from her.

"No, what I mean," Ellie persevered, "is how are you really doing deep inside?"

"I guess I'm holding up. There's so much happening right here on the surface I haven't had a minute to think about what you call the inside."

"How's Ocean coming through the whole ordeal?"

"He's fine, I guess. With all the things to be done I've hardly seen him. He's at Dred Scott most of the time, but when I see him he drives me nuts."

"I'd like to hear more about the ways he drives you nuts."

"It's his moods. He hides under the table or bed for hours on end. He won't talk. The only thing that interests him is television and records. He turns the volume way up whenever I'm on the phone. I start to yell, then I feel guilty. I don't know what to do."

"Well, Blessings," Ellie Pearl said, "you know the most important gift we can give our children is to make ourselves happy."

The well-dressed lawyer's hand came to rest on Blessings's sleeve. "I don't mean to change the subject or be indiscreet, but are there any new men in your life?"

Blessings laughed. "Are you kidding? With the way I look and the crazy way I dress, the only men I attract are crazy, and I've had enough of those. Besides, who has time? Stopping all the bad stuff around here is a full-time occupation."

"You know, you really are quite attractive and could do a lot for yourself if you wanted to." Ellie looked at Blessings's faded down jacket, loosely fitting corduroy jeans, and cheap sneakers.

"I'm not interested in men. I've given up on them, and they've finally given up on me. I'm a lot happier now. I just don't think about it anymore, I keep busy with other things."

"A little makeup, just a little, would do wonders for your skin, which is really quite beautiful . . ."

Blessings blushed. "Are you kidding? Do you have any idea what they put into makeup? I wouldn't put that stuff on my face for anything, practically right in the eyes, which are connected to the nose and could go into your throat, which means it could get into your system. My hands are all rough, and no amount of had cream would make them soft enough for men to want to hold. Not me, forget it, I've had it with crazy men."

Ellie, combining certain techniques of interrogation she had learned in law school with what she felt she had absorbed of Shawn Luftman's gift of sensitivity, pursued. "You know everyone must have some kind of emotional life. It's only natural, part of our need for intimacy. It's really none of my business, but I do care for you, and I don't mean to pry, but tell me if you want, are you involved, uh, involved with any women?"

"No," Blessings said sharply, "I'm not into that either. Anyway, who ever said women are less complicated than men. I just don't have time for either, and don't miss it. There are more important things right now, like the way they're screwing up the city, the environment, and then there's the arms race. Which reminds me, I'm supposed to man the Beacon Nuclear Hotline in fifteen minutes." Although Blessings had hardly begun to eat the cream cheese raisin wheat germ pita sandwich she was holding, she leapt from the bench where the two women had been sitting and she crossed Ho Chi Minh square half-running and chewing at the same time.

The funeral itself was a sad affair. Things started badly almost as soon as a tall red-haired man, introducing himself as David Burns, founder and director of The Necrobiotic Society, asked to meet briefly with Blessings right before the service. He asked a few general questions about the deceased, where he grew up, what he did, who the other members of his family were, then presented Blessings with a bill for six hundred forty dollars. She looked aghast.

"But you promised," she blurted.

"I'm very sorry, Mrs. Winter, to have to inform you of a slight cost overrun, but our estimates are only approximate. Sometimes the actual bill comes in under. This time, unfortunately, the total is slightly more due to our own increased costs. You see, we try to be as nonprofit as humanly possible. Now, I understand there's a little musical presentation."

"That's right," Blessings said, and she handed him a small cassette that Wharfield had placed in her hand only minutes earlier. She was depressed by what had turned out to be David Burns's crassness, but restrained from further protest. Organ music began to play out of cheap loudspeakers placed on either side of the plainly decorated room.

The few who had come to pay their last respects to Moses Reed were scattered in clusters around the Necrobiotic Chapel of the Pines. Luftman, who had promised to attend, sent a lavish bouquet instead. Reed's sister, a corpulent woman with thick glasses, a wide-brimmed hat, and the highest heels Blessings had ever seen, had come all the way from Ohio. She sat in the front next to her mother's wheelchair and sobbed throughout. It was, apparently, fear of someone in such obvious pain that discouraged the two or three disheveled residents of the Traymor, whom Reed had known only vaguely, from moving any closer. In the rear on the other side sat Wharfield, Trenton, and Leon Zimmer, a baby-faced man in a sweat suit whose blond curly hair, the graying ends of which seemed to be frosted, gave him the appearance of a transvestite who had selected the wrong wig. They were joined halfway through the service by Norman Elson, a college professor dressed in baggy chino pants and a tweed coat which hung loosely over his thin frame. He insisted on shaking hands with the others before taking his place. Ellie Pearl sat alone, inattentive to the formality of the funeral, staring instead at Ocean who had taken refuge under the bench across the aisle from mother, grandmother, and aunt. A few others were scattered about the room.

David Burns, whom Blessings realized bore an uncanny resemblance to the Universal Life Church bishop who had married her and Moses, stepped ceremoniously in front of the barely assembled gathering. He spoke at first of the difficulty of living, loving, growing, and communicating in Beacon Land, then announced with a glimmer of glee that the special topic for today was exclusion.

"The life taken from us too soon is an example of the plight of the little man." Burns spoke as if he had known the deceased since childhood. "Moses Reed was consumed by an all-consuming consumerism practically unavoidable in our declining world." The red-headed funeral director proceeded to dwell with such self-righteousness upon the evils of his competitors, that even Blessings was embarrassed. Worse, he seemed to have forgotten the musical offering. Blessings motioned by wiggling both hands cupped to her ears.

"Ah, yes, as testimony to the life of Moses Reed we will listen to some of the music he loved and that will help rhythmically to heal the loss we all feel." Burns stepped over to Blessings's seat, and, bending down, whispered in her ear, "Not too long, now, I've got another party coming in at 11:45." He left the room and in a matter of seconds the warm bass tones of the Persuasions emanated, crackling, from the loudspeakers on either side.

Wharfield had managed, without Reed's tapes, to assemble a number of his favorite songs. As agreed with Blessings, some had a more or less religious flavor. The Persuasions were followed by Marian Anderson singing "In the Upper Room," and Wharfield had recorded the traditional spiritual "Swing Low Sweet Chariot" as the penultimate musical offering.

David Burns, assuming it was the last, moved to the back of the room and began to fuss with the fixtures that would have allowed immediate exit through the rear double doors. He was disturbed when the tape did not stop, but continued with the one song that Blessings had insisted upon, a mass gospel rendition entitled "Be Encouraged." This was the only record that was not part of Wharfield's large collection. He had purchased it the day before on the way to work. It was one of Reed's favorites and served, at least in Blessings's mind, as a theme song of what in retrospect might be seen to be best in the years of their marriage.

As the Florida Mass Choir repeated the plaintive refrain for the last time—"life is sometimes disappointing, and those on whom you depend when you need 'em can't be found"—Burns pushed against the rear doors so violently that the small clusters of mourners were shocked out of whatever redemptive effect the music might have had.

The band of neighbors from the Traymor slipped out quietly. Wharfield, Trenton, Zimmer, and Elson stayed seated, talking in the back until Reed's sister wheeled her mother down the aisle. They offered their sympathy to the older woman while Moses's sister tried to retrieve Ocean, who had emerged from under his bench only to retreat once more. She hardly noticed the unlikely band of middle-aged men whom she had never seen before.

Blessings had not budged from her seat. As perpetually in motion as she usually was, she was at present transfixed, tears running down her cheeks. She had made a decision listening to the music, a decision she knew her respectable friends, as she liked to think of them, would disapprove.

Blessings had vowed then and there, before the coffin of her ex-husband and under the hypnotic tones of the gospel train, to find Reed's killers if it took her the rest of her life.

Reed's ashes were remitted to Blessings, who intended to scatter them at the foot of the natural geyser in the redwood groves of Canaan where they had been married. For the time being, however, she wedged the little urn among the supplies she had once assembled in the pantry on Earthquake Preparedness Day. She was so busy in the weeks and months that followed that the bug man came to his final rest between a bottle of pure spring water and a can of refried beans.

3

MC PHAIL AND THE LADIES LEAGUE

■ One evening around the time of the Winter-Reed divorce, in fact, three years before Reed's death, Rory McPhail, President of the Beacon Board of Adjustments, left the playground of Dred Scott Elementary School. In the Volvo he had had since student days he raced to pick up his wife, who worked as a volunteer support coordinator in the Beacon Ecological Trauma Center. McPhail was a half hour late, which he knew would irk Lucille.

"Do you have any idea what time it is?" she greeted him.

"Not exactly. Am I late?"

"You know we've discussed habitual lateness and what Shawn says it means in interpersonal terms, I mean the hostility . . ."

"I remember, I'm awfully sorry, I really am." McPhail leaned across the stick shift to kiss Lucille on the cheek. He could see in the light of oncoming cars a gray film poking at the roots of her thick blond mane. The thought that his wife dyed her hair repelled him.

"It means, if you would not interrupt, which Shawn says is also a form of aggression, that the person who's late assumes his time is worth more than the person he keeps waiting. It's antisocial. There's no getting around it."

"I'm not sure it means all that, but I'll try to be on time."

"I can assure you it does. Where were you anyway?"

"Had to visit Dred on business, which ran longer than anybody expected. How was your day?" McPhail hoped to reorient the conversation.

"Completely draining emotionally. We saw several of the families from Bay Point. You know, the ones who discovered they were living on a toxic dump. They're very decompensated. We're working to help them learn to trust the environment again with some pretty heavy ecological role play."

"How about the twins?" McPhail asked.

"I called. They've started dinner. Hope it's not overdone by the time we get there."

"That's good," McPhail was relieved that matters had at last taken a forward turn, even at the risk of burned dinner, "because I'm supposed to meet with the Chief at seven."

"Again tonight?" Lucille snapped. "I think, and Shawn agrees, that you may be unconsciously avoiding your family."

"I'm not, but something came up at the last minute. It must be important or Horton would not have called."

Lucille grew silent. Without speaking another word, in fact, the McPhails crossed Beacon. They were lucky to find a parking place in front of the simple wood frame house on Friendly Street.

McPhail hugged his teenage sons perfunctorily. He noticed the kitchen strewn with unpacked boxes and bags delivered that afternoon from the Beacon Farmworkers/Homeowners Food Cooperative. Rifling through the packages, McPhail's narrow shoulders, concave chest, and long spindly arms combined with his prematurely gray frizzy hair to give him the appearance of a hungry marmot sifting through some poor camper's knapsack. He lifted great chunks of cheese, sacks of trail mix, quarts of natural cashew butter, and gallons of raw acidophilus milk before finding what was evidently the object of such a fervent clawing search. McPhail held a long strip of cashier's tape up to the light.

"I don't want to criticize anyone," he exclaimed, looking at Lucille, "but do you think we might exercise a little control? We seem to pay more for a week's groceries at the Coop than if we shopped at one of the big corporate food chains."

"Of course we do," Lucille snapped, seeing through Rory's attempt to exculpate his own guilt at being late and leaving early by blaming her for spending too much on food. "It costs money to be socially responsible. You're the one who forbade us to enter supermarkets. If you think we're spending too much, then why don't you attend the order seminars?"

"Don't be silly. You know that's the night the Board meets." McPhail headed for the cabinet in the hall between the sampler embroidered with the word *Peace* and the hanging macrame planter. Taking out a small wooden box, he removed a marijuana cigarette which he consumed with bored efficiency.

"Come on, Dad," Che McPhail yelled from the kitchen as soon as he smelled the familiar smoke, "will you ever quit?"

"No reason to. Most fathers drink martinis when they come home. Just ask your friends. And you know what industry that supports. I've a right to a little relaxation after a busy day. Besides, the money helps feed Latin American peasants."

"And drug dealers."

McPhail, holding smoke in his lungs, did not respond. In a matter of seconds he seemed less like a nervous marmot rooting for food than a koala bear that had just been tranquilized.

"Dinner's ready," Che informed everyone, and the McPhails sat down to a meal of stuffed croissants and organic yogurt.

"Anything new at school today?" the now solicitous father asked.

"Not rilly," Fidel McPhail, slightly smaller and more finely featured than his brother, said. "You know, the same old stuff. We had the most boring assembly during the first period, and my three study halls were a rill drag. Oh, one funny thing happened in the cafeteria. You know that fat kid Sierra, Sierra Caldwell, like toadilly bloated? Well he's always eating other people's sandwiches and like toadilly gagging. So today, Max Weiner, the kid I told you about whose father sells bagel chips, Max packed a sandwich made out of peanut butter, dog food, and hot pepper. Sierra bit into it and like toadilly choked. We almost died laughing. It was toadilly rawsome. It rilly was."

"Very funny." McPhail forced a smile through lips so tightly pursed around his flush babyish cheeks that he appeared to be smirking.

"How about you, Che?" The McPhail twins, born not terribly long after Rory and Lucille had visited Cuba, were named after the heroes of the Cuban revolution.

"Nothing much."

"Nothing happened, all day? How about your lunch?"

"I didn't get lunch today. A bunch of us were going to buy falafel when the black kids shook us down. No lunch money, no lunch."

"Listen, Che, we must reach an understanding. I wish you wouldn't talk that way. It doesn't matter that the kids were black. I mean, you don't have to use the words 'black kids.' Caucasians sometimes behave exactly the same way. Most of the really big crime—I'm talking about million-dollar corporate rip-offs—are committed by whites."

"Is that why they call it white-collar crime?"

"Don't get smart. I'm serious. We shouldn't think black or white, only different."

"Whatever you say, Dad."

Just then there was a loud knock. Fidel opened the door behind which stood a large braless woman in an Indian print dress and sandals laced crisscross halfway up her exceedingly hairy shins.

"If it isn't the earth mother!" Che blurted.

"I thought we agreed not to use that term," McPhail snapped.

"Did you get hold of the plumber," she bellowed, "because he never showed up here."

McPhail swallowed. He had been so busy all day that he had forgotten to phone about the leak in Katy Dawson's shower. He had tried the day before to fix it himself. Having failed, and broken the turn-off valve in the process, he had been forced to shut off the water in his tenant's apartment.

"I'm sorry, I wasn't able to reach my plumber," McPhail lied. "He's usually so good about calling back. Do you think it can wait until tomorrow? I'll phone first thing in the morning."

"The kids haven't bathed in two days, and this business of running to the outside faucet to wash dishes is like camping. It's getting to be a drag."

"Why don't you bring the kids up here and bathe them?"

Katy Dawson shook her head.

"Lucille will call right away, won't you, hon?" McPhail was angry at himself for having forgotten, and even angrier at having to call the emergency plumbing service which charged time and a half. He relit the little butt of marijuana and held the smoke in his lungs while Lucille called the plumber and the twins washed the dishes. Forgetting her anger, Lucille took her place on the sofa beside him.

"You're especially uncommunicative tonight," she began. "The plumber is not such a big deal, and Che was only talking the way kids talk."

McPhail folded his arms and brooded.

"You needn't withdraw like that," she said.

"Yes, of course, you're right, we'll survive one more repair, but I will not tolerate anyone speaking like that in my home." McPhail thought of himself as extremely tolerant, though his weak point was imagining that anyone might not be exactly like him.

McPhail could not be tender or consoling without at the same time patronizing those around him. He never lost his temper, nor did he ever lose control of the situation which left Lucille feeling manipulated and furious. Until a few years ago she would yell, but the louder her voice became, the more self-possessed McPhail seemed. That only made her madder. Sensing that something was wrong, she had suggested that they enter couples therapy.

"It wouldn't be appropriate. I'm not the one with the anger problem," he said. And even after Lucille McPhail began seeing Luftman, Rory continued to ridicule her. "It's just not politically correct," he chided. "Therapy is an insidious form of repression. It's like the army."

"But Shawn thinks I'm freeing everyone a little by freeing myself."

"Nonsense," McPhail retorted sharply, "it's the thought police."

Lucille was consoled by Luftman's suggestion that what she felt to be McPhail's condescension was in reality a way of defending himself against feelings. "I'm sure it's not that he doesn't love you," the sage therapist offered, "he's just trying to avoid being close. He probably has some of the same fears as you, but men in general are less good at being open about their emotions. Do you think we could enroll Rory in our men's tenderness project? There's a new session about to begin."

In spite of the fact that Lucille sensed how anxious Rory was not to be late for his meeting with Beacon's Chief, she had decided to broach the subject that for a long time had been a bone of contention between them – exercise. Before therapy she had hardly been conscious of her body. As a result she had gained weight. But alerted by Luftman to the importance of body image, she began secretly looking at herself in the mirror. Lucille asked Rory what he thought of jogging.

"Jogging," McPhail offered, "is too public a display of concern with the body."

"What about tennis? Shawn says I should learn a sport."

"Too middle class."

"What do you want?" she responded. "When you start to get middle-aged you're bound to get a little middle class."

"Progressives," McPhail said firmly, "should not be so narcissistic. Remember, we were in on the ground floor of the movement."

"You may be right, but I've grown fat since we stopped marching in the movement. We don't even walk anymore. I'm not asking for much, just a little body movement." Lucille didn't realize how much her wit, of a kind of which McPhail was incapable, vexed him.

Lucille paused. "I think I've found a solution to our exercise difference," she announced.

"What's that?" McPhail asked.

"Jane Fonda has opened an exercise studio downtown, and they're offering discount memberships if you sign up right away. You know as well as I do the money would be going to the right people."

This argument, Lucille knew, would be hard for Rory to resist. He quickly consented, permitting her to register on a trial basis as long as it were such a worthy cause. She was delighted and couldn't wait to tell Luftman, even though she also knew that the idea of exercise still rankled that part of her husband whose unwillingness to compromise with the establishment had made her love him in the first place.

"Shit," McPhail thought, "I said I'd be there by seven, and she wants to talk about sports."

McPhail stopped at the corner of Fleetwood and Ellis. He walked to the rear of the house only to be startled by Chief Jerome Horton, a barbecue fork in one hand and a can of beer in the other, standing on the terrace. The Chief, a giant of a thin man with skin so pale and eyes so light that he could have passed for an albino, was grilling a steak.

Horton's appearance was all the more startling because of his pointed, almost kidney-shaped, ears and because of the fact that, save a tuft right below his lower lip, he was completely hairless. McPhail was not the first to wonder if he shaved his head or was actually bald. Had McPhail dared to ask, he might have learned not only that Beacon's leader tonsured himself daily with an electric razor, but that he waxed his smooth pate as well. Horton was wearing a black bulky sweater and designer jeans. Alternately illuminated and shrouded by the flames and smoke of his hibachi, he reminded McPhail of the logo of the devil on his favorite can of ham spread.

At Horton's side stood Eric Tucker, his aide and constant companion. Tucker's long blond hair, streaked almost white in places and immaculately combed, his sky-blue eyes and slightly babyish, artificially tanned face gave him the air of an aspiring movie star. Many were of the opinion, in fact, that Tucker's appeal to members of both sexes should have destined him for the role of the city's highest elected official. Few, however, realized that he was shy and preferred Beacon's smokeless political back rooms to the public view. Nor was it generally known that Tucker had been a crack trainer for EST where, by indoctrinating others, he developed considerable skill at manipulation, before himself undergoing a progressive political conversion.

Tucker had managed Horton's victory which some in Beacon regarded with disbelief. Beacon's own Rasputin concocted for his man, who was the ne'er-do-well youngest son of one of the city's oldest and richest families, a sterling character and a noble life of public service, omitting, of course, any mention that he had been sued for divorce on the grounds of physical abuse or that he had once been tried for a crime he didn't commit. The fact that Horton had not completed high school was easily remedied after the election by bestowal of an honorary degree from Beacon High.

McPhail started to explain why he was late.

"Rory, Rory," Tucker said somewhat paternally, "no one cares what you were doing all day. By the way, how are the wife and kids? Still leading the good life?"

"Is that all you wanted to know?"

"Why, no, actually," Tucker continued, "the reason we called you in is that Jerome and I think it might be useful for you to set up a little tea party with the milk and cookie ladies. You know the ones I mean?" McPhail nodded. "Everyone knows how fond they are of you, and you know how influential they are where children are concerned. We thought you might use your charm, your considerable charm, to convince them of the advantages of a little, let's say, restructuring of Beacon's schools."

"I'm listening." McPhail looked at his hosts.

"What we have in mind," Tucker obliged, "is something that's been tried in other countries but never in the U.S. Jerome and I are convinced it would be a sign of progress if progressives could carry it off in Beacon."

"I'm afraid I don't understand," McPhail protested.

"Rory, let's not get impatient. Curiosity can kill . . ."

"We're gonna take the children," Horton grunted from behind another spurt of flame. McPhail looked puzzled. "We're gonna take them out of their homes and put them in the schools where they belong."

"We must proceed slowly," Tucker cautioned. "Musn't use words that might upset people unnecessarily. You might think of presenting it to the League ladies in terms like 'an exciting new program for childhood development' or 'redistricting.' Now I've been doing a little research in the books, and it seems that schoolchildren can't be reassigned without consulting the community first."

"That's what the book says," Horton added.

"So we're going to need the Board's cooperation," Tucker said.

"I can arrange a hearing anytime you want," McPhail volunteered.

"I don't think a big public meeting would be useful, not right now at least," Tucker replied.

"Then I still don't get it. The Ladies League would be about the last ones on earth to accept the idea of kids living away from home. They're a bunch of middle-class housewives whose whole life is children."

"That's a lot of crap," Tucker responded sharply. "You know as well as I do that most of them send their kids to day care all day anyway. Besides, I've run a little check on the League ladies, and it turns out that their children are in high school now. So they might be convinced to help restructure the lower grades. You can tell them for now that their little preciouses won't be involved. It's for younger children, and only in the flats."

"What about Stafford?" McPhail asked.

Horton cleared his throat. "The superintendent's tit is in the same ringer as the League ladies. You couldn't find a stupider one if you looked. His boys will give what's her name, the one who sits there knitting all the time with the radio on her ears . . . ?"

"Shirley MacGregor," Tucker assisted.

"Yeah, that one. Stafford's ready to give her and her friends enough information to knit themselves into a nice tight knot." Horton lifted the dripping steak from the grill. His head glistened in the leaping flames.

"What Jerome means," Tucker said, "is you don't have to worry. Stafford will cover whatever comes along. All we're asking of you is to get out there and make sure the ball gets rolling, just not too fast."

"I'm still not sure . . ." McPhail hesitated.

"You'll do great," Tucker insisted. "Now I know how anxious you are to get back to the comforts of home." Horton, who had begun to cut his meat, took a large bite of steak.

"Rory," Tucker said, "this packet contains all you need. Read it before you start. And, uh, just one more thing. It'd be better at this stage if we moved kinda quiet like. Okay? That means you might want to hold a tea party away from the board room, and no public meetings. Do we understand each other?" He sat down at the table with Horton as McPhail skirted down the pathway separating the Chief from his neighbors.

Horton finished his steak and dumped one more dirty dish into the sink already piled high with the remains of several such bachelor evenings. He made a couple of phone calls while his aide, like a general plotting a difficult campaign, sifted through letters and memos, occasionally drawing a long red line across the maps spread before him on the floor. Almost as soon as Horton hung up, the inseparable companions crawled into Tucker's low-slung sports car and disappeared into the mild Beacon night.

McPhail was greeted at home with a piece of bad news. The plumber, who arrived shortly after he had left for Horton's, in the course of fixing Katy Dawson's leak, had detected the presence of dry rot behind the wall and basin.

"How bad is it?" Lucille asked.

"Hard to tell," the overalled man with a pipe said. "I'll fix the leak if you want, but you'll have to pull the tub if you want to take care of the rest. The little I can see from here runs clear under the house." She paid him the eighty dollars minimum and went upstairs.

As Lucille feared, Rory descended into a funk. "The house has been nothing but trouble," he began as he always did.

"Come on, Rory, just because our progressive friends think it's too bourgeois . . ."

"I said at the time we were selling out by buying in. If we had listened to our instincts instead of your father, we wouldn't be in the mess we're in." It was true. Lucille's father, a wealthy insurance executive disturbed by both his daughter's and his son-in-law's lack of visible income, had purchased the house on Friendly Street for them with the understanding that it would be maintained.

"Just a minute," Lucille replied, "whose idea was it to convert the basement into a rental unit? Who? Mr. Politically Correct!"

"I was opposed to owning property right from the beginning. But as long as we were here, I thought we might do our bit to relieve the housing crisis, that renting could even be a progressive act, if we found the right tenant."

"And who did you find? Some hippie who played the drone all day and cooked curry all night. Then who? You remember the one who didn't pay rent for a year and wouldn't move? The one who took all the appliances while we were at the beach?"

"We couldn't evict him. Think of what our friends would have thought. Besides, he found us Katy."

"Nice of him to move his cousin in after cleaning us out."

Rory sensed that he had been beaten, which permitted Lucille a more conciliatory tone.

"Look," she suggested, "we can stand here and argue all night about whether or not we should have bought it or whether we should have rented out the basement, but that won't take care of the rot. I know it'll cost, but we'll make it through. I could ask Dad for another advance from the trust fund."

"Oh, no, I'd rather sell on the spot. No more money from your father's corporate corruption," McPhail said.

"I know how you feel. We've been through all this before. But I'm sure we could find an appropriate person."

"The appropriate people charge twice as much," McPhail objected.

"That's because many of them are educated. They know what their labor's worth. Besides, they have a right to live like everyone else." And as Lucille tried to convince Rory that they could have the dry-rot in their basement fixed without risking either bankruptcy or compromising their ideals, she walked to the phone table in the hall. Opening the Yellow Pages, she encountered what seemed like the obvious solution to their problem. There, under the heading *Pest Control,* among the myriad of promises of free inspection, confidential consultation, control of rats, mice, roaches, spiders, fleas, silverfish, odor, and rot, stood the promise of Moses Reed, which had, in fact, been written by Blessings: "Safe Environmental Improvement. Professional Fumigation Support. Preserve the tranquility of your home through the sensitive rehabilitation of unwanted insect species."

"Look at this," she implored. Indeed, it was like a vision, an apparition that comforted the antiwar leader turned property owner, then landlord. The McPhails phoned Reed and made an appointment for him to come over the following day.

Reed remained under the house for a long time. Maneuvering alternately on his back and belly, he could see that water had been leaking from Katy Dawson's shower for months, maybe as long as a year. What began as seepage must have become a drip and then a flow of some proportions since it ran along the mudsill of one whole side of the house. To complicate matters, there was evidence of beetles. McPhail was incredulous, whereupon Reed, who was used to such reactions, urged the worried homeowner to accompany him on an expedition under the joists of his slowly but surely disintegrating home. Lying under a beam filled with the little pinpoint holes made by the postpile beetle's excursions in and out, Reed banged his fist across the roughly sawed wood. Fine dust poured out like confectioners' sugar from a sieve, a small cloud landing in McPhail's mouth.

"Ptt, ptt," he spit wildly like a cat trying to rid itself of a particularly distasteful hairball, "is this stuff poisonous?"

"No, it's perfectly harmless," Reed reassured him, "but you can never predict how far it goes, and that means fumigation." He shined his flashlight into the dark space between the floorboards which overlay the joists and the outer wall. "No telling where it stops."

"Will toxic chemicals be involved?" McPhail asked.

"Yes, actually we'd use a deadly gas. But don't worry, you'll be out of the house, and there are no permanent effects."

"Whew," McPhail sighed, "my wife's an ecological support coordinator, and she doesn't allow any toxic chemicals in the home."

Reed found it difficult to understand how the man lying on his back next to him could hope to eliminate dry-rot and beetles without the aid of strong medicine, but he let things stand. He had had no jobs for over three months, and was anxious to begin.

"Perhaps you want to get other bids, so here's my number if you want to get in touch." Reed knew that any termite specialist in Beacon would offer the same advice and that others were more expensive.

"That won't be necessary," McPhail replied. "You're the one. You may begin as soon as you like. I want you to know how pleased we are to place our house in the hands of an ecologically conscious exterminator. And if there's anything we can do, please let us know. My wife Lucille and I would like you to feel at home. Feel free to visit upstairs whenever you like, and if there is something special you like to eat, we can make arrangements to keep it in the fridge."

Reed wondered if he might be getting himself into some kind of experimental sexual scene of the type he had heard existed in certain quarters of Beacon. He was reassured by noting they didn't even have a hot tub, and that—he had heard—was the first sign.

Reed drew up a contract and started bringing over the necessary equipment as soon as it was signed.

Later in the week of McPhail's visit to the Chief, Blessings Winter was in the backyard cultivating organic compost when Ocean appeared on the deck.

"Bibi," he shouted, placing one hand at his ear.

"Who is it?" she asked. The child simply shook his head. "Tell them I'm coming." She wiped her hands on an old pair of pants hanging on the deck post, then ran up the stairs into the half-finished kitchen, its plumbing exposed by unclosed walls, the cabinets still without doors.

"Goddammit, Ocean, have you been eating sugar again?" She grabbed the remains of an empty packet of sugar of the type dispensed in restaurants, all wet and sucked empty at one end. "How many times do I have to tell you, *no sugar,* and that means none!" Blessings picked up the receiver dangling from the phone on the far wall. "Hello, sorry," she gasped, "I'm out of breath, just ran in from the backyard, and my kid was eating sugar. Who is this?"

"Blessings, this is Barbara Wolfe, president of the Beacon Ladies League. I have some good news I'd like to share with you. You remember, we spoke about the possibility of your joining? I wasn't too sure at the time how flexible our entrance requirements really are. But I've consulted the others, and I'm happy to inform you that we voted at our last meeting to waive the entry fee for younger women who might not otherwise be able to become one of us. As you know, we play an important role in all kinds of local affairs."

"Oh yes, of course, that's why I asked to join. I thought my experience in day care . . ." She covered the phone with one hand and shrieked, "Goddammit, Ocean, you turn down that racket right now or you're grounded for the rest of the day. I mean it. One more like that and you're docked for good." The boy had been holding a portable video game in one hand and a microphone in the other. The buzz of racing cars radiated stereophonically from two large speakers on the floor.

"Sorry for the interruption," she uncovered the mouthpiece. "I could hardly hear. Now, what were we saying?"

"Actually," Barbara Wolfe continued, "I'm empowered to ask you which of our special areas of interest would suit you best. We run large general meetings and sponsor smaller subcommittees too. These gatherings are much more intimate, as you can imagine. Let's see, we have groups involved in voter registration, education, gardening, public affairs, tennis, golf, photography, the arts, self-discovery, and self-expression."

Blessings, who didn't like sports and had never had a hobby, suggested that her expertise in child care made her uniquely qualified for the Education Committee. "I also have a son in the first grade," she added.

"Yes, that would be perfect," Barbara Wolfe said. "And very timely. Right now the League is involved in a very important project with Beacon's children. In fact, we're meeting at my house this Wednesday for lunch. If you can make it, I promise a little surprise, but you must keep this to yourself. You see, after lunch we've been asked to to the home of one of our city's most important people. That's right, he wants our opinion. I do hope you can attend." Blessings wrote the address in pencil on the bare wall, then stormed into the bedroom.

"Okay, give me that thing, right now. That's it." She grabbed the still buzzing triangle of plastic with what looked like a pair of binoculars sticking out of one end. At first, this present from Moses on the child's birthday had pleased her. But as Ocean had learned to make it buzz louder and louder, and then to hold it up to a microphone which amplified the roar of racing cars throughout the house, she began to see the Tomytronic 3-D Thundering Turbo as a form of electronic hostility extending the tension of the last year of their marriage even beyond divorce. She threw it against the wall. Two small batteries popped out and rolled across the floor. The boy let out a scream and buried his face in the covers of the unmade bed. Blessings rebuttoned the side of her overalls and returned to the backyard.

On the day of the Ladies League meeting, Blessings drove to the Wolfe residence. This large, white stucco, vine-covered and tile-roofed house was nestled in a crease of the hill where Beacon fades into the dusty wasteland of the Great Central Valley. There the Education Committee welcomed their youngest member. In nervous anticipation of their after-lunch visit, they joked like adolescent schoolgirls.

"Rory McPhail's about the cutest elected official this town's ever seen," exclaimed Edie Conglin, a short, trim woman with brightly dyed red hair and a large wen on the back of her neck.

"You don't remember Ed Cummings," responded Barbara Wolfe, "City Manager back in the early sixties. Now that was cute."

"Sure, I remember Ed. All I'm saying is that Rory is cuter. Anyway there's no beauty contest between them, and I'll tell you something else. Rory's so smart that he can explain the workings of the Board so that even I can understand them. We've talked many times on the phone," the proud Mrs. Conglin announced. "Honestly, I don't know what the Board would do without him."

"Well, they'd better start making plans, because a lot of people around Beacon would like to see him in higher office. Who knows? Maybe he'll be our next representative." Barbara Wolfe looked around to register the pleasure on the others' faces. Opening and closing her mouth to expose a set of expensively capped teeth, she resembled a blinking lighthouse. Shirley MacGregor glanced up from her knitting and removed one earphone from her ear, a familiar signal that she acknowledged the gravity of their little civic secret.

"I don't know if he should go that far so fast," Edie Conglin cautioned, "I think personally that he'd make a good Chief. That's enough for now. He's so gentle too."

McPhail was, at least publicly, a gentle soul. He had developed a public persona most remarkable in the impression it conveyed that he was listening. It didn't matter to whom he was talking. That person felt that he or she was the only person on earth, or the only one who mattered. Tucker had sensed immediately how useful such a talent could be. He approached McPhail, the househusband who knew how to diaper and talk down to children, to run for President of the Board, knowing that the enormous confidence his man inspired would be an invaluable tool. The Ladies League adored the bushy haired McPhail, who often acted like a child in need and who, unlike their husbands, made them feel he cared.

McPhail was a facilitator, gifted at creating the impression of harmony between people in conflict by avoiding, almost as a principle of nature, direct discussion of any issue that risked becoming controversial. If, for example, someone wanting to build a second unit in violation of the city zoning code were brought by objecting neighbors before the Board, McPhail, after consultation with

Tucker, would ask simply if they were aware of the housing shortage in Beacon or in the country as a whole. He would press to know if those standing before him were personally opposed to affordable shelter for the homeless. And since the very nature of the question prevented anyone from responding in the negative, the matter was quickly resolved to the satisfaction of the party who would build and would also probably feel inspired to make a donation to the Progressive Action Party.

Few realized the importance of McPhail's voice in convincing those who pleaded before him to sacrifice their own interest for the sake of the greater good. Slightly nasal, a bit grainy, and with just a trace of whine, McPhail's speech was above all inviting. It made him seem accessible, even vulnerable, in a way that paradoxically comforted those who listened spellbound. McPhail's voice was a mouthpiece that not only complemented Tucker's reclusive braininess, but that planed the roughness of the Chief's own style. He was a siren, luring irresistably a docile citizenry to do the bidding of the Board. As the general planners of the lives of the inhabitants of Beacon and the final arbiter of their disputes, no matter was too small or too large for the Adjustors, who were fortunate enough to have as their head a man as seductive as Rory McPhail.

McPhail greeted each of the League ladies as they came through the door, and they in turn introduced him to Blessings. He could not have known, of course, how impressed the congenial group was at the sincerity of his plea.

"You may have wondered," he began like the narrator's voice on a high school science film, "why I invited you here today. It's because of your experience in certain matters and because, frankly, the city once again is in need of your help. The problem I am talking about," he paused as if about to let them in on some deep secret, "has to do with Beacon's children. Your expertise in such matters is well known, and I thought I would seek your advice before making the slightest move."

"While it's true," Barbara Wolfe responded excitedly, "that the League did do a study some years ago, I'm not sure it's still up to date."

"Ladies, I would like to be able to level with you from the start." McPhail looked at each one. "No one could have predicted four or five years ago the present situation, and the future remains uncertain. This is why I would like for us to try to forget the dusty old books and reports and to think together of the children. Let's close our eyes and think hard of the next generation." The League ladies were charmed to be asked to close their eyes in the presence of Rory McPhail. They remained perfectly silent for what must have been a minute, entranced.

When they began to open their eyes, McPhail continued in a congratulatory tone that suggested they had all already accomplished a great deal of business. "You know the Board of Adjustments is ultimately responsible for the welfare of our children. We have been advised by Superintendent Stafford that Beacon's progressive educational system has not always lived up to his expectations." The ladies moved collectively to the edges of their armchairs. "So let's put our heads together, just you and me, and imagine for a moment the high school. Superintendent Stafford suggests we should perhaps consider, and mind you I'm not sure I agree, but he suggests we should consider cutting programs there."

"What kind of programs?" Shirley MacGregor suddenly removed both earphones.

"We might think, for example, about tailoring the counseling and career options," replied McPhail, who knew Shirley MacGregor's husband was a counselor at the high school.

"Oh, dear," chirped Edie Conglin, who in reality had no idea what McPhail was talking about.

"Unthinkable, ridiculous," said Barbara Wolfe, whose own husband worked in the administration of a nearby teacher's college. "Why, just this fall our son Monroe had to wait for over two weeks to see a counselor, and by then he was behind in two courses. Absolutely ridiculous," she repeated.

"I know how strongly you all must feel," McPhail said calmly, "but let's not try to personalize the situation. Let's keep our minds open and look at other options. We might, for example, look at the high potential program. You know it is coming under increasing attack from a certain element in the community. I won't mention any names, but some of the primary parents consider it a luxury."

"I think I speak for everyone when I say that would be a mistake." Barbara Wolfe again took up the standard. "There's only one high school in town, and it is our duty to keep it strong. I think I speak for all of us when I say we would fight that hook, line, and sinker. Am I not right, girls?" The League ladies nodded as a group. The obviously pleased Mrs. Wolfe smiled her lighthouse smile, removed her shoes, and folded her legs on McPhail's faded velvet sofa.

"If you feel that strongly about it, then we should certainly look at other options." McPhail glanced around to make sure he had everyone's attention. "What would you say about the possibility of redistricting at the primary level?"

The Education Committee of the Ladies League breathed a collective sigh of relief. Of their number, only Blessings had a child in the primary grades.

"What if, just what if," Barbara Wolfe pursued, "Beacon were able to create an educational foundation like Goshen? My husband and I had dinner the other night with one of the people involved over there, and I'm sure he would be glad to give us lots of ideas. Just think, we could organize a series of gala dinners and write to foundations. Then we might think of a voluntary tax. It would be hard work, but I know we could do it. And think of it, we'd be getting in on the ground floor. It would be our idea."

Blessings, hearing the word foundation, could no longer keep still. "The last thing we need is to get big corporations messed up in Beacon's schools," she blurted. "All you have to do is look at the names like Rockefeller and Ford to know they're corrupt. The next thing you know they'd want to dictate what we teach." McPhail looked stunned. "Now I have a lot of experience in this kind of thing," Blessings continued, "we had exactly the same problems running Nature's Child Day Care Center where we came up with some really creative solutions, things you'd never think of if you're thinking about foundations. I'm talking about really grass roots kinds of things like ways of saving energy and recycling paper."

Reed, who had been under McPhail's house since early that morning and who at that very instant was wedged in the tight crawl space between the furnace and the foundation, could hear people speaking upstairs. No one, however, could have imagined his surprise at hearing his ex-wife lecturing the Ladies League about how to run Beacon's schools. At first he thought there must be some mistake, he must be dreaming. But then the familiar shrill voice again penetrated the floorboards.

"Instead of the power trip of a foundation we could form our own food commune. At Nature's we saved money by buying peanut butter and cheese in bulk. It wasn't the commercial stuff they sell in big supermarkets either. We installed low-watt light bulbs and adjusted school hours to fit daylight savings, we could lower the thermostat in classrooms, and I forgot to mention setting up a phone tree to save postage."

The ladies, taken aback by the boldness of Blessings's intervention, tried to steer the conversation back on course.

Blessings sensed having made a blunder. A group as prestigious as the Ladies League was not ready for such innovative ideas, she thought, and so she grew quiet.

McPhail, who pretended to listen and even to take notes, said simply, "These are all excellent suggestions, but we should be careful not to move too quickly. I think Blessings is on the right track. Perhaps we should think of reducing our budget first. I'm not sure Beacon is ready for a private foundation that might have negative social effects."

"Whatever do you mean?" Barbara Wolfe asked.

"Well, for instance, like separating privileged and underprivileged children and making the underprivileged also feel disadvantaged. We have a commitment to all our children, don't we?" This was one of McPhail's questions designed to make anyone who might even think of answering in the negative feel like an axe murderer. "If I might make a suggestion," he pursued, "how would it be if we explored together the idea of program consolidation?"

"What's that?" Jessica Flowers asked.

"It means a regrouping of resources, and maybe even a rethinking of some of the ways we handle the education of the poorer element of our population in the lower grades. Superintendent Stafford has some excellent ideas along this line, and I would like to invite you personally to meet and work with him. This, ladies, is where we should go from here."

"I think I speak for all of us," Mrs. Wolfe repeated in a lowered voice, "when I say that we are available to help with whatever the community needs."

"I knew I could count on you," McPhail replied. "Do you think we could form a subcommittee to study the questions that have come up this afternoon? And could this committee report back, say, at your next meeting? I am at your entire disposition. I must warn you, though, some of the material you will encounter may be confidential, and we will all have to be extremely discreet. We can learn together how to trust one another."

They agreed, and with even greater zeal than might otherwise have been possible, for Jessica Flowers, Edie Conglin, Shirley MacGregor, Barbara Wolfe, and Blessings Winter now constituted a special subcommittee of the Education Committee of the Ladies League. They would have a secretary, consult with Superintendent Stafford, and represent the community at large public gatherings. But most of all, they would get to meet in the privacy of their homes with the irresistable President of the Board of Adjustments who had taken them into his confidence.

Reed was still stretched out motionless on his back. "And I

thought they were into kinky sex," he muttered to himself.

McPhail had no way of knowing that at the very moment he was meeting with the ladies of the League, Chief Horton received the visit of two men. Both were wearing three-piece suits. One carried a briefcase, the other a large portfolio.

"Welcome, gentleman. I'm not sure you know my aide, Eric Tucker, do you?" They shook hands.

"Please, sit down." Horton motioned toward two chairs facing his desk. "Now, what's on your mind?"

Dave Porter, a mustached man with a shaped razor haircut, pulled several sheets of paper from his briefcase and folded them on his lap. "Mr. Chief, as you know, the Truscott Corporation has plans for the development of Beacon, plans that could assure the financial well-being of the city well into the next century." As Porter spoke, Victor Nelson opened the portfolio resting against the arm of his chair. He spread a series of architectural drawings across one edge of Horton's large mahogany desk. Tucker rose from where he had been sitting and hunched over the bluish sheets.

"Mr. Chief," Porter continued, "we're frankly a little concerned about the slowness with which matters are proceeding."

"Let's see what we have here," Horton said with a mock seriousness obvious only to his aide.

"What you're looking at, Mr. Chief, are the Truscott plans for the downtown area on which now stands the, uh, old Blackstone Hotel."

Tucker and Horton pretended to be interested.

"Truscott is thinking in terms of an office complex with its own shops and exhibition hall." Nelson lifted the top drawing to expose an artist's renderings of several elegantly landscaped office buildings surrounded by busy people in suits with briefcases. "Over there," said Nelson, pointing discretely, "we would like to add a complete health and fitness center. Then, if you will just follow me long enough to consider these last couple of sketches," he shuffled the large sheets draped over the edge of the desk, "you will see a series of apartment buildings, small model cities within the city. This project alone could transform Beacon into the liveliest town in the region."

Horton turned toward his aide. "What do you think?"

"What you're proposing will change the entire scale of the city, and there may be serious objections from some quarters about destroying one of Beacon's architectural treasures," said Tucker.

"You mean the preservationists?" Porter asked. "Even they know the Blackstone's in ruins and that the land's, well, frankly, not maintained."

"It may not be manicured like some people's front lawns," Horton replied, "but there's folks use it as a park. They live in there at night. Besides, gentlemen, Beacon is a very progressive town. We take seriously questions relating to nature. The minute word gets out we're even thinking of touching the land around the Blackstone, we'll be bombarded down at City Hall with all kinds of people from the Sierra Club and, what's the name of the bunch with the whales . . . ?" He hesitated.

"Greenpeace," Tucker said.

"Mr. Chief, the Truscott Corporation is prepared to invest a billion dollars in Beacon, and I don't have to tell you what that would mean in terms of taxes and jobs, not to mention beautification. Think of it, your name could become synonymous with the rebirth of the city. I'd like you to take a look at one more sketch. This drawing, made especially for you, is what you would see from right here where you sit." Porter made a studied sweeping gesture as if to indicate that in a mere matter of months Horton would be able to see the Grand Canyon from his window.

The two men from Truscott looked up expectantly from their clearly drawn dreams.

Tucker cleared his throat. "Speaking for the Chief and the community, and without going into the problems connected to the Blackstone, I can tell you that there are some pretty big hurdles to cross before we could even think of putting up buildings that size right in the middle of the city. Like the Chief says, this is a democratic town where a lot gets done out in the open, in public meetings."

"Let me try to understand," Porter said. "Are you telling us that Truscott may not be able to build in Beacon?"

"We're not exactly saying that," Tucker said, "only that it's going to take some doing and maybe a little push from City Hall."

"What exactly are we talking about?" Porter asked. "The Truscott Corporation is very anxious to get started, and I feel we could work very nicely together. May I ask you to look at the timetable we've developed?"

"We're getting a little off track," Tucker replied, "or at least we're jumping the gun. Personally, I'd like to hear more about ways of working together, since I think that's where we might find solutions to the details that would be profitable to all concerned and that might take us beyond the impasse of city bureaucracy." He smiled. "We understand that the bureaucracy limits us all."

"What do you have in mind?" the vice-presidents asked in unison.

Horton took over from his aide. "There are a number of special projects of great interest to the city that might be helped along by the Truscott Corporation."

"What kind of projects?"

"Well, education for one. We'd like any building downtown to benefit Beacon's kids." Horton's gaze fixed upon the two vice-presidents. "Then," he hesitated, "there are a couple of other projects I would prefer to keep to myself, if you don't mind."

After a short silence, Tucker pressed gently, "What do you think, gentlemen?"

"Well, the idea is a little novel for us. I've frankly never heard of anything like it before. We'd have to take it back to our financial people. I'm not sure how they'll react. But just so I can prepare things, how much would you say we're talking about?"

Everyone, including Horton, looked at Tucker who hesitated. "I'd say we're talking something in the range of five, six, could go as high as ten."

"Million?" Porter gasped.

Tucker nodded.

"That's a lot of money."

"Gentlemen, that's what it'd take to improve our view from City Hall. When you come to think of it, this is peanuts compared to what Truscott stands to make. I'm sure the people up top will see it that way. They shouldn't mind a small outlay for public relations. That's your job, isn't it?" Tucker took an exaggerated glance at the business cards Porter and Nelson had extended upon entering. "Smart business people like Truscott might even enjoy doing well by doing a little good. Now, if there are no further questions, the Chief has a busy schedule . . ."

"Just one thing," Porter added, "when do we have to let you know?"

"There's no big rush, except I thought you were the ones anxious to get started. Take a week to think it over, and give us a call," Tucker replied. The aide stood up to shake hands with the vice-presidents, who hastily gathered their drawings and left.

"Are you sure we have to use that much on a bunch of middle-class brats?" Horton asked as soon as his guests were out the door.

"Would you rather give up Beacon to gentrification?"

"To what?"

"To people with regular jobs and foreign cars, who like to eat in French restaurants. You know the kind, moving in with families.

Don't worry. Chiang's plan is the only way of getting the liberals out of hills, short of burning their houses down."

"Then run it by me again."

"It's simple as pie. First, we make the wrong element want to leave by threatening something that all their guilt won't be able to resist. It could be anything, but messing with the schools is easy enough. These folks are so busy anyway eating croissants that they won't notice until it's too late. Then we move in. You'll see. It's foolproof, and Truscott is footing the bill."

Horton sat there rubbing his bald head.

Porter phoned the very next day to say that the Truscott Corporation had approved the program of public relations they had discussed. Tucker was delighted at the ease with which the "big boys" were willing to part with such a large sum, and, within the hour, had called a meeting of an organization virtually unknown except to its members. Indeed, though the directors of Beacon's Capital Exchange saw each other socially at various Party functions, they had gathered formally as a group only once—to ratify the articles of incorporation Tucker had drafted. Because each had in his or her way also participated in every politically correct movement since the sixties, they were at first suspicious of any organization with the word *capital* in its name.

"We're about as far from capitalists as you can get," one complained.

Tucker laid to rest their qualms. "You must understand," he explained, "that we are reversing capital, turning it around. That's why we use the word *exchange*. Business can be used for both good and bad ends. There's a difference between big corporate capitalism and the creative use of money in service of the right cause."

"Sounds like you're selling out," another objected.

"No," Tucker had insisted, "you have to understand we need our own source of funds, our own expertise, and our own record of success if we are going to defeat the other side and accomplish our progressive goals."

"But what about the money? It doesn't exactly grow on trees," Larry Newton, once head of the Peaceful Freedom Party, asked.

"You let us worry about that," Tucker replied, as gradually, the members of Beacon's most militant fringe were converted to what only a short time before, in the absence of even the remotest hope of capital, they had denounced as "socially irresponsible," "repulsive," and "sad."

"The reason for tonight's meeting," Tucker began, "is to announce a piece of good news. The Exchange has acquired the means to actually implement progressive action. But we will have to work hard to make it happen."

"Where's the money coming from?" interrupted James Meyer, a slim, freckled man with tufts of graying hair. To one side of a large bald spot on the top of his head could be seen a reddish scar.

"The money is to be provided by Truscott Corporation," Tucker informed them.

"The Truscott Corporation," spurted Pam Sidel, "they're the worst pig developers in Beacon Land. Have you been to Goshen lately? Have you seen what they did? Well let me tell you. Downtown is nothing but one big commercial center, a fucking mall with little shops selling running shoes and truffles."

"We have to keep in mind," Tucker said, "that we are different. This is Beacon, and we're about to achieve what the government and the developers can't or don't want to do. We are forcing them to take a step in our direction. Whoever thought we would be able to harness the huge wealth of the Truscott Corporation in the service of the movement?"

"What kind of development are we talking about?" Newton asked.

"Housing for starters, nonprofit community organizations, progressive businesses, offices for the right kind of groups."

"Like us?" asked Irving Caplow, a bearded man slouched in an armchair with a hat over his eyes.

"Like us," Tucker said, "but others as well."

"Where we gonna put our project?" Newton pursued.

"That's not decided yet," Tucker replied. "We're looking at a number of options. But I wouldn't worry about that. Now that we've finally obtained the wherewithal to be truly progressive, the where is just a detail."

"Okay," Newton conceded, "but I don't get why we're here right now."

"We're here because there are some things I'd like to ask you all to do in the coming months to make sure we stay on course."

"Like what kind of thing?"

"Nothing very serious or taxing, but still important. We are obliged to hold a few public hearings. The wrong people may show up with silly objections, and we could get bad press. I would like to make sure that we all turn out to present the correct side."

"Oh, no, you mean you want us to speak in public in favor of the Truscott pigs like we're a bunch of right-wing toadies?" Pam Sidel said. "Not me, I won't. It's too embarrassing."

"I'm not forgetting anything, Pam," Tucker said. "We won't even need to mention Truscott for some time. But you must remember that what we're really doing here is turning the big corporations against themselves, and that's a radical move. In fact, that's what the movement means today."

"What kind of objections are we talking about?" asked Newton.

"Well," said Tucker, "let's pretend that the people, say, who live around the old Blackstone Hotel show up and start to complain that we're ruining their neighborhood. All you have to do is get up and show them how selfish they are. That won't be hard."

"Isn't that where Leon Zimmer lives?" Caplow asked.

"Right across the street."

"What fun it'd be to get his little yuppie ass," the slouched man exclaimed.

"I hear you," Pam Sidel said, "but I still don't like the idea."

"Look, Pam," James Meyer took over, "It sounds like Eric is talking millions, and what's not to like when millions are involved?" Meyer, who lived in a basement on welfare and food stamps, seemed to light up like a bulb. Indeed, the scar on his head glowed like a hot mesquite coal, and he grew as silent as Caplow.

Tucker seized what he sensed to be a certain momentum. "Just wait," he promised, "until you catch a glimpse of all those good middle-class citizens whimpering and whining about the impact on their environment of what you would think is a skyscraper. You'll get a chance to call them racist too. Don't worry. You won't even have to mention Truscott. Besides, you won't be alone. We plan to turn out a lot of the right kind of people."

"Are they really racists?" Pam Sidel asked.

"I'm not sure they're really racists, but more what you would call segregationists or separatists," Tucker replied. "Please, let's not quibble over words. We've got business. You should be hearing from me soon."

In democratic Beacon, citizen participation was the watchword, and during the next few months Tucker saw to it that there were even more public meetings than usual. On any given night, the civic-minded resident might select from among half a dozen, including the weekly audience of the Board of Adjustments and the regular gatherings of any number of its appointed satellites: the subcommittee on schools, on traffic, on mental health, on the environment (with its special subgroups on toxic waste, water, and air), on the deregulation of gender; the task forces on aging, on sexism, on specism; the delegation to advise the Board on foreign policy, on zoning, on rent control; the planning office and parks commission; the university liaison committee; the police review board; the licensing and facilities commissions; the panels on human resources and welfare, and on the handicapped; and the list went on. Each committee also hosted meetings of its budget review body as well as of the subcommittees that handled relations with comparable groups in other towns.

Blessings Winter tried as best she could not to miss a single gathering of Beacon's key civic bodies. After her divorce she was frantically driven toward as many political, social, and spiritual organizations as she could scrape together the dues to join. Often the modest entrance fee was the only impediment to membership, an obstacle overcome, as in the case of the League, by special waiver. At one point Blessings belonged to so many groups that she could not possibly have attended all the meetings in a month. But time was of no consequence. She would show up at two or three in a night, a dozen in a day. Sometimes, for example, she would begin with a late morning planning session of Students for Irish National Liberation. She would excuse herself with the familiar abrupt "Bye, got to run" in order not to miss a luncheon with La Leche League. She then ran to Planned Parenthood, leaving early for an appointment with the steering committee of New El Salvador Tomorrow. By dinnertime she found herself at a rally in support of MASH, Mothers Against Sexual Hassle, ending the day with a session of late-night Hellerwork at the Shiatsu Center.

No pocketbook could have held all the membership cards Blessings kept in a carton under the bed. No personal secretary alone could cope with the amount of bulk mailings she received daily and most of which remained unopened. No one on whom others depended for everyday needs could possibly have juggled such a great variety of appointments and still maintained even the semblance of sanity, which Blessings was able to do only because the frenetic pace of her outer life was so in keeping with a deep internal fracture.

In the course of a complex child-care arrangement by which Reed was to pick up Ocean halfway through a hearing of a subcommittee of the Beacon Domestic Violence Task Force, he screwed up the courage to ask his ex-wife what she was doing in McPhail's living room the preceding week.

"Are you following me around?" she asked.

"No, I just thought . . ."

"Well don't think, at least not about that. I'm involved in a lot of things, and where I go is my business. Anyway, it's a secret project, and we're not allowed to say anything about it."

"Who's the we?" Reed asked.

"The Beacon Ladies League. Listen, I've already said too much, and I've got to get back into conference. Here's Ocean." She kissed the boy on the cheek. "Bye."

It was during another such meeting, the biweekly session of the traffic subcommittee of the Clean Air Commission, that Blessings first learned of the plan to build on the site of the Blackstone. As was Tucker's habit when there was a particularly delicate matter that risked attracting public outcry, he buried it in the most unlikely, but nonetheless credible, committee possible. This way no one might afterward claim that the issue had not been debated. Tucker was also careful to hide the actual substance of such proposals behind the technical language of seemingly innocuous bureaucratic procedure. Thus, an undisclosed corporation's designs upon the Blackstone site were buried in an item on the official agenda which read Redevelopment of Census Tract 55423, and which proposed to free from traffic a block-long alley where delivery trucks often lingered, thereby eliminating noise and pollution. When the time came for questions from the public, someone asked where this particular piece of property could be found. The actual street address made Blessings's ears perk up. She knew that one of the parents from Nature's Child lived right across from Tower and Saturn, which was also right up the street from Ellie Pearl.

Early the next morning Blessings phoned the woman who was handling her divorce. The still sleepy Ellie Pearl phoned Leon Zimmer. Both were surprised that there should be any discussion of plans to build near them without consulting them first. Rather than panic, however, they decided that Zimmer should call Tucker, who had been a classmate of his at Bountiful State University. Their conversation was both alarming and encouraging.

"Frankly, Leon," the Chief's aide confided, "Beacon needs to enlarge its tax base. No decision has been made, but I don't know how much longer the city can hold out. You have my assurance that nothing will be done without consulting the community first."

"Oh yeah," Zimmer said, "what kind of guarantee have we got?"

Tucker hesitated. "Look, how about if I arrange a meeting between the President of the Board of Adjustments and the group of your choosing. That good enough?"

"Doesn't mean fuck," Zimmer insisted, "I want your word you ain't going to meddle around my turf."

"There are forces, Leon . . ."

"Forces, shit," Zimmer yelled into the receiver.

Leon Zimmer's neighbors had grown older, more settled. Many had married, purchased a house, earned professional credentials. Those who had children had also traded their early model Volkswagen bugs for Volvo station wagons and Vanagons. And yet those who dwelled in those few square blocks between the Blackstone and the fancy food shops to the north were united by a certain nostalgic righteous feeling that for the most part remained more sensed than spoken. It was, for example, signaled in the way they dressed, in the bumper stickers displayed on cars, in the insouciance with which they cared for their lawns, and especially in the foods they ate.

An especially acute doctoral student in sociology, in fact, seized upon this particular subculture as worthy of study and wrote a masters thesis entitled "Hippies into Yuppies: A Microsociological Study of Postmodern Urban Culture." "One feels in the area of Beacon tract 55423," she wrote by way of introduction, "a sense of shared history. A surprisingly high percentage of the interviews conducted show that this upwardly mobile segment of Beacon's population expresses satisfaction at having reached an average mean age of 42 without having, in the phrase used most often, 'been co-opted by the system.' "

The neighbors met in the comfortable living room of Ellie Pearl where they formed an association. They agreed that anyone, whether property holder or renter, living within a ten-block radius of the Blackstone could join. In addition, there would be corresponding members or friends, among whom they counted Blessings who not only had alerted them to the danger in the first place, but who was in contact with a number of important local organizations and who also lived on the edge of their neighborly perimeter. When it came time to choose a name, they rejected several suggestions containing the word Blackstone which, they felt, would appear too oriented toward a single issue or piece of property and not sufficiently politically aware. They opted instead for the Urban Awareness Alliance for Neighborhood Preservation. With such a name, they were convinced, the battle was already half won. The Chief and the members of the Board, in the face of such concrete evidence of solidarity, would be forced simply to recognize their mistake.

Just to be sure, however, Zimmer accepted the offer to meet with McPhail.

Leon Zimmer lived in a small bungalow behind a large and once stately brown shingle which, since giving up his part-time position in a small real estate firm, he rented to students. Zimmer, like McPhail until the time of his election, was one of the growing number of househusbands whom another sociology student writing on "The Sexual Politics of the New Man" now estimated at between fifteen and twenty percent of Beacon's adult male population. He was married to Karen Zimmer, herbal consultant to Beacon's finest gourmet restaurants and to its alternative medical establishment.

The President of the Board of Adjustments, a man who had perhaps changed even more diapers than the ex-broker, arrived before anyone else. Several small children were crawling back and forth between the kitchen and the hall.

"Come on in. Give me a sec, Rory. I'm two down and one to go." Zimmer referred to his infant son on the changing table and to his toddler daughters, one of which was headed toward the space heater.

"Hold on there, young lady, where do you think you're going?" McPhail asked young Keri Zimmer. "You'll get burned if you go any farther." Then, picking her up, he carried the child under one arm to the back room where Zimmer was down on his hands and knees next to the bed.

"Can I help? What are you looking for?"

"The goddamn Handiwipes. Once they can walk, they shove everything all over the fucking place at least once a day." Zimmer fished with a lengthened coat hanger a cone-shaped container of premoistened towelettes from under the dresser.

"Oh, you use Wipe and Dipes?" McPhail seemed anxious to make comradely chatter. "Lucille and I found Wet Ones to be better, they're less mess. Also biodegradable, according to people who are into eco . . ."

"Look, just leave me alone for a sec while I take care of business. I'll be right out."

McPhail had a sense of just how long Zimmer would be and took the opportunity to look at the bookshelf on the other side of the chimney. Falling upon a number of volumes that could also be found in his own living room, *The Greening of America, Zen and the Art of Motorcycle Maintenance, Creative Parenting, Games People Play, The Portable Nietzsche,* McPhail felt somewhat more at home. Not wanting to be caught browsing by the steering committee of the Urban Awareness Alliance, however, he quickly sat down.

Zimmer returned from the bedroom. "Help yourselves to coffee. French roast on the left, water-decaffeinated Jamaican on the right. The others will be here shortly." Indeed, several members of the Urban Awareness Alliance slipped into the room before McPhail could pour himself a cup.

"Look, Rory, we've been through a lot of stuff together, haven't we?" Eliot Friedman, head of Beacon's Free Rent Coalition, said. "You remember draft counseling at the high school, don't you? And the time we were arrested together at the antinuclear rally? Now, there's some heavy shit coming down in Beacon, and we've got to work together to stop it, right?" McPhail remained impassive. "I don't have to to tell you that the Truscott people have hired a bunch of sixty-thousand-dollar-a-year men in gray suits, ties and all. They're trying to sell a slick package, but there's no way we can let them do it." Friedman's remarks were interrupted by the arrival of Ellie Pearl, Blessings Winter, and Beth Hansen, head of Beacon's largest child care organization, BONKERS.

"On what grounds do you think the city should turn such a permit down?" McPhail asked with feigned seriousness. "You know the Blackstone's been closed for years. The building's decaying. It's a hazard. Why the revenue alone . . ."

"Cut the shit," Zimmer blurted. "We're talking about my side of town."

"Let's not be parochial, Leon," Walter Carroll, editor of *Groundroots* magazine, interrupted. Then, glaring at McPhail, he said, "Think of the big picture. To begin with, these people won't stop at just one building. I know them. They want to develop the whole downtown, fill it with high rises, parking lots, condominiums, hotels. If the Board lets Truscott in, they'll be sanctioning our intervention in South America. That's right, the blood of thousands would be on your hands. I can't believe Beacon would let itself fall into the hands of the CIA like that, because that's what we'd be doing."

There was a moment of silence during which Zimmer thought he saw McPhail take a deep breath, which was a good sign.

Suddenly Blessings jumped from her lotus position on the floor. "This may sound crazy to you, but I thought everything was okay until a friend who's been working on these things tipped me off. The big developers don't care about Beacon. All they know is that land is cheap, and they can make money by turning it into another Goshen. A skyscraper right in the middle of town will cut out light for the children. It wouldn't stop pollution. It would attract an undesirable element to our neighborhood."

"Could you be a little more specific?" asked McPhail, who was at first surprised to find Blessings at the meeting of the Urban Awareness Alliance as well as the Ladies League, then delighted by the commodious confusion she seemed to spread wherever she went.

"I mean the people who'll shop in all the cutesy boutiques. Conservative people, housewives with dyed hair, people in American cars that are not energy efficient and make exhaust, cigarette smokers. I can show you figures."

Ellie Pearl tried to calm Blessings who by now was gesticulating wildly. The self-possessed lawyer was like an attentive cook turning off the burner beneath a whistling steam kettle. "The fact is," she said, "that no one has ordered an environmental impact report, and until one is done, the application for a building permit is premature."

"Ellie's right, there's no provision for day care," Beth Hansen added.

"Yes, of course. I would be the first to agree with all that has been said," McPhail offered. "But the one thing you must realize is that the city can no longer afford to let this opportunity pass. Building would provide jobs for the poorest segment of the community—the unemployed, blacks, single mothers, workers. You must believe me when I say that I have given the matter a great deal of thought. Real progressives must favor progress . . ."

"Progress shit," Zimmer blurted, "these people have connections to the Mafia. They're coming in to fuck up our neighborhood. Do you call that progress?"

"Leon, let's not think only of ourselves. We must not let selfish interests ruin this chance to help the people most hurt by the arms race," McPhail said.

"What?" Zimmer asked.

"I'm speaking of the fact that the money that should be spent here at home is going to the military. Personally, I do not favor approving the permit, but I think you can see why some members of the Board might. I can assure you I would never allow a building of the kind you see in downtown . . ."

Blessings let out another burst of steam. "Wait a minute," she chortled, "you allowed a fast-food restaurant across from the Crocker Bank, and they are serving the kind of sweet, greasy food that rots people's minds. They're creating killers. Then you let them put in an adult bookstore that's breeding rapists. Here, I've made some copies of an article that proves pornography encourages rape." She began passing out stapled sheets.

"Rape, rape, I know nothing of rape, and we ought to know nothing of rape," hummed Bobo Dam Dass, a small, dark man with a shaved head. He had arrived late and was sitting, legs and arms crossed, next to Blessings. Dam Dass, author of the highly acclaimed *Meditation and Real Estate* and head of the Dharma Commune, was the guru of gurus, a man so peaceful and learned that he was considered the godfather of Beacon's spiritual community. Hundreds flocked to his biweekly course on miracles. McPhail respected the Reverend Dass, as the Chief referred to him, because he controlled the "meditational" vote. One word from the little man sitting on the floor, Tucker had often joked, and thousands would hum to the beat of a different mantra.

"The best defense is not to attack another's position, but rather to protect the truth," he chanted. "It is unwise to accept any concept if you have to invert a whole frame of reference in order to justify it. This procedure is painful in its minor applications and genuinely tragic on a wider scale."

"What the fuck is Bobo saying?" Eliot Friedman whispered to Zimmer.

"I've never understood a word the man's uttered, but he's on our side. That's what counts. Besides, he knows real estate, and we're talking like big buildings."

"Listen," McPhail repeated, "no one is more concerned than I am, and you can rest assured that I will see personally that the Board takes your feelings into account. But we have to balance the interests of everyone in the city and do what's best for all. Maybe the best thing for now would be to form a committee, a task force to present the neighborhood's point of view."

"Oh, good," Blessings broke in, "I already have experience doing this kind of work." She referred, of course, to her participation in the subcommittee of the Ladies League Education Committee, though she could neither divulge its nature, having been sworn to secrecy, nor its outcome, since the subcommittee had yet to meet.

"If you could perhaps give us some kind of assessment," McPhail persisted, "it would come in handy when the Adjustors have to decide. You know as well as I do that the matter will be settled tomorrow. You have my word that nothing will be done without your input." The President of the Board stood up, and, pretending to be late for an appointment, nervously withdrew.

"I don't get it," Zimmer blurted the moment he was gone. "First he struts in here early acting like Mr. Rogers, then he's got so much to do he can't stick around long enough to hear us out. There's dirty dealing going on, and we've got to find out what it is." But Zimmer had hardly finished speaking before the others, pretending to be at least as busy as McPhail, also departed. Only Blessings remained.

"Leon," she said, "I think I know something that may help out, but you've got to promise not to tell a soul."

Zimmer took both her having stayed after the others and the tone of intimacy in her voice as signs of seduction and began to fondle her hair.

"Cut it out, Leon," she objected. "Get off your male power trip long enough to think about something real, but remember, you've got to keep it quiet." He desisted, lighting a marijuana cigarette and holding his breath while Blessings revealed the secret of her meeting with McPhail and the Ladies League. "Next week," she confided proudly, lowering her head to where Zimmer might have touched it once more, "we're supposed to meet with Superintendent Stafford."

"What's the connection?" Zimmer asked.

"All I know," Blessings responded, "is that McPhail is in both places."

"He could say the same about you."

"I know. Only he's got the power. He's the head of the Board, and I'm just a community organizer."

"You're probably right. But it's not McPhail. They've got to be using him for the deals they're cutting higher up. Listen, I don't want you to say a word to anyone else. I've got an idea." Blessings's eyes glistened, since there was nothing she liked better than telling a secret in exchange for learning one.

"We've got to figure out who's doing what. So, I'm going to give you a little list of questions to ask when you get all cozy with Stafford and your conservative friends. Maybe you and I can diaper McPhail."

"Cut it out, Leon, I'll have you know I was admitted to the League on a scholarship, and they put me on the Education Committee because of my day care experience."

"Okay, okay, so you know about kids. Big deal. There are a whole lot of things we need to know to break this thing. For now, you keep mum, and I'll be back in touch as soon as I can find out who's jerking us off."

In the week following McPhail's meeting with the Urban Awareness Alliance, the Ladies League gathered in the Superintendent's office.

"I'm so glad you could come in to talk to us today," Stafford greeted them. "I've asked the other members of the team to join us." He introduced Dr. Frank Hines, Dr. Ron Rossman, and Dr. Paul Szbad. As soon as they were all seated the man purported to be the secret hand that ran the district, Glen Chiang, entered almost unnoticed and, without being introduced, took his place in the rear.

Stafford opened the deliberations on a familiar note by explaining that their job was to educate the children of Beacon, but that this had become increasingly difficult in recent years due to a lack of cooperation on the part of certain parents who had grown too independent. "In order not to waste your valuable time, I've asked our planning expert, Dr. Hines, to give us a more detailed account of just where we stand." Stafford smiled the smile of an infant passing gas.

Hines, a man whose ruddy complexion bespoke high blood pressure and whose pork chop sideburns, prematurely gray, signaled worry, was so short that when he rose from his chair it was hard to tell whether he was sitting or standing.

"What we have here is a situation that has been declining over a number of years. The district is like me, it has been eating too much and needs to be trimmed. Things are out of control. Worse, Beacon has developed a two-tiered educational system where children in certain neighborhoods are getting a better education than other children across town. We see this in the yearly test scores analyzed by Dr. Rossman. And the teachers can see it in the classroom." Hines's head oscillated with self-congratulatory pleasure like one of those spring-headed turtles on the dashboard of a teenager's car. "Now that isn't fair, is it?" Hines looked at the League ladies who, with the exception of Blessings, had all visited the beauty parlor that afternoon and on cue shook their variously frosted, permed, colored and curled heads to the rhythm of the bobbing turtle. "What are we to do?" Hines asked. "For that we must consult the education professionals." With the feigned enthusiasm of a TV game show host presenting a new contestant, he said, "I turn the floor over to Dr. Ron Rossman."

Rossman resembled Hines down to the gray, slightly irridescent polyester suit he wore and which indeed they had purchased together at a Macys two-for-one sale. "Uh, yes," he began, "this is a particularly thorny question that educators have wrestled with since the beginnings of the Academy in ancient Greece."

"Pardon me," interrupted Blessings, "but could you tell me what problem we're talking about?" She pretended to be taking notes.

"Yes, of course. We're speaking about the age-old problem of unequal achievement. The pattern has degenerated in Beacon to what we professionals call a cycle of downwardly mobile expanded expectations. If, for instance, we provide additional programs for the disadvantaged, the parents of the advantaged hire private tutors. If we create smaller classes for lower achievers, the same parents put their children in private school. This is what Dr. Hines means when he says the situation is out of control." The staff looked appropriately sad at Rossman's rehearsed horror. "Now, for the first time in history," he continued with an upbeat, "we have the opportunity to conduct an exciting educational experiment that would make the advantages of private boarding school available to all."

"What do you say, ladies?" Stafford asked with authority. "Can we count on you to help us out?" The League ladies, anxious to show that they were on the inside of an important secret that they would have a role in making public, again nodded in unison.

"Let's be clear," Stafford inquired, "are we talking about the high school?"

"No," the Leaguers echoed in chorus, "in our opinion the place to start is in the lower grades."

"Ladies, you have anticipated our thinking entirely. Quite frankly, I was at first a little skeptical about your ability to assimilate such a mass of complex material, but you've surprised even an old hand like me. Now my staff has certain recommendations, but we wouldn't think of submitting them to the Adjustors without your approval. I must warn you, though, the information we will be discussing is highly confidential."

"You don't have to worry about us," Barbara Wolfe assured him, "the League has a long tradition of confidence." The others were practically drooling to know what lay before Stafford in the orange folder marked *For Your Eyes Only, Not For Reproduction.*

"My staff's recommendation is that we submit to the Board of Adjustments a plan of resource reconfiguration that would include relocation of children to two primary sites in the flatlands, of course. Ladies, I believe we have an opportunity to make a real difference for Beacon's children, and I believe the community is ready for the change, although I know that once a zone is named, objections will be raised." The women of the League were relieved that none of the proposed "experimentation" would take place in their neighborhood. Only Blessings seemed outwardly perturbed. Barbara Wolfe could sense her body squirming, and, after the awkward outburst at McPhail's, dreaded whatever the League's newest member might say. For her part, Blessings, remembering the coolness with which the ladies received her initial suggestions, did hesitate ever so slightly before drawing from the knapsack which served as handbag the list Zimmer had given her.

"You will have to excuse me," she began, "but I'd like to know the answers to a few questions." Stafford looked surprised, but, to the chagrin of the others, encouraged her to proceed.

"I'd like to know first how many people participated in this decision?"

"I'm afraid I don't understand," Stafford interrupted. Blessings repeated the question a little faster.

"What would you say, Frank?" Stafford turned toward Dr. Hines who was now bobbing his head up and down like a horse doing number tricks in a sideshow. "There must have been five or six," the Superintendent concluded after a pause.

"How long did it take?" Blessings again read from her sheet.

"I can see you are new at this," Chiang said, taking over. "If you had been following district affairs for as long as some, you would know that this is an issue we've been batting around for years. It didn't just come out of the blue." Stafford looked relieved.

Blessings persisted. "I guess I mean, how long did the decision take this time?"

"In my estimation," Stafford scratched his head in the guise of thought, "and this is only a guess, it took forty to fifty hours."

Blessings pretended to take a note, then, looking again at the page before her, "Who was involved?"

Stafford gestured toward everyone in the room.

"No one else?" Blessings asked.

"Just us," Stafford assured her jokingly.

"Let's see, then," Blessings continued, "there are five people here, and it took, you say, fifty hours, five times fifty is . . ." She hesitated. "Does anyone have a calculator?"

"Two hundred and fifty man-hours." Stafford, sitting back in his chair, seemed genuinely proud merely at the mention of such a considerable effort.

"I would like to see your documentation."

"What do you mean?" Chiang asked, perceiving that Stafford was still too pleased with himself to respond.

"I'm not exactly sure," Blessings said. "Maybe you could give me a copy of the folder there." She pointed.

"Oh, I'm afraid that would be impossible," Chiang assured her. "It's not a document that's accessible to the layman in any case."

"Layperson," Blessings corrected him. "I would still like to be able to to study anything you have on paper." She glanced at the list Zimmer had given her. "I mean like any kind of memorandum, minutes of meetings, that kind of thing." The polyester bureaucrats leaned forward in their chairs and stared at Blessings with a disbelief so total that she began to wonder what sacred taboo she had transgressed now.

"You don't seem to understand, Mrs. . . ."

"Winter," Blessings blurted. "It used to be Winter-Reed, but I don't have time to go into that."

"You don't seem to understand," Chiang replied, "that the district doesn't operate in such a formal manner."

"You mean you don't write anything down?" Blessings asked.

"We do, we do. We're all former teachers, and we write on the blackboard," Frank Hines, pointing to the wall behind Edie Conglin, offered enthusiastically. "Then there are the notes and pieces of scratch paper we throw in the trash." Chiang seemed to be glaring at him. "Uh, I'm sorry, I mean that we recycle. Someday you really ought to come back and let us tell you about the district's recycling program."

"I'm really interested in recycling," Blessings replied, "and I could put you in touch with some people who are doing some exciting recycling work. But do you mean to say that you make big decisions like this just by sitting around and talking?"

"I'm afraid so," Stafford admitted. "You must understand that we're no different than any other district in the state. Don't forget too that we're experts who've been around a long time, and we have certain feeling based on past experience."

"You mean you decide big things like this on feelings, just like me?"

"You simply don't have our experience," Stafford said. "Besides, you must understand there are certain pressures . . ." Chiang looked menacingly at the Superintendent.

"I see," Blessings avowed.

Barbara Wolfe, who could hardly contain her anxiety at the acrimonious turn the conversation had taken, tried to put things aright. "How long do we have?" she asked.

"Ron," Stafford picked up the cue, "what kind of lead time are we talking about?"

Rossman carefully studied his calendar watch. "We should plan on a time frame of not more than two weeks. We want to be able to generate a proposal for the Board by the end of January."

"Is that sufficient, ladies?" said Stafford. "Good. I'm so glad you could come in to see us, and I look forward to seeing you again, say, two weeks from today. Remember, now, if you have any questions, please don't hesitate to call. I'm glad to talk with you anytime, and that includes weekends and nights."

Blessings had been knocking for some time and was about to leave when she heard footsteps shuffling toward the door. Zimmer opened the screen. "Jeez, it's you. I was just dozing. Come on in."

"Don't you ever change your clothes?"

"Oh, so we're getting personal. What do you mean?"

"I mean it looks like you slept in your clothes, that's all."

"No, I changed back into these just for you."

She stepped into the living room which was almost as disorderly as her own and smelled of old marijuana cigarettes. Realizing her gaffe, she said, "I know what a pain doing clothes can be. I've been so busy lately that I've had a load of wet laundry sitting in the washer for a week. I just haven't found time to put it in the dryer."

"Oh, yeah, I bet that one smells good. Listen, why don't we just take our clothes off and smoke a little dope?"

"What about Karen?"

"She's away on an herbal consult. Won't be back until tomorrow morning."

"Honestly," Blessings blushed, "you men are into such power trips."

Zimmer grabbed her hand.

"Come on, Leon, I'm not into that, really I'm not."

Like a reprimanded child he pulled back. "Okay," he pouted, "what's up? Like what happened at the meeting?"

"You must promise to swear never to say a word to anyone that I told you. Do you promise?"

"Okay, okay. Christ. Did you find out who it is? The questions?"

Blessings nodded her head. "They're doing it with feelings. Glen Chiang, I think he's the one running the show even though he doesn't say much, claims there's nothing written down."

"What about the Blackstone?"

"Never came up. They've got nothing to do with it."

"Wrong. Same bunch. They all take orders from up top."

"No, really, Leon, they seem okay. I mean how can you be okay when you work at an unhealthy job in a stuffy office like that? I think they have health problems, but they seem interested in making boarding school available to everyone."

"Interested in what?"

"They've got some kind of plan. What did they call it? Something like reconsolation, or reconciliation. They're reassigning pupils, that's it, at a couple of schools. They talked so fast, and I had to work so hard to get my questions in, I couldn't really catch it all."

"Which schools?" Zimmer asked.

"Leon, come on, you can't expect me to remember specifics, not at that level at least."

"Wah, you want to play twenty questions? Did they mention East Rock? That's where my kids will be going, if I can ever get them out of diapers."

Blessings thought for a moment, then shook her head.

"Whew."

"Leon, you're so paranoid. There's nothing to worry about now that I'm working with the League. Listen, I'm late for a meeting already. Gotta run. Bye."

Before Zimmer had finished muttering "Shit, they're still out to get us," Blessings was gone.

4

ANIMAL ABUSE

■ Zimmer stood in the Café Aroma waiting for a bearded man wearing a hat made of inverted gloves to finish talking on the phone. As depressed as he had been by the meeting with McPhail and by Blessings's visit, he was now just as excited to be leading the campaign to preserve the Blackstone, which at first consisted of contacting the Adjustors. This was not easy, since each had an aide to screen visitors. Zimmer's attempts to phone them at home had fallen for the most part upon taped messages and unfulfilled promises to return the call. He would try once more in the half hour between visiting the supermarket and the opening of the bank. In his excitement he rapped on the phone booth with a dime.

"Hey, man, what's the rush?" the disheveled man in sandals snorted. Zimmer caught a glimpse of his tattered serape under an outer garment closest in texture and shape to a long coat made of fur and reeds punctured by an occasional feather. Around his neck was a choker of sharks' teeth interlaced with spoons, their curved ends flattened and spread across his chest like some ancient silversmith's rendering of the sun.

"Do you know there's a five-minute limit on calls when people are waiting?"

"Why so uptight? I'm talking to my ole lady who's about to score a lid." He slammed the door in Zimmer's face.

When he finally got into the booth, which smelled of stale smoke and breath freshener, Zimmer tried to reach Joel Steinhammer, only to fall again upon his recorded message: "Joel and Bill welcome your call with gentleness and compassion. Since they are unable to . . ."

"Too busy humping," Zimmer muttered and slammed the receiver down.

The café was jammed, but just then a bearded man with brightly dyed orange hair and a pink tank-top was gathering his things at a table near the front. It was not until he stood up that Zimmer realized the man was wearing a dress. And it was not until he drew still closer that he could see the rouge-covered cheeks that had begun to sag.

"It's all yours, sweetie," the man said as Zimmer moved in to claim the table.

Zimmer removed his sweat shirt and put it on the chair where the man's pocketbook had been. He took his place in line. As he moved closer to the cash register, on which a sign read *We Serve Only Politically Correct Red Wine,* he stared at a table of heavyset women in T-shirts, overalls, and engineer boots. Some had hammers and chains hanging from wide leather belts of the kind worn by weight lifters. Each had placed a helmet under her chair. The ladies were playing cards and chewing big wads of bubble gum.

Zimmer was surprised to find a couple seated at his table when he returned with his cappuccino. The man glared at him.

"Hope you don't mind," the woman said, "it's getting kinda crowded, y' know, and like nobody's got too much space, like y' know."

"No. I mean, okay," Zimmer replied, realizing there was not much choice. In fact, he did mind, and the more he sat beside them, the more he objected. The man wore his hair in a long braid, which had started to gray. His skin was rough and dark in a way that bespoke neither outdoor work nor sun-filled leisure, but self-abuse. He continued to stare with eyes that looked like two cigarette holes burned in an army blanket. He was missing several teeth. The woman, who had begun to rub his arm, seemed to be holding him back like a pent-up animal. The man started to slobber.

On his way out Zimmer brushed against an overweight woman dressed like a Renaissance minstrel with a billowy velvet hat and plume. She was blowing bubbles, one of which stuck, then popped, on his cheek. The crowd, which had been watching, laughed. Zimmer would have responded angrily had he been less stunned by what he saw through the Aroma's plate glass window. Gloria Martinez, aide to the President of the Board, stood talking with another woman in front of the Wild Flour Bakery. Zimmer knew that getting through to her might hold the key to influencing McPhail, but he didn't want to plead his case, or even ask for an appointment, in front of anyone else. A chance encounter like this could ruin his chances.

On this particular morning Gloria Martinez had run into the wife of one of her husband's law partners, a woman in a pink jogging suit who stood munching a whole wheat croissant. The two stood talking until the woman put down the bag, did several awkward stretches against a nearby telephone pole, then jogged off, still chewing. Zimmer, who could still feel the cool bubbles popping on his neck, emerged from the Aroma and followed Gloria until she turned the corner between the herbal bookshop and the bath boutique. Stepping into a phone booth, he made a note: "Walks to the Wild Flour on Thursdays."

Zimmer spent almost every waking hour learning what he could about the lives of Beacon's Adjustors and their aides. He took note of their comings and goings, their past histories and family situations, their passions and pet peeves, the little details of their daily lives. Zimmer made it his business to inquire into McPhail's past, his wealthy in-laws, his pioneering househusbandry, the litany of his rental woes. He interviewed the McPhails' first tenant, whom he tracked down with the help of a former real estate connection. The man who had refused to pay rent was now vice-president in charge of mutual fund sales at Socially Responsible Investment Associates. Zimmer learned all about Gloria Martinez's trust fund, her first two marriages, her and Alan's unsuccessful attempts to conceive a child, and her depression. He learned of Bernice Dever's struggle to become an accountant and even acquainted himself with some of the clients whose income taxes she prepared every spring. He knew about the accident which had left Joel Steinhammer paralyzed from the waist down and about his relationship with Bill, who was in charge of Beacon's public park system.

On the basis of such intelligence gathering Zimmer surmised a general pattern of personal instability characteristic of the Adjustors, not the least important aspect of which, he felt, was a certain betrayal of youthful progressive ideals. But there was nothing here that was of much use in the present situation. After all, just about everyone in Beacon had his or her own private failure or unrealized dream. Almost everyone had made at least one life change. Alas, Zimmer could find nothing with direct bearing upon the struggle against construction at the Blackstone.

On days when he was not on any particular track Zimmer loitered in the park across from City Hall. Walking around the block, moving from bench to bench, hiding behind the pigeon-stained statue of Ho Chi Minh, he registered the movements of the enemy, hoping to catch a glimpse of Truscott executives on their way to perform some act of wild corporate corruption. Instead, he saw nothing even slightly suspicious and only an occasional familiar face. He knew the schedules of many of the regulars who had dealings with the city. Walter Carroll visited the Beacon Clerk in the early afternoon to pick up the press packets for various public meetings and to research articles for *Groundroots*. Tucker, who arrived early, came out of the building at 11 A.M. to visit a friend at the local newspaper office. He always returned with lunch in a paper bag and on most days would repeat the routine before supper. The Chief, who entered through the rear door, was never at work before early afternoon and would leave in his official car before anyone else.

Zimmer spent a good deal of time on the phone talking to those who had known the Adjustors in some previous incarnation or were simply friends of a friend, anyone who might throw light upon the thinking that would go into the decision on the Blackstone. At other times he stalked the Adjustors whose activities were not nearly so predictable as those working at City Hall. He depended upon chance sightings in the course of his spot-checks of their homes, and on their rare appearances at publicly announced meetings.

On one such occasion Zimmer called upon Blessings. Keri had a cold, the weatherman had predicted rain. The solicitous father was reluctant to take children to a gathering that might require rapid movement and thus risk losing them in the crowd. Blessings, who objected at first, gave in once he disclosed the importance of his mission. The Down With Animal Abuse rally slated for that noon was sure to draw a number of Board members because the Chief was slated to be the final speaker.

By the time Zimmer arrived at Bountiful Plaza a crowd had gathered in the open area between the falafel vendors and the fountain where several dogs were alternately swimming and shaking themselves off on the students sitting along its outer rim. Behind them a small band of men and women with shaved heads and long orange robes were chanting and jumping up and down. Between thumb and fingers they clapped little cymbals to mark the rhythm of their ecstatic dance. Several women stood on the side with children who, except for sucking their thumbs and an occasional glimpse of a disposable diaper beneath the orange robes, were the miniatures of their parents. Two of their fellows of indeterminate sex stood in front of a large plastic garbage can from which they dispensed to any passerby brave enough to grasp an extended paper plate divine food, a yellowish curdled substance resembling scrambled eggs mixed with curried croutons.

"Christ," Zimmer thought, "you would have to put me in a trance before I would touch that shit." All around incense curled into the air from slim sticks burning on the pavement.

At the far end of the plaza rows of tables occupied by people of various religious and political beliefs formed an almost ceremonial corridor in front of Founders' Gate. Students and street people could be seen arguing, as they did every weekday at noon. The lines of people circulating back and forth between the hopping Buddha dancers and the archway leading back to offices and classrooms seemed oblivious to the presence of some of the most illustrious members of the animal rights community. All around signs were being waved attesting to the conviction that mankind is responsible for centuries of abuse of species other than its own: *Stop the Torture Now, End Factory Farming, Zoos are Prisons, No More Fur, Lab Animals Never Have a Nice Day, Join the Veal Vigil, Support the Bronx Zoo 5, Animal Labs are the University's Auschwitz.* To the left, tacked high on a tree, one could still read *Off the Pigs,* a sign clearly left over from another demonstration.

Michael Bridgeman, president of the Beacon Animal Rights Coalition, seized the microphone. "We have a very exciting and full schedule this afternoon. It is a privilege, a real privilege, to introduce our first speaker, Dr. Edward Keyser, former campus veterinarian and now head of the Pavlov Brigade, who will speak about his experiences in animal labs."

A small man with a red kerchief around his neck stepped to the podium. Dr. Keyser, who had been fired because of a scandal having to do with the falsification of research data, spoke with the righteousness of a lawyer defending himself against the charge of bribing judges. "My fellow human beings—and I use the phrase with shame because of the inhumanities we inflict upon our fellow beings—try to imagine, if you can, the following. A helpless, six-week-old chimpanzee is taken from his or her mother. He or she is imprisoned in a dirty cage which is never, I repeat, never, cleaned. Then he or she is released only long enough to travel to the surgical table where he or she is strapped down and anesthetized. His or her skull is opened and electrodes, painful electrodes are inserted into the brain. The animal's head is held in place by braces which are more instruments of torture than scientific tools. He or she is prevented from sleeping, defecates on him or herself, and dies a slow death at the hands of his or her oppressors. And why? So that some biology student can get a Ph.D., or some professor with a high salary can publish another article. Ladies and gentlemen, we are all responsible for the animal death camps in our own backyard. Yes, the buildings and sheds where the merciless slaughter takes place are just to the east of where we are standing right now."

Bridgeman informed Dr. Keyser that his time was up and again took his place on the steps of University Hall. "We are privileged to have with us today," he said, "world-famous antispeciest, Tank

Mountainfire, founder of the Bloodroot Café and president of Mothers Against Sexual Hassle."

Zimmer had heard of Mash, the group responsible for ferreting out cases of sexual harassment among the university's notoriously lecherous faculty.

Tank took the microphone by its stand and thrust it between her legs like a weapon.

"My topic for today is hunting and rape," she announced to thunderous applause. Her fellow Mashers were stomping their booted feet and whistling, straight fingers in their mouths. "Hunting is a sport. The animal killed is literally a 'game.' But the hunt has sexual trappings as well. We are told 'she wanted it,' 'she lured him into it,' 'she captured his heart.' The same story is told of animals: they are overpopulated and must be killed for their own good. And as long as we're on the topic, I want to say a few words about rodeos. Like pornography or the circus, the rodeo is viewed as an innocent form of amusement. Pornography enacts the ritual domination of women, and the brutalization of rodeo animals celebrates the acts of violence out of which our country was born. I'm talking about the taming of the Wild West. All the tools of sadism are on display: whips, spurs, brands, the tying and binding. People who would never dream of paying someone to beat their dog or cat pay to see grown men torment horses and steers. The cowboy is a sadist in disguise. And if I have time, I would like to say just one final word about prostitution and supermarkets." She looked at Bridgeman who pointed to his watch.

"Okay, it'll be quick. In patriarchal society, both women and animals are consumed as flesh. Men buy women's flesh in pornographic magazines, sex shows, and houses of prostitution. The dead bodies of animals are bought from supermarket shelves. Men are predators in pursuit of edible female flesh—a chick, a bird, beaver, pussy, a piece of ass. Women are treated like animals, like dogs, and we at Mash are here to put an end to that."

As she stepped away from the speaker's podium an honor guard of heavyset women resembling Tank—except for the fact that some had orange hair and many had oversized safety pins in their ears—formed a ring around her. A few hecklers, no doubt fraternity boys, made chimpanzeelike sounds on either side. Suddenly, one of the women carrying a chain yelled with a voice that needed no microphone, "You'd better crawl back to your animal house or wherever you came from." The honor guard of Mash escorted their cherished leader to a row of waiting motorcycles which could be heard roaring off in the distance as Bridgeman again took control.

"Now that we have heard the voices of science and gender, we've reached that part in our program reserved for a more spiritual perspective."

Tank Mountainfire was followed by none other than Bobo Dam Dass, who was presented in his incarnation as the head of Buddhists Concerned for Animals.

"There are vital energies in every living being," the orange-robed spiritual master assured his listeners. "These energies merely take a different form within each of us. This means that we must all work to recognize that the difference between man and the other species is accidental, insignificant. When we abuse an animal, we abuse ourselves. Besides," he cautioned, "we are all reincarnated many times, and any one of us might come back next time as the baby chimpanzee or the rodeo animal that we've heard about this afternoon. I want everyone to think about this the next time you even think of taking your children to the circus or eating meat. It could be you or someone you love." Bobo Dam Dass returned to his seat, folded his legs under his robe, and began to rock back and forth.

Bridgeman announced in a tone of high seriousness that the Chief of Beacon, a supporter of Animal Rights from the beginning, would say a few words. Horton, wearing a Mao hat and dark glasses, stepped to the podium. Eric Tucker, like a ventriloquist, stood not ten feet behind.

"My fellow citizens, first off, I'd like to thank you for inviting me out here today. Like our host said, I was in on the ground floor of animal abuse, there from the first. And that's because, as you've heard, there is no difference between America's war on animals and its oppression of people. America's zoos are animal prisons. The torture in our animal labs is just a domestic version of what this country is doing in Central America and in the Middle East. I'm not going to speak long, but I just want to say this: we broke the sound barrier, we sent a man into space, even to the moon. Now it's time to break the species barrier. I want you to know that I'm with you one hundred percent. As Chief of Beacon, I'll do all I can to fight for freedom wherever there's oppression." There were loud cheers. The animals had clearly won the day.

As the crowd on Bountiful Plaza dissolved, Bridgeman pleaded for everyone to boycott fur and to observe antiveal week. Zimmer profited from the chaos to move closer to Horton, who was shaking hands with his animalist hosts. The Board members and their aides were quickly surrounded by solicitous citizens. Gloria Martinez listened inattentively, trying to keep an eye on Eric Tucker.

Finally, she could stand it no longer. She excused herself and caught up with Tucker in front of the University Art Museum. There they agreed to rendezvous at her house later that afternoon.

The purchase of the enormous house on Lincoln Street had been a great source of tension for Gloria Martinez and her husband, Alan Modell. They had argued bitterly when the opportunity presented itself to acquire the palatial Georgian from an estate that Alan was handling. Gloria could not understand how anyone could possibly want to live in a home which, even by the standards of Beacon's prosperous northside, seemed to dominate the entire neighborhood. She maintained that it would be considered too upper middle class by her friends in the Progressive Action Party. She wanted one day to be an Adjustor and feared that a mansion might hurt her chances of getting on the Board.

"Nonsense," Alan responded, "just think of all the parties you will be able to give for the Party. Why you could turn our home into a center for fund-raising. It's the perfect place to organize. There's plenty of room for an office of your own. Besides, this part of town has produced more than its share of Beacon's politicians. Chief Bradley used to live somewhere around here, and Assemblyman Peterson is from right down the street."

"I hear you," she responded, "but what you really mean is that this house suits all your lawyer friends."

"Now wait a minute, just a minute. If what you call my lawyer friends had not contributed to your pet causes, we wouldn't be standing here talking about what the voters think is too big or too small for the Martinez-Modells."

"It's in terrible shape," she pointed out in a desperate attempt to make him change his mind.

"But it's a grand old place. We could fix it up, taking our time, of course. And we're lucky, we've got the money. Why not take advantage of it? Lots of partners have bought older homes and know the best workers around."

"Oh no, just a minute. I don't care if every lawyer in town has bought a white elephant and restored it, I'm not going that route. I don't want this wreck in the first place, but I'll be damned if I'll let your right-wing friends dictate who works on my house."

"Just because people you don't like breathe, that's no reason to stop breathing. Listen, if you're so concerned, why don't you take care of it yourself?"

The Martinez-Modells bought the mansion on Lincoln Street, but the quarrel did not end there. Gloria, convinced that Alan had outsmarted her, deliberately delayed taking care of even the most basic structural work. His gentle encouragement had no effect. Late one evening, however, after a particularly tedious Board meeting, her defenses were down when she overheard Horton taunting McPhail about fixing up his basement. She empathized with his embarrassment; and, knowing that the Head Adjustor would only hire the most appropriate tradespeople, she inquired discreetly once the room had cleared.

"He's really terrific," McPhail assured his aide, whispering as if they were still discussing some important piece of Board business. "The big companies are all such rip-offs. We looked the longest time, but it was worth the wait. The company's small, but they're independent and one hundred percent correct." That was all Gloria needed to hear.

Moses Reed, having repaired the damage to McPhail's foundation and retiled his tub so that Katy Dawson could bathe her children, passed into the service of Gloria Martinez and Alan Modell, whose sagging foundation and frame were filled with dry-rot and bugs. Not only was fumigation a foregone conclusion, but the entire house had to be raised by means of an intricate system of braces and pneumatic jacks.

Reed had not been at the Martinez-Modells for more than a week, when Gloria received Eric Tucker. She was not exactly unaware of the exterminator's presence in the shallow dusty space below the living quarters, but she was still dizzy with excitement from the noon rally when Tucker arrived.

Opening the door, the still attractive woman with long strawberry blond hair, full red-glossed lips, and sensual skin that had begun to wrinkle only slightly about the mouth and eyes, pulled Eric Tucker inside and in the same motion locked the double bolt. "I thought you would never get here. I waited and waited. What took so long?" whispered Gloria Martinez, who was dressed in a knee-length pink kimono with a bird of paradise on the back.

"The boys in City Hall slapped a meeting on me at the last minute. Anyway, here I am, and that's what counts, isn't it? You know I'm worth the wait." Suddenly Gloria grew quiet and put a finger to pursed lips.

"What's with you?" Tucker asked.

"There's someone working under the house, so let's go upstairs."

Tiptoeing up the broad wooden steps of the central staircase, the two aides turned into the guest room where they began what would have been just another of their occasional encounters were it not for the heating vent that transmitted, yea, that amplified, their bizarre carryings-on.

Just as suddenly as Gloria had grown silent she began ferociously hugging Tucker who had not yet taken off his coat. "Hey, what you doing, baby, clawing all around like you're looking for something I maybe got and maybe don't. Quit that scratching."

"But you promised."

"Maybe I did. But you know nothing comes easy. You're gonna have to work."

"Come on Eric, don't be mean. I've been waiting so long," she pleaded.

"Now hold on just a sec, wait right here, cause first, baby, you're gonna eat a little dirt."

"God, I love it, I just love it when you talk like that." She began feeling his pants, front and back, as though she were patting dry someone who also happened to be fully clothed.

"I know you do, but like I say, you're gonna get down in the dirt for this one, cause, bitch, I'm gonna do you like a dog. So you get down on all fours and start panting, and I'll be ready in a jiff."

Gloria quickly took off her kimono and lowered herself on hands and knees. Tucker removed his clothes. Positioning himself behind, he penetrated her from the rear. She began to moan as he grabbed her no longer trim hips. They moved rhythmically for a short while.

What was going on in the second floor bedroom resonated throughout the ventilation system of the still half empty house like the echo chamber of some medieval castle.

"Okay, bitch, now I want you to bark."

Gloria let out a little whimper.

"Shit, I know you can do better than that. You sound like some tiny poodle with a fancy haircut and a bow on its neck. I said bark!" And he thrust so hard from behind that she let out a scream.

"Good, that's better. Now start scratching the dirt like you're looking for a bone." She began to bark louder, and, as Tucker reached the paroxysm of his own pleasure, she was still scratching the thick pile of newly laid carpet with her painted nails. Spent, he withdrew and lay at her side. She moved to place her head on his still heaving chest. After some time she began to rub his arm with the back of her fingers.

"Cut it out," he protested.

She kept on caressing.

"Okay, if you're gonna have it your way, hand me that fancy belt of yours. We're gonna put you on a leash." Gloria was anxious to please the man who was not only responsible for her exalted position as aide to Head Adjustor McPhail but whom she also loved. She reached up on the bed and removed the sash of her kimono which she handed obediently to Tucker. He tied it around her neck.

Tucker patted Gloria. "Now we're going for a little walk." He led her in circles around the room. Red blotches, the traces of rug burns, appeared on her knees. "Come on, Eric," she pleaded, "it's really starting to hurt. Besides, it's making marks that Alan will see."

"That's what you're all up tight about, huh?"

"I'd like to leave him out of it, if you don't mind. Remember what we agreed."

"Then I want to hear you say it up front—that no one, not even that fancy lawyer husband of yours does it like Eric Tucker, cause he runs this town."

"It's true, Eric, it's true. Oh, it's so true."

Gloria repeated his words, then, exhausted, fell to the floor. Half leading, half dragging, Tucker pulled her toward the closet where he tied the end of the sash to the doorknob.

Tucker dressed while Gloria watched adoringly.

"Oh, Eric," she said, "I wish it could last forever."

"That was good enough for now," he said, reaching into the pocket of his jacket and then throwing in her direction a package about the size of a vial of perfume. "Here's the nose candy you ordered."

The embarrassed exterminator knew what it was like to work under the houses of people who, once he had disappeared into the basement, forgot about him altogether. He was used to the routine dramas of family life and on occasion had even been the aural witness of more painful scenes of domestic violence. This was not the first time he had witnessed lovemaking nor had sustained the embarrassment of adultery. Yet nothing he had ever heard matched the bestial antics of Gloria and Tucker.

Reed tried shifting the locus of his scraping and sawing to some less audible place in the cellar. He made several trips on all fours dragging behind the screws and pods of jacks, the levels and shims that he would need to prop up a badly sagging rear wall. On one such venture he was startled by something moving suddenly in his path. Retrieving the flashlight from his overalls pocket, he pointed its beam in the direction of the movement only to see a rat disappear under what must have been a hole in the sheeting of the first floor.

Once he had deposited his tools where he would begin anew, Moses took a deep breath. He smelled something unpleasant. At first he thought it was simply earth and rotten wood which, when wet, can give off a rancid odor. Shining his light again, Reed noticed that the Martinez-Modell's main sewage line which passed no further than a yard from his feet was ever so slightly cracked. A stinky puddle, white and crusted around the edges, had seeped into the surrounding dirt.

A few minutes later the toilet flushed. Reed could see the moist patch swell like an engorged sponge. "The folks upstairs may run this town," he thought, "but they still shit like everyone else, and they don't give a whiz about who's sitting in the dung."

Except for the maps of Central America on the walls alongside several brightly colored serapes and a sombrero that was coming unraveled along its edges, the El Pueblo Bar, Restaurant, and Cultural Center might have been any of the chic upscale establishments of Beacon's gourmet ghetto. Mariachi music came from the bar which was surrounded by cane stools. Posters supporting causes of every kind were tacked so thickly around the door that the official bulletin board reserved for announcements resembled a mattress held together with tacks.

Tucker recognized the waitress, a good-looking woman named Terri Kantor. Her long, stringy hair cascaded in all directions over her thin peasant blouse. She wore a small guitar earring in one ear and a compass in the other.

Tucker told her that he was waiting for friends and that they would be having beer.

"Oh," Terri replied, "then you should know that the El Pueblo has the largest selection of Third World beers in all Beacon Land."

Tucker's guests took their places and, after some consultation, ordered one Cuban, one mainland Chinese, and one Albanian light.

Martin Wasserman, a balding, pudgy man who had attended a small nursing school in the Midwest, had worked in convalescent homes before going back to complete a degree in geriatric psychology. He had drifted up and down the coast, finally settling in Beacon where he ran first a series of self-help seminars in personality improvement, then had opened the area's first adultery rehabilitation clinic, which had succeeded until mounting pressure from the licensed psychotherapy community and rumors that Wasserman had himself never been married forced its closure. It was then that Wasserman, in need of another livelihood, turned to the members of the Progressive Action Party whom he had met in the course of his adultery work and who, after that November's election, were in a position to be of assistance.

Wasserman quickly became the Party's expert in psychological matters. He handled delicate negotiations and even advised the higher-ups when it came to convincing those who might think about straying from the Party of the virtues of team spirit. Because of his experience with the convalescent, they placed him at the Helen Keller Center for Special Living. There Wasserman both lived and kept an eye on the other residents, pushing them when necessary toward what he referred to tactfully as "small displays of civic duty," which consisted mostly of getting them to appear at large public meetings. As of late Wasserman had taken on a number of delicate assignments.

For such complicated jobs he usually took along Howard Greer, a small, bleary-eyed black man whose chronic drinking problem had facilitated his recruitment into the Party which, as in the case of Wasserman, allowed him to live in one of its safe houses.

"What's happening, boss?" the pudgy Wasserman asked as soon as Terri arrived with their order.

"Gentlemen, there are some important things about to happen in the city, and the Chief and I would like to see them go through without any hitches."

"What kind of things?" Wasserman asked.

"What kind of hitches?" Greer echoed.

"Fellows, there's no secret and not much to tell. A respectable company with backing wants to build downtown, and we are kindly disposed to the project. There are, however, a few neighbors who are trying to do all they can to block it. We would like to avoid trouble, if you know what I mean."

"Uh, not exactly," Wasserman muttered.

"Come on, Marty, you're a bright boy. Look, these people call themselves . . . Shit, I don't know what, they change their name so often. Neighborhood activists, community organizers. They think they're progressives, liberals, with a dose of ecological bullshit thrown in just for fun."

Greer laughed.

"One thing's for sure. They start to whine like babies whenever anyone wants to touch their little half acre, unless it's for a nature park with underground garage, no chemicals on the lawn, and biodegradable playgrounds for all their little brats. So, it'd be helpful if you could round up some of the right kind of people to speak at the Board of Adjustments next Wednesday night."

"Like who?" Greer asked.

"Well, you might think about arranging a good minority turnout for starters, paid guests, of course."

"Just say the word. Streetwise, hardcore probationers, fly guys?"

"The mix is up to you, Howie. But remember, twenty, and no more than fifteen bucks apiece. Understand?"

"You got it," Greer said.

"Marty, do you think you could bring a few friendly faces from the Center? Some handicapped support might come in real handy. Don't worry, we'll supply transportation and soft drinks."

"We don't use the word *handicapped.* The residents of the Keller are *other-abled* or *specially challenged.*"

"Okay, but let's not have too many with the bad speech like last time. People will think we're running a freak show. Besides, they have no sense of time. McPhail, bless his heart, can't keep 'em to the limit. And if you could get grandma, that'd be terrific. She's my favorite."

"I'll do my best," Wasserman promised. "How about some money for my people? You know costs . . ."

"What costs? They already live at our expense, and you do too. Don't forget it. The least you all can do is to show a little gratitude. Or, look at it this way, we're providing a night's entertainment for people who don't get around much anymore. You're running an other-abled escort service."

"All right," said Wasserman, shifting his eyes toward Howard Greer.

"Good. Oh, I almost forgot. There may be some talk about children Wednesday night. We could use a little support there too."

"What do we know about children?" Wasserman asked.

"Doesn't matter. We'll have people there. Take your cue."

Wasserman and Greer finished their drinks and left.

Tucker asked Terri Kantor for the check.

5

THE PROFESSOR

■ Linda Elson, hair wet and still in her robe, struggled to fasten the pants of a wiggling child. The legs made of four rows of snaps kept coming apart as she at first misaligned one side and then the other. "Goddammit, Dylan, why aren't you doing this while I get ready?"

"Because I've dressed Alex three times this week, and Rachel's only done it twice," the robust preteen said.

"So what? You should be willing to help while your father's away. Besides, I can't stand all the counting. Is Rachel up and dressed?"

"I'm sure she is, and I'm sure she'll beat me to the good cereals too."

"For Christ's sake. If there's a cereal you both like in the variety pack, let's buy the big box." A dog scratched at the front door. "Let Nietzsche in, will you?"

"Why do I always have to do it?"

"Just do it," Linda Elson shouted. Dylan stormed out of the bathroom and stomped down the staircase of the Elsons' large house whose dark redwood paneling gave it a warmth that forgave its ill-defined spaces.

Linda stuffed Alex's legs into an infant seat attached to the round kitchen table. She cut a banana in small parts and placed them before the screaming child. Dylan returned and, at the stove, proceeded to spoon and spill pancake batter onto the grill, the butcher block counter, and down the crack in between.

"Be careful, will you?"

"I'm doing my best. I do this every morning, and Rachel isn't even downstairs."

"Is she still asleep?"

"Probably."

Linda raced through the laundry room and yelled up the back stairs. "Time to get up, fast. It's late. The bus will be here in twenty minutes."

"Okay, okay," a child moaned. "I'm tired, I hope you know."

Back in the kitchen the pancakes were now smoking on the grill. "Turn that down, will you?" Dylan, who had forgotten about them, shoved a spoonful of yogurt in Alex's mouth. "I'll take over now. You watch the stove."

Rachel, a slender ten-year-old with long brown hair and braces, pushed the swinging door. "Good God," Linda said, "you're not dressed, and don't forget to comb your hair. Go on now, get the brush and hurry."

"Here." Rachel shoved a piece of mimeographed paper toward her mother. "Sign this."

"What?" She read the reminder to the parents of children at Audubon School that there would be no classes next Wednesday in observance of International Women's Day. "Christ! That's just great."

Dylan flipped three charred pancakes onto a plate and looked up. "What now?"

"Nothing, just get breakfast on the table."

"Come on, I want to know."

"It's just that I forgot school's closed next Wednesday for Women's Day."

"What's wrong with that?"

Linda laughed. "Nothing. It's just that women have struggled hard for equal rights in the workplace, and to celebrate it, they make us scramble for day care so we won't lose our jobs. It seems like they take a day off every week."

"What's wrong with that? We can take care of ourselves."

"I don't like the idea. Now, eat quickly and collect your stuff."

"I can't find my backpack," Rachel whined.

"Where did you put it?"

"I don't know. If I did, I wouldn't be looking for it," the half-asleep child snapped.

Linda darted upstairs, returning with the tattered purple bag in one hand, her own straw pocketbook, manila folders protruding from the top, in the other. "It was under the pile of junk on your floor. If you would just put it in the same place at night, we wouldn't go through this every morning. Never mind. Now, where do you two want to go on Wednesday? I'll call today." Without answering, the older children, alerted by the roar of a bus down the street, scrambled for the book bags lying on the kitchen floor.

Linda turned to see Alex climb out of the infant seat and across the table where, knees and elbows in a trail of buttery syrup, he was stuffing the rest of her burnt pancake into his mouth. She picked up the sticky infant and wiped his hands and face. "Come on, let's go upstairs. Mommy has to finish drying her hair."

Linda Elson double-parked near the corner of Luxemburg and Rose. Running around the car, she lifted Alex from his car seat and headed toward the rear of the brightly painted clapboard house. There she handed Alex to Terri Kantor who, when she wasn't working at El Pueblo, ran Wonderland Day Care. In fact, when Blessings Winter closed Nature's Child many of the parents switched to Wonderland, which also meant a shift from early ecological education to Latin-American cultural enrichment.

Terri took the wiggling two-year-old in her arms. She wrestled its mouth up to her own and, closing her eyes, took a deep breath. "Uh, oh," she said with a singsong, "what did we have for breakfast this morning? We've been cheating, haven't we?"

Linda, embarrassed, tried to explain. "We were in an incredible rush, and the batter was already made when I got downstairs. You know Norman is away, and what with trying to get everyone dressed, fed, and the lunches made."

"I definitely smell the telltale signs of maple syrup," Terri interrupted. "You know how hyper sugar makes the children. You may go off to work, but we bear the consequences."

"I know, I know, but they love it, and it's . . ."

"It's a disaster. I see I'm going to have to agenda maple syrup for the next parents' meeting. In the meantime, please, please, try to give Alex something more nourishing in the morning, something that will not make him so wild and maybe even scar him for life. He hasn't been playing with transformers, has he?"

"With what?"

"You know, transformers, action toys that turn from warlike machines into macho-type monsters. They tend to excite children just like syrup and give them bad male images. Our society would not be so violent if . . ."

"Look, I'm in a big hurry. Could we discuss this later, or like you say, agenda it for the parents' meeting? I've really got to get to work." Linda did not want to offend the woman to whom she was about to entrust her youngest child.

"Sure. I really didn't mean to guilt trip you or anything, but you know how careful we must be." Several children pulled at Terri's long Panamanian skirt.

Linda, who felt like a contract murderer late for a hastily planned crime, took advantage of the distraction. She kissed Alex, whose body did exude a sweetish odor, and found herself back in the car turning off the hazard lights before realizing that she had forgotten to tell Terri she would be picking up Alex early. "Shit," she thought to herself, "that cucaracha brought up early pickups and late arrivals at the last parents' meeting. You'd think they were going somewhere. I'll call later."

By the time Linda sat down at her desk in the basement of Sisters Hospital a pile of phone messages had already accumulated. Two doctors' offices had called about test results, a woman wanted information about the effects of secondary smoke on her eleven month old, the suspicious husband of a couple Linda had seen the previous week called to inquire confidentially if there were any way of telling from amniotic fluid if his wife were carrying another man's child. A slip marked *Urgent* left no other message than that someone should call as soon as possible. Linda dialed the unfamiliar number, and, after some hesitation, a young woman who identified herself simply as Sunrise revealed hesitantly that she was about to end her pregnancy by drinking a mixture of mushrooms and herbs.

"You've done just the right thing by calling here," Linda assured her, "but please don't take anything. You could do yourself real harm. Now give me your address, and I'll be there in half an hour."

Sunrise, a flower child of eighteen, lived in a large house which had in its time served as the headquarters of one of Beacon's most famous communal living groups. When, in fact, *Newsweek* magazine had ventured a major piece on alternative lifestyles of the sixties it was to the Lhasa Commune that the journalists turned. Bobo Dam Dass, before founding the Dharma, had even resided within the now decaying structure whose walls showed traces of a brighter past in the writing and faded psychedelic colors which still could be seen on the surface of the badly peeling paint.

Linda pushed through a beaded curtain into the shabby room strewn with pillows. There was a distinct smell of incense mixed with odors of various exotic foods and dirty clothes. Two walls were covered with faded Indian printed cloth tacked at frayed corners, while the other two were bare except for a monochrome picture of what must have been their spiritual leader, ears protruding like question marks on either side of his glistening shaved head. The hardwood floor, no doubt once covered with carpets, was pitted by burn holes and stains. The girl was sitting on madras bedding that looked like it had not been changed in years.

"Tell me if you can what's going on." Linda took off her heavy felt cape.

"I'm scared, I know I shouldn't be talking to you." The girl seemed frail and was extremely pale.

"Scared of what?"

"Well, if my polarity person, you know, ever found out I was talking to anyone from a hospital, like . . . he's like away this morning. I'm pregnant, and like I can't handle a kid. I'm really scared." She began to cry.

"And so you were thinking of terminating?" Linda asked.

"Of what?"

"Of terminating. It's a nice way of saying abortion."

"Right. My polarity person, like his name is Rex, took me to a woman who he said knew about women's things. She gave me this to drink." Sunrise held out a small mustard jar filled with a greenish oily mixture. Linda unscrewed the top and could detect a strong paint-like odor without even raising it to her nose.

"Listen," Linda said, "I'm really glad you called. It's hard to tell what's in here, and I would hate for you to swallow something that might harm you." She slipped the jar discreetly into her purse. "Now, let's see, can you tell me how pregnant you are?"

Sunshine sobbed and nodded that no, she couldn't.

"We can calculate, if you like." Linda withdrew a small round calendar from where she had placed the jar. "Let's see, when was your last period?"

Sunrise sobbed harder. "I don't know, like I'm real irregular. Sometimes it comes and sometimes it doesn't. But I never thought I would get pregnant. Rex promised I wouldn't. He said it wasn't in my chart. Oh, I'm scared."

"Your chart?" Linda asked.

"Rex did my stars. He told me an Aquarius couldn't get pregnant by a Cancer, that's him, when the moon was in Gemini. Oh, he's going to be so mad, he'd just kill me if he found you here."

"Don't worry, we're not going to let that happen." Linda felt as though she was comforting one of her own children and for an instant regretted having yelled at them over breakfast. "But this is a big decision. Are you absolutely sure you don't want to have a baby?"

The frightened teenager shook her head.

"Well, then, either we can arrange for you to terminate safely at a hospital, or, if you were willing just to go through with the pregnancy, we could arrange to have the baby raised by someone else. You know there are lots of parents who can't have children and who would take very good care of your child." Linda put her arms around Sunrise who was now shaking. She held her for some time until, glancing at her watch, she decided it was time to leave. Writing down her number, Linda made Sunrise promise not to do anything without calling her first.

Linda dashed back to Sisters. She picked up the charts lying on the counter in the ultrasound room, but before she could read the name on the top file, a pregnant woman in a grayish hospital gown, standing with arms folded and legs spread by the dressing room curtain, reminded everyone that it was her turn.

"On deck," one of the nurses whispered.

Sheila Singer had decided, as she had told Linda during their counseling session the previous week, that her body was up against the biological clock, and it was time to have a baby.

"What does your husband think?" Linda asked.

"Oh, I'm not married," Sheila replied.

"Then what does your partner think. Babies are a lot of trouble, you know. It's easier when there are two to share the burden."

"That's so middle class," Sheila retorted sharply. "Most men are such babies anyway. A husband or whatever you call it, a partner, would just be one more child to take care of. It'd be like having twins." She giggled.

"I'm sorry, but I have to ask this for the family history that is part of genetic counseling. Will the biological father be involved?" Sheila said nothing.

"Do you know the father?" Linda pursued.

Sheila moved her head in such a way that Linda couldn't tell whether she meant yes or no.

"Can I ask if this is a multiple partner pregnancy? Are there several possibilities?"

Sheila continued shaking her head from side to side. "Actually," she volunteered after a brief pause, "it was Tank."

"I beg your pardon."

"Tank Mountainfire is my partner. She'll be coming with me to the amnio."

"But she's not the father," Linda pursued.

"Not what you call the biological father, though she did make me pregnant."

"I'm afraid I don't understand."

"You see, she did it. We got the sperm from Lifebank."

"I see." Linda wrote on the chart "artificial insemination, Beacon Feminist Women's Health Collective."

"Did you select the Erickson option?"

"Tank used a turkey baster. It was fantastic sex."

"Maybe I'm not making myself clear. You know many people involved in same sex pregnancies these days are choosing to eliminate male from female sperm, and I just thought . . ."

"Oh that," Sheila smiled proudly, "of course. Tank and I wouldn't know what to do with a boy. We're having a little girl named Bette if you want to put that on your chart."

On this, the day of her amniocentesis, Sheila Singer was accompanied by a stocky woman in striped overalls and a T-shirt reading *A Woman's Place Is Anyplace,* whom she presented as Tank Mountainfire, her patient advocate. Tank's purple spiked hairdo glowed like an old-fashioned nickelodeon under the fluorescent lights.

"I don't really think you'll need an advocate," one of the nurses said. "The procedure is not all that threatening."

"I consider any handling of my body by the medical establishment to be a hostile intervention, a form of rape. That's why I've brought a support person with me." Sheila turned toward Tank who placed a hand on each of her shoulders and began to rub her neck. "Besides," she continued, "sticking a big needle into the serenity of my pregnant uterus is unnatural, and I want to be surrounded by people I love and who care for me."

"It may be unnatural," the nurse said firmly, "but if you really wanted to be one hundred percent totally natural, you would not have come here today for the test. You would have risked having an abnormal child, which at your age is a real possibility. That's nature's way. It's not too late to back out if you like."

"No, no, go ahead, but I want Tank with me through the whole ordeal."

"That's fine." Linda, anxious to avoid an argument, took over. "Let me describe the procedure to you. First the physician will locate the fetus by ultrasound. You'll actually be able to see a picture of your baby on the screen."

"What's the radiation level?" Tank interrupted.

"There is no radiation," Linda replied.

"Oh, no, you can't pull that one on us. I know better than that."

"Honestly, there is no radiation. The picture works by sound, by sound waves, and there's no evidence of risk," Linda assured Tank who was by now rubbing Sheila's large belly.

"Let's continue. The physician will press a drinking straw on your abdomen to make a mark where he will place the needle."

"Wait, wait, stop right there, my God." Tank folded her arms and turned toward Linda and the nurses. "Aren't there any women physicians on the staff? Speaking for Sheila, who is under heavy emotional stress right now, I would really prefer someone more in touch with women's bodies. I'm sorry we didn't think of it before, but I really must insist."

"I'm afraid there are only men. The doctor performing amnios today is Dr. Abrams. If you would like to discontinue the procedure then we can stop now."

Tank folded her beefy arms, spread her legs, puffed up her cheeks and glared.

"Okay, once he has located the fetus, Dr. Abrams will insert the needle and draw two tubes of fluid. You shouldn't feel much, and the whole procedure usually doesn't take more than five minutes. I must ask you, though, to let us know if you feel anything unusual like contractions in the next few days."

Sheila Singer had ceased listening. Tank had slipped over her head a pair of foam-rubber earphones which she withdrew from one of her large overalls pockets. "The first side is whales," she whispered to Sheila as the three women moved into the sonography room lit only by a diffused dim bulb in the ceiling and the flickering of luminescent screens. Tank carried the recorder attached to Sheila's ears like a plasma bottle above a moving emergency stretcher.

The ultrasound technician rubbed a cuplike device over Sheila's pregnant belly, now more pronounced as the rest of her body sank to either side. Looking at the screen, she narrowed the circling motions of the cup until slowly it came to rest upon the outline of a fetus which appeared on the screen like the grainy quadrant of a coarsely cut phonograph record lit dramatically from the thin edge. "All set," she announced. Dr. Abrams, who had, in fact, overheard the conversation between Tank and the nurses, stepped into the room and gazed at Sheila, who, lying on the table, resembled a porpoise with earphones. He moved toward the screen, looking all the while at the streaky visual display.

"What's that little circle?" Tank asked.

"That's the baby's head. It's big, isn't it?" Dr. Abrams said. "But you know what they say—like mother like daughter." Linda and the technician laughed. Sheila, lulled by the lapping of waves, did not notice.

"Dr. Abrams likes to joke," Linda interjected. "You get used to it after a while."

"That was not one bit funny," Tank snapped. "If you think this whole ordeal is a positive experience, you are wrong. I'm here to protect Sheila, so let's cut the sexist patriarchal remarks and get on with the bodily invasion. That's hard enough. One more like that, and we sue for malpractice."

Dr. Abrams made a couple of indentations on Sheila's swollen belly. Without looking, he extended one hand to receive the sterile needle while with the other he rubbed iodine over the marks. Then, without further ado, he plunged the long needle a good three inches into her stomach. Sheila suddenly jerked, as if she were ascending from the bottom of the sea. She let out a loud whimper and began to wriggle. "Steady now," Dr. Abrams insisted, "we don't want to hit the little genius in your womb now, do we?"

"That's it!" Tank walked menacingly toward the intensely concentrated physician. The nurse who had been holding an empty test tube ready for the second vial of fluid stepped between them.

"Calm, calm, ladies. Let's not get excited," Dr. Abrams urged. "It'll all be over in a jiff." Sheila settled back into the world of underwater mammals. In a matter of seconds, Dr. Abrams removed the filled tube. A little brownish liquid spurted from the top of the needle, which he quickly capped.

The sight of the amniotic fluid startled Tank. She turned away and moaned weakly. Losing consciousness, she slipped heavily to the floor, more like a seal than a whale.

"Oops," said Dr. Abrams, "another nervous dad. Would one of you get the smelling salts? Although, let's see, why don't you wait a moment before using them, okay?"

In the Sister's Hospital cafeteria Linda took the nearest empty table. Setting down her pocketbook, briefcase, lunch tray, and a styrofoam cooler, she picked up a copy of the *Tribunal*. The news section was missing, but she began to leaf through the classifieds, the personal ads, and the public notices.

Her eyes had just focused upon the agenda of that Tuesday's meeting of the Board of Adjustments when, by the kind of coincidence that makes one sometimes think of one's life as a film, Alan Modell, who on several occasions had served as the Elson family lawyer, set his tray down at the same table. They had consulted him most recently, just before Norman's departure, because the nervous college professor—convinced as usual that he would not survive round-trip jet travel—insisted on drawing up a will.

"Mind if I join you?" he asked.

"Not at all. What brings you to Sisters?" Linda asked.

"Just grabbing a bite before taking depositions. Our firm is handling a malpractice suit. Your unit, as it happens."

"What is it this time?"

"A hot tub birth defect."

"Go on."

"It's like this. Couple comes in for an infertility workup, doctor tells them the thing to do is relax, so they have intercourse in the hot tub. They've spent years getting pregnant, so when they do, they refuse an amniocentesis, and the child is born retarded. Now they're suing."

"Sounds like the retardation is hereditary," Linda quipped.

"Say, is Norman still away?" Alan Modell asked.

"Funny that you should ask. I'm on my way to the airport to pick him up as soon as I drop off this morning's fluids." She patted the little styrofoam box at her feet.

"Has it been hard without him?"

"It was at first. But we've managed. It's almost routine now. If you forget the emotional side, things are not too different from when he's there. Men are lucky to have wives to pick up the slack." Alan Modell thought he detected a slight sharp edge.

"If you're thinking of Gloria, you can forget it. She's been so busy since getting involved in politics I hardly see her anymore."

Linda felt awkward. She meant to flatter the man who was responsible for their family interests, such as they were, but realized she had touched a raw nerve. An uneasy silence punctuated the conversation as she searched desperately for a topic that would relieve the embarrassment they both felt.

"I know how busy Gloria must be," she said, "but she's playing such an important role in local affairs." She pointed down at the newspaper. "I was just reading about the Board's next meeting."

"There you have it. She's always at some meeting or other."

"What's this about an experiment in early childhood development?" Linda asked. "Norman's been involved with the schools. It's about the only thing he does besides work." She felt relieved, as if Norman's frequent absences, and almost constant distraction, might somehow equal Gloria's neglect. "This must be new."

"It is. I don't know much except that it has to do with housing children. Gloria mentioned something about boarding school. She knows the details. Let's see, you're in the Audubon district, aren't you? I don't think it would affect you, then."

"I can't believe this," Linda replied. "Yesterday a note came home saying the schools would be closed on International Women's Day, and now you say they want to house children in the schools?"

"From what Gloria tells me that's right."

"It's not my domain, but I know Norman will be anxious to find out all he can. Do you think Gloria would mind if he gave her a call?"

"I'm sure she wouldn't."

Placing an assortment of plastic utensils back on her tray, Linda Elson picked up her things and balanced them in the direction of the kitchen. Alan Modell lifted the *Tribunal*.

Norman Elson's reunion with his family went better than expected. After living alone for four months while teaching at another university, he feared the sudden responsibility and routine that family life implied. Linda, on the other hand, had to her surprise grown increasingly independent of the man she felt so often stifled her in imperceptible ways as long as they were together. Another two months, she had thought to herself on the way to the airport, and she would have been just about ready to go it alone.

The Elsons always argued in the time surrounding leavings and returns. She bore the brunt of his pathological fear of flying, which cast a spell of explosive gloom for weeks preceding departure. He, in turn, felt abandoned whenever she traveled. Linda was convinced that Norman did little things, made insinuations or withdrew, to sabotage her infrequent trips to professional meetings or to see old friends. But most of all she feared the usual quarrelsome couple of days following his return when he would no doubt inspect the house to see if it had been maintained, verify bills and check receipts, quiz the children for telltale signs of neglect, oversleep and then spend too much time on the phone. He would, in short, make her feel like his housekeeper, babysitter, and accountant, and make her wish that he would leave again.

This time Elson remembered the advice of their marriage counselor. "We can," Shaw Luftman had said, "always imagine petty dissatisfactions that blind us to the positive." The phrase had struck Elson at the time as a good example of the banality of psychology. "The man sounds like a fortune cookie," he remarked to Linda upon leaving the office. Yet the advice stuck in Elson's mind. Indeed, on several occasions recently it had worked. And Linda, in her tactful way, reminded him that fortune cookies are not so bad after a Chinese meal.

This time Norman Elson purposefully avoided any mention of the weeds that had overtaken the yard, the dog whose eczema had remained untreated, the dust and bills that had accumulated in his absence. Instead, he showed appreciation for the sign the children had made welcoming him home and for the meal that was waiting. And that night, once he and Linda were alone, Elson confided how pleased he was that they had weathered such a long separation. They made love decorously and fell asleep.

Unused to the quiet of the suburbs after months in an apartment on a busy city street, Elson woke up. He remembered an old dream that had not occurred since the days of his first marriage.

He was with his parents in a European train station on the border between ill-defined countries. The customs officials asked for their papers. His father quickly offered his, but Elson, overdressed and confused by the seemingly limitless abundance of pockets in his overcoat, bush jacket, and pants, could not find his passport. He began to sweat. The train was about to leave. His father called to him. He was overcome by a mawkish feeling. And that was when he always awoke.

Elson tried reading and, in fact, managed to get through twenty pages of an article on pins as cultural object in nineteenth-century America before drifting off. When he awoke again he picked up the personal advertisements in the *New York Review of Books.* Some of the ads amused him. "Indian man seeks woman for sex." "WJM lightly into bondage heavily into food seeks WJF with same healthy appetites." Elson always looked for the announcements that he could recognize as having been placed by a friend. He imagined being able to answer every ad, maintaining a secret correspondence with people he had never seen. Most of all he fantasized about having himself placed such an ad, forgotten, and then receiving letters from lonely women in every state. The letters all craved a "40ish professor, excellent sense of humor, tough on himself and on others, soft inside, sensual, discreet, married but free for daytime dalliance and travel." Elson fell asleep safe in the knowledge that, as his Aunt Esther used to say, "a Jewish boy'll be Pope before such a ting should happen."

Elson spent a quiet weekend unpacking, puttering around the house, reading, talking on the phone. He was surprised to find himself genuinely pleased to return to the town that for so many years he had considered temporary, ignorant of history and heedless of time, a place where it was impossible to plant roots, invest, consider dying, and call home. Oh, he was aware that most people living around him were capable of managing perfectly well, but he had always distanced himself from that possibility. Elson considered himself different, more consciously evolved—morally deeper even—than the ordinary inhabitant of Beacon. "Most people here," he once maintained before a class on literature and personal experience, "remain so ignorant of other worlds that they are forced to invent themselves anew each morning."

"Like what's wrong with that?" an eager freshman asked. "It's a way of staying young."

"I appreciate the spontaneity of your question," Elson replied, "but men have wrestled with this very issue since the dawn of time.

Someday you will recognize that there are no easy answers to life's insolubles."

"Like I don't see the problem," the student insisted. Elson noticed the others twisting in their seats.

"The problem is that we have fabricated in Beacon a universe that contains a large element of fantasy. It isn't fully real because many people choose to remain blind to the inescapable difficulties of existence."

"This is getting really abstract, like totally suspended. Gimme a break."

"I beg your pardon."

"I mean could you give like an example of what is real?"

"The basic fact of our existence is that we will die," Elson answered. "And although no one can predict the exact moment of his or her death, the knowledge of this fact creates an emptiness in our everyday life. Now if we try to fill that emptiness with easy solutions . . ."

The student again raised his hand. "So what's an easy solution?"

"I was just getting to that. Easy solutions are the kind of ready-made answers that we see around us everywhere. Anything that gives people the impression that they no longer have to think—new religions, worship of the body, herbal remedies, drugs, meditation, jogging, psychotherapy, obsession with eating just the right foods, self-help seminars, blind dedication to faraway social causes with no awareness of what charity means at home."

"How about devotion to the intellectual life?" the student asked.

"That's different, but I don't have time to go into why right now." Elson began to perspire. "Now, if I may continue, the error attached to thinking we can eliminate empty space from our lives is that we eliminate at the same time empty space for others. This has ethical implications, since it means that we see ourselves as failures unless we can convert other people to our point of view or they can convert us to theirs. Does everyone understand what I mean by the intolerance implicit to the illusory elimination of tragedy?"

Before anyone could answer, the bell rang. The giggling group of blond students in T-shirts and brightly colored bermuda shorts lifted an assortment of beach towels, frisbees, and balls from under their seats and skateboarded to the swimming pool. That evening Elson bragged to Linda over a glass of chilled Chablis that he had injected a necessary antidote of anguish into young lives poisoned by bliss.

On Monday Elson pumped up the tires on his bicycle and rode to the university. There he found a large stack of second-class mail, parcels, publishers catalogues, announcements of forthcoming meetings, promotional copies of scholarly books, postcards from students studying abroad. A memorandum from the department reminded Elson that he was to teach two courses in the coming semester, "The Artist and Society in Twentieth-Century France: Marcel Proust" and a graduate seminar on "Theories of Comedy from Aristotle to Freud." The courses pleased him because they would be occasions for the discussion of obsessions that were dear to him – the body, sex, and laughter. Of course, he would be dealing with personal obsessions objectively and in the third person. Elson was not like some of his colleagues who bared their souls in class, not like one of his own professors who had explored in every course, regardless of subject matter, his tortured relationship to his mother and to the first two of his three wives.

Elson caught himself laughing. He began to wonder what it was he found loathsome in the stereotypical tweedy professor yet acceptable in himself that could account for this sudden burst of lightness. He withdrew one of the 3 × 5 cards he always kept in his pocket and made a note: "Humor and the perception of oneself in the act of perception. Relation of laughter to the erogenous zones, to orgasm? How is it that the places on the body most sensitive to being tickled are the very ones with the greatest erotic potential? And if they are the same, why does tickling prevent arousal? Are feet an exception? Foot fetishism and humor, intersecting zones within the psychoanalytic canon. Worthy of at least an article." Elson laughed even harder, this time at his note. How funny, he thought, that someone would actually pay me to do what amuses me most: to read, write, talk about reading and writing, to laugh, and to read and write about laughter.

Elson went about the petty tasks of organizing the semester. He posted office hours and prepared the syllabi and bibliographies that would guide him and his students through the coming months. He had cleared his desk sufficiently by midafternoon to begin composing the lecture that would serve as an introduction to his graduate seminar. "Scholars have long noted," he wrote on one of the yellow pads he kept beneath his desk for when note cards would not suffice, "the historic association between comedy and deformity. Plato emphasized the 'kinship of the ridiculous with what is morally or physically faulty.' Aristotle claimed it represents a 'kind of failing or defect which is not painful or injurious to others.' Later rhetoricians such as Demetrius and the author of the *Coislinian Treatise* insist that 'the jester ridicules faults of mind or body.' Comedy is rooted in the defective, in Aristotle's representation of men as 'worse than they are'—in the partial and particular as opposed to the universal of tragedy."

There was a loud and very deliberate knock.

"Come in." Elson could hear what sounded like scratching at the base of the door, which opened, closed, and opened again. Gradually, a woman sweeping a cane back and forth entered. As the door started to swing back another hand pushed from outside and a scruffy, quite pimply student in an air force jacket came into the small cubicle as the woman's cane felt its way along the bookshelves toward Elson who stood up. "Are you together?" he asked.

"Groovy question," the man replied. "Yes, we're very together."

"I mean are you accompanying . . ."

"Yup, this is Debbie, and I'm Barry, her sighted aide. She's interested in taking your course on artists in the twentieth century. Debbie, who was rocking back and forth, refused Elson's offer of a chair.

"Tell me, have you taken other courses in the department?"

"Are there prejudices?" Barry asked.

Elson seemed not to understand.

"You know, man, like things you gotta do to get in the class."

"Oh, prerequisites. No, there are none, but I do like to have some sense of each student's background in the material."

"This is Debbie's first course in the department. She doesn't speak French, but the class is in English, right?"

"True enough," Elson confirmed, "but you know this is a course which does involve a certain amount of looking at slides. We're going to study impressionist and cubist painting, and I just wondered . . ."

"Groovy, no problem," Barry interrupted, "I know what you're thinking, but I plan to come to class and describe the slides to Debbie."

"That's fine with me," Elson assured them, "then there's the question of books. I know all the readings have been translated into English, but I'm not familiar with what's available in braille."

"Hey, man, no problem. I plan to read them out loud."

"Good. I'm glad that's resolved. How about the term paper? You do realize there's a certain amount of writing required."

"No hassle," the man repeated. "Debbie and I have everything worked out. She'll tell me what she wants to say, and I'll write it down." The amplitude of Debbie's rocking grew shorter, its rhythm quicker, as enrollment seemed increasingly possible.

"Okay," Elson said, "if Debbie, I mean you both, think you can handle the work, it's fine with me." Debbie turned, cane extended, and began foraging toward the door. Since she had not said a word Elson wondered if she were not also mute.

Elson was frankly pleased at the unusualness of the arrangement which would present a teaching challenge, and he returned to the yellow pad. "That which provokes laughter always involves a cutting short. This is a point stressed over and over again by those who have undertaken the task of writing about humor. Kant claims in *The Critique of Aesthetic Judgment* that 'laughter is an affection arising from a strained expectation suddenly reduced to nothing.' George Meredith maintains that comedy is the function that allows compression of whole sections of the Book of Ego into a sentence, volumes into a chapter. Freud insists at considerable length that jokes contain a short circuiting of the psychic."

Elson stopped on the way home to see his oldest and dearest friend whom he had missed while away.

"Come in, come in, look at you dressed like a storm trooper." The two men embraced. "Well, how was it?"

Hans Weil, having left Germany before the war, could never get over his friend dressed in a leather motorcycle jacket and wearing a helmet. The metal clips at the cuff of each pant leg made it appear as if he wore boots.

"Hans, it was like the old joke, you know the one that goes . . ."

"Don't tell me," the bespectacled white-haired professor interrupted, "the Jews may not have killed Christ, but they sure tortured him to death."

"That's it, you don't forget a single one." Elson was pleased. "You know, we're getting to be like the one about prisoners."

"Don't tell me, you mean the one about numbers. The prisoners have been locked up together so long all they have to do is say the number and everyone laughs."

"That's it," Elson repeated.

"Only we used to tell it about passengers in a train, you know the famous joke train between Cracow and Lemburg, and there was one more twist. When it came time to laugh at the number and nobody does, one of the men in the compartment asks 'why?' Another replies, 'He told it badly.' "

"That's a good one," Elson laughed. "I wonder if that train really carried travelers, or if people only bought tickets to listen to the jokes."

"You know, I'm so old and these jokes are so familiar to me that sometimes I wake up in the middle of the night convinced I told them to Freud." Elson made a mental note to fill out a card. Hans

Weil as a young student indeed knew Freud and had invited him to lecture at the University of Heidelberg.

Elson and Weil briefly reviewed the last few months, then agreed to have lunch later in the week. Riding home, Elson wondered what it was about Hans that so reassured him. He knew it was something deeper than humor, yet the funny, unseizable thing about laughter was that there was nothing more serious. Was it Weil's age? His relation to a past that transcended the superficial culture of Beacon? Could an exception like Hans undo all the rules, like one just man in Sodom?

After supper Elson enjoyed a game of Ping-Pong with his older children before retiring to the bedroom to read. Linda, who was watching a dramatization of the holocaust on educational TV, asked if he would like to join her. He studied the screen long enough to see a German officer and a Jewish woman about to consummate the love affair which united them against prevailing historical winds.

"When I want soap opera, I'll watch during the day. This is obscene," Elson said.

Elson returned to watch the eleven o'clock news, which he did every night for reasons not completely unrelated to the program that had held Linda's attention earlier in the evening. Elson dreamed about the holocaust far more than he admitted. The confusion of tragedy with melodrama was the very kind of situation which, he was convinced, had led to catastrophe in the first place.

Watching the news on television at least once a day was Elson's way of remaining on guard lest anything like the holocaust should happen here. He remembered Hans Weil's stories of work at the Heidelberg Institute for Social Research in the early 1930s, work which, even before the invention of television, convinced him and a handful of scholars to leave before it was too late. Otherwise they wouldn't have been standing there this afternoon telling jokes, Elson thought.

Elson removed a 3×5 card from his packet. "History is a kind of joke told by survivors," he scribbled. "We're getting beyond the erotic and even beyond the physical. If the proximity of laughter and death is demonstrated by the momentary loss of consciousness during laughter, does the fact that we laugh at the dead indicate moral superiority? The difference between surviving the joke, with the feeling of suddenly being reborn, and surviving history may be the space of the ethical imperative. Worth at least a footnote?"

"Our in-depth feature this evening," the gray-haired announcer promised against a background of dramatic trumpet music, "will be a follow-up visit to the Rawhide Ranch." Suddenly the camera shifted to show a woman pushing a shopping cart up the aisle of a supermarket and filling her basket like any other shopper. She wore dark glasses, bright orange slacks, and a floppy sweater covered by what at first appeared to be a fur stole but which, upon closer inspection, turned out to be a leather horse collar. It was not until she rounded the corner between the paper products and the vegetables that one could see that she was attached by reins to a man, himself clothed in leather and wearing studded bracelets, who was steering her around the market like a horse and plow.

"What the hell is this?" Elson asked.

"You probably couldn't get good craziness like this back East. Come on, let's cuddle," said Linda. When Elson didn't move, she went on. "I visited one of the old communes the day you got back, and some of the same people who used to live there are now up at this Rawhide Ranch."

The reporter referred to "the heaven and hell of the S and M lifestyle."

"Lifestyle," Norman blurted, "lifestyle, my ass. That's a word I'm glad not to have heard for a few months."

"Quit being so cynical. Just because things are harder back East doesn't make them more real. Let's watch."

"What exactly is your philosophy of love?" the earnest young woman reporter asked the studded man. The scene had shifted to the headquarters of their living group.

"It means that we are very committed to experiencing life as fully as possible. And since many of us have discovered that life's pleasures are the same as its pains, we have decided to eliminate as many false barriers as possible. To us it's not natural to separate things that go together." Several straggly haired, remarkably obese women in long dresses and bandanas moved around in the background. They were struggling to keep a herd of excited children away from the television camera.

"What about the other residents of Burneyville?" the reporter asked.

"They objected at first. We took a lot of flack, you know, nasty looks and obscene phone calls. They even tried to get the health department to shut us down. But they couldn't. I think they've grown used to us now. We don't have much to do with them, and they don't bother us. We pay taxes like everybody else."

"How do you support yourselves?" the journalist asked.

"A few of us work at outside jobs, but we also run a mail-order business."

"What kind of business?"

"We specialize in the manufacture of progressive sexual aides."

"Could you explain to our television audience what that means?"

"Well, I could show you. Britt!" he called to one of the obese women who waddled toward the camera. "Listen, Britt, run to the shed and bring back a couple of samples. Be sure to get a few of the leather goods. Don't forget you know what. And hurry up, you understand."

The reporter, obviously intrigued by the militaristic tone, asked if such brusqueness were usual.

"Oh, yes," he replied. "I'm one of the S's, the leaders. The M's love discipline, they need it. We've tried other ways, but this is the only thing that makes them happy. They're miserable without it." Britt returned, arms filled with an array of exotic sexual paraphernalia.

Elson made a mental note that he could use this in his course. It was one thing to read about scenes of bondage in Proust, but something else to actually see the equipment. Elson wished he had a VCR and could record this to show the class how relevant Proust still was.

"Here we have a few old standbys, standard whips," the man explained, "both long and short. Take a look at the fine leather work on this beauty, which is only nineteen ninety-five. We also make a full line of both men's and women's clothing. These are some of our offerings for the spring." He held up a pair of leather pants so slim in the leg, Elson thought, that you'd have to have been in a concentration camp to fit in.

"Of course we can whip up any of our leather goods to order in rubber," said the man, "if that's your thing." Several of his harem, which was waiting attentively in the background, giggled. The more their leader talked, the more evident it became that he was basically delivering an advertisement. Except for the studs, he reminded Elson of his uncles in the garment business. The reporter gradually caught on and tried to shift the subject but the man in leather quickly held up a small oblong object that demanded explanation.

"What's this?" said the reporter.

"I knew you would ask, you devil. We're very proud of this one, new this year. It's our mask." He picked up what looked like a black football covered with zippers. Sticking his hand inside, he inflated its collapsed sides to dramatize the fact that, placed over the head, the zippers would fall wherever facial orifices were to be found, horizontal ones for the eyes and mouth, vertical for the nose, little triangular patches for the ears.

"Would you mind demonstrating?" the reporter asked.

"I can't personally, it's not my thing, but I can have it shown. Britt, you've been naughty, now come over here at once and put the love mask on. I mean now. Let the people have a good look." Britt did as she was told.

"Love must be blind," said the reporter, obviously pleased with herself.

"Some people see the world through rose-colored glasses, others through zippers," the man said.

"Who orders this one?"

"Oh, you'd be surprised. People from all walks of life, mostly men, of course. Would you like to see our tack room? That's where we store our private collection of love equipment." The camera shifted to a small barnlike structure with an assortment of whips, bridles, boots, and collars hanging from the walls.

"Enough," Elson protested, "I'm not used to Beacon yet. In fact, how would you feel about getting out of here?"

"What do you mean?" Linda asked.

"I mean leaving, moving, raising our kids in some sane place where little cults don't grow in the soil like weeds, where every meshugah who can read shaves his head, sticks incense up his nose, declares himself God, and expects the whole world to follow by night."

This was the old discussion that had led to Norman's spending a semester in the East. She could not tell if he were serious, but even if he were joking, she took it personally. It meant he was blind to what was genuinely fulfilling in their lives. She had been convinced that by living temporarily somewhere else he would get any idea of moving out of his system.

The interviewer announced that this evening's presentation would be followed by a panel discussion. The scene shifted back to the studio where four experts on human sexuality were assembled in order to discuss the S and M lifestyle with members of the television audience. No sooner had the moderator given the number than the phone began to ring.

A woman from middle-class Goshen wanted to know if such sexual acts really hurt. A man from the more liberated Canaan wanted to know exactly where the Rawhide Ranch could be found. Yet a third from progressive Beacon wanted to know if his impression was correct that the poor and elderly were excluded. It was then that Elson, who had begun to tune out, recognized a familiar voice. Linda, who could hardly contain her discomfort at seeing their marriage counselor, Shawn Luftman, on the screen, had hoped that Norman wouldn't notice. It would only serve to aggravate his culture shock and to affirm him in the belief that they should leave.

"Holy shit," Elson exclaimed. "I'm not in town seventy-two hours and here's Luftman pulling one of his sexual media stunts. This place is nuts."

"I knew this would happen, just when things were going so well. I just knew it."

6

NEW AGE HOSTILITIES

■ As the chambers of City Hall filled with excited citizens, the Board of Adjustments gathered in a small room off to one side. The existence of these private meetings was no secret. They were referred to publicly as "executive sessions," meaning that Eric Tucker would meet with the Adjustors to prepare them for the difficult decisions that lay ahead.

Tucker cleared his throat. "I want you to listen carefully," he urged, "we've got some very important business tonight. A couple of small things first–electroshock therapy, some old lady who didn't register her house with the rent board, several foreign policy items. Use your judgment here. O'Reilly will lead." Tucker referred to Harold O'Reilly, Beacon City Manager. "If you feel you're getting into trouble, table it. Now comes the good part, the schools. Stafford will make a report, and he'll introduce the Ladies League. They've been working together, so I don't foresee any surprises. We'll end with the application from Truscott who'd like to build downtown. Here you could take some flack, but we've got the situation pretty well covered."

Tucker, picking up a long stick like an art historian about to begin a lecture on a particularly detailed painting, pointed at the closed-circuit TV monitor mounted on the wall. "Now," he said tapping the screen, "I want you to be able to recognize the right people. You'll hear from the progressive community, which has really turned out for this one." He pointed to the members of the Capital Exchange sitting toward the rear. "And there'll be some new faces." Moving the pointer to the other side of the screen, Tucker identified Greer, who was furiously distributing signs to a group of young black men. The placards read *Frustrated Revolutionaries, Closet Racists, Neighborhood Nazis, Jobs for the Poor, Environmentalists Love Trees More Than People.*

Tucker then pointed to a half dozen or so well-dressed businessmen entering the room. "Here are the representatives from Truscott. Don't hesitate to call on them if you need any info, they've got it all in those little briefcases. Remember, if things get hot, they can always come back. And, speaking of hot, don't underestimate the so-called community activists who've been screaming all over town. Tonight's their night."

The Urban Awareness Alliance was gathered around Zimmer, who was joking about the three-piece, sixty-thousand-a-year men that Truscott had trotted out for the occasion. He seemed ebullient, confident, and, as Ellie Pearl whispered to Blessings, even a little light-headed. He was pleased to see that old friends from the movement, James Meyer, Larry Newton, and Pam Sidel, had shown up to fight the good fight. He checked once again with Blessings to see if there was any truth to the rumor that the Blackstone might be spared. She kept darting back and forth between the Urban Alliance and the Ladies League. Moving nervously behind the row of connected seats, Zimmer rubbed Walter Carroll's shoulders like a solicitous fight manager about to send the man he had trained into the ring. To his right a somewhat less cheerful Karen Zimmer was busy trying to retrieve two-year-old Keri from where she had wedged herself under the seats for the third time. Watching her was Beth Hansen, considered by some to be the foremost authority on child rearing in Beacon and who wore a T-shirt that read *Dare Care Not Warfare.*

"I don't mean to intrude," Beth said tactfully, "but Keri seems to show the early signs of a slight hyperactive thing. Nothing to worry about, of course. These are the active years, I mean after they learn to walk but before they can talk. You might want to think about enrolling her in one of our Terrible Two Seminars at BONKERS. We also run support groups for parents who want to be able to handle their child's seminar experience more effectively. Just a suggestion, you know, but you should give it some thought. Keri seems like a really bright kid with fantastic motor skills. What she's doing is only normal."

"Thanks," Karen replied, "I'll think about it," and with Keri in her arms she dashed off after Jason who had discovered the tangle of wires hanging beneath the table from which the weekly meetings of the Board of Adjustments were broadcast to the citizenry. Just then the Adjustors emerged from their executive session and McPhail, striking his gavel, announced with his usual nasal but firm tone, "The Board is now in session." Nobody moved.

"Please, please, take your seats," he insisted, "we are about to start." The buzzing civic interest groups slowly took more manageable shape.

"We have a lot to do this evening, so let's try to keep on schedule. I see that many of you have come to discuss the Truscott permit, and we have scheduled it as early as possible, as you can see, item D. But we have a few matters of business that must be taken care of first if you will just bear with us." McPhail paused before announcing in a slightly more formal tone, "Item A, consideration of a ban on electroshock therapy in Beacon."

The Adjustors listened first to a petition from the Committee Against Electroshock, which attributed most of the world's ills since the discovery of electricity to this barbaric medical practice, then to testimony of several doctors who vouched for its effects.

"We don't know why it works," a man dressed in a white coat informed the Board, "but it does. And specialists only use it for severe depression when all else fails."

"What about the negative side effects?" asked Bernice Dever.

"The most pronounced side effect is short-term loss of memory," the medical man replied. "I would just like to add, since I see my three minutes are up, that if Beacon outlaws electroshock, it will just drive patients to seek it elsewhere. Besides, you ought to consider whether city government ought to enter into matters of medical expertise."

"The Board is responsible for all our citizens," Adjustor Dever informed him sharply. "Personally, I would like to hear from the people involved. Is there anyone here tonight who has actually had electroshock?"

A wiry man with long matted hair, glazed eyes, a string of beads around his neck and bells around his ankles, raised his hand, grunted, and announced that he had brought a group of former mental patients who were willing to share their experiences with the Board. Like Bruegel's allegory of the Blind Leading the Blind, he told the ragtag band of fellows where to sit and when to deliver, in the monotonous tones of the brain damaged, the little speech that each had more or less learned for the occasion. Unfortunately, and perhaps because of the side effects of electroshock, none could remember much about that which they denounced. In fact, their very inarticulateness was used as proof of the insidiousness of the practice, as the spokesman for the Committee Against Electroshock, in a fiery speech, compared the doctor in the white coat to Joseph Mengele.

"I beg your pardon," Bernice Dever interrupted, "I'm afraid some of us don't get the literary reference. Just who is Joseph Mengele?"

"He was known as the Angel of Death at Auschwitz," the man informed the Board, "an animal, one of the greatest torturers history has ever known."

"Thank you for the clarification," she replied. "Quite frankly, I am outraged and saddened that in this day and age we could permit such a thing. I propose that we ban electrocution. And yes, folks, the slip was intentional, because that's what we're dealing with. And I also move that we appoint a committee to study medical torture in Beacon."

"Second," Joel Steinhammer chimed in, and the prohibition passed unanimously. President McPhail asked City Manager O'Reilly to look into forming a special task force on local torture as part of the Human Rights Commission.

While the Board of Adjustments debated electroshock, a small bus with the words *Gifted Transportation* printed on its side stopped at the entrance to the Helen Keller Center for Special Living just long enough for Martin Wasserman to jump aboard. He personally directed the series of subsequent stops before a dozen or so doors, the lowerings of the lift, the delicate transfers of wheelchairs, the awkward positionings, and careful strappings once the people were on board. As the door shut for the last time and they settled for the short ride to City Hall, he stood, hands cupped, like a counselor at a summer camp for overly sensitive teenagers.

"I don't make speeches," he began, "but the Board of Adjustments is very anxious to have some input tonight from Beacon's other-abled community, input about one of the most important building projects to come along in years. So please speak as strongly as possible in favor. Feel free to ask all the questions you want, like what kind of provisions the Truscott Corporation, they're the builders, has made for the specially challenged. Ask how many jobs there'll be. And if you're wondering what all this has to do with us, just remember, the Truscott project means a lot to the city in terms of the kind of revenue that keeps the Keller running. Any opposition to it is a direct attack on you and on the other-abled everywhere. That's all I have to say."

When the bus pulled up at the side entrance to City Hall, a swarm of women in jeans and lumberjack coats immediately descended upon them. They wheeled the manual chairs and held forward the little stick switches fastened to the armrest of those lucky enough to be motorized. Together they made their way up the outside ramp like an army of miniature tanks, treading into the rear of the auditorium as the Board proceeded to the domestic and foreign policy decisions for that evening. The Adjustors officially registered their disapproval of the national defense budget and declined participation in a federal disaster readiness program.

"The government is the disaster," Bernice Dever interjected solemnly. Gloria Martinez began to laugh uncontrollably and had to retire to the small room from which Tucker had been observing the proceedings. She watched on the TV monitor as the Board granted sister city status to yet another Nicaraguan village, condemned Israeli settlements on the West Bank, and passed a resolution making it illegal to own, transport, or to test nuclear weapons in Beacon.

"Point of clarification," Bernice Dever said. "I want to know if the last item includes irradiated food."

"Of course," McPhail informed her. "Let's move on then to the last two items, a report on Beacon's children and the application to build on census tract 55423. McPhail looked at his watch. It was already nine o'clock. "Superintendent Stafford, may I ask you to present your findings to the Board."

Stafford, who shuffled laboriously up to the microphone, seemed more fatigued than usual. His polyester suit hung in ample eddies over his amorphous body as if there was an extra yard or two of cloth on both sides of jacket and pants. Little semicircular layers of sallow flesh were suspended under each eye. Even his normally raspy voice seemed to contain more than the usual number of folds as he again recited the long litany of the woes of the Beacon schools, declining test scores and enrollment, and uncooperative parents who thought they knew more than the teachers and the Board.

"What is your recommendation?" McPhail asked.

"Mr. President," Stafford bellowed with the bonhomie of a retired circus clown working a preschooler's birthday party, "it is our recommendation that children currently attending certain elementary schools to be designated be given the opportunity to participate in an exciting educational experiment. Beginning next fall they will be housed—that is, lodged and nourished—at suitable relocation sites. There they will be educated in accordance with the progressive guidelines adopted by the Board at its last meeting."

McPhail thanked Superintendent Stafford. "Now's the time for input from the community," he added. "We're fortunate to have with us tonight an expert in educational matters because of her long years of service with the Ladies League."

The League ladies, who were sitting in a group and had been chatting amiably all evening, wiggled and chirped with excitement as Barbara Wolfe, looking back twice at her constituency, walked slowly toward the podium.

"Christ," Zimmer whispered to Carroll, "she looks like she just stepped out of a Brooks Brothers catalogue," an obvious reference to the pale yellow shirt, plaid pleated skirt, cardigan sweater, polished loafers, and pearls she wore in prim contrast to the beads and ankle bells of the band of former mental patients.

The civic-spirited Mrs. Wolfe spoke confidently about the League's hard work over the last few months and of how it had come to a difficult conclusion. "The community of Beacon had been living in a big house for a long time, and certain rooms in the house are not in order," she warned. "We can no longer afford to live on such a grand scale. I'm sorry to say it, but we're all just going to have to live in a smaller, more orderly house from now on. We're going to have to learn to cooperate with each other. The Education Committee of the Ladies League, after extensive consultation with Superintendent Stafford and the Board and many hours of soul searching, recommends adoption of the Superintendent's plan."

"Thank you. Let's call the question." McPhail banged his gavel. "All in favor, say aye." Beacon's ruling troika echoed in chorus their President's last syllable. "Very good. Then the Board will recess briefly to discuss specific sites."

"Good work," Tucker congratulated the Adjustors in the TV room. "You're doing fine. Soon the opposition will pack it in with their precious little children. So, go on out there and do like we rehearsed. Oh, Rory, I forgot to mention that Suki wants to make an appearance, so if you could make a spot."

The Adjustors emerged, and McPhail banged his gavel repeatedly. "In executive session," he announced, "the Board has adopted an ambitious program of early childhood development that will forward the principles of urban democracy. Part of this plan involves the relocation of all school-age children at the following sites. Pupils now attending Audubon and East Rock elementary schools will, beginning next fall, no longer live with their families but will be housed at Dred Scott."

The simultaneous gasps coming from the well-dressed matrons of the League and from the community activists of the Urban Awareness Alliance created a powerful stereo effect.

"What's this shit," Zimmer shouted. "First you wanta turn my neighborhood into a dump, then you're gonna meddle with my kid. This ain't progressive, it's corrupt, fucking corrupt shit." The red-faced leader, who had begun to sweat profusely, was now standing on his chair against which he was banging the heels of his heavy wooden clogs. His supporters tugged at his sweat suit.

"Sit down," Blessings pleaded. "Don't blow it on this one. I'm on the Education Committee of the Ladies League, and we'll be able to work from the inside. Right now we've got to save ourselves for the Blackstone. Please, Leon."

McPhail banged his gavel so constantly during Zimmer's outburst that the community leader's words were barely audible. "If you cannot behave so that the Board can conduct its business," he insisted, "I shall have to have you removed." Police officers stationed at strategic intervals around the auditorium began to converge toward Zimmer, who was now squatting hunchbacked on his chair. Under the increasingly firm tugs of Blessings, who had managed to locate the drawstrings of his sweat pants, he crawled down like a performing circus animal leaving its stool. McPhail motioned for the officers to desist. "The Board recognizes Barbara Wolfe," he said.

"I'm afraid there's been some mistake," the Leaguer said calmly. "In our deliberations Audubon was never mentioned."

"That's because it's your neighborhood," Pam Sidel shouted from where she was seated, surrounded by the Capital Exchange. "The Audubon parents are too rich. They need to be taught a lesson. Why I've even heard that some of them are Republicans . . ."

"Please, please," McPhail implored in a feigned attempt to restore order once Pam Sidel had made her point, "we must stick to our agenda."

"It is true," a stunned Barbara Wolfe continued, "I live near Audubon. I have also worked with the school district as part of the Ladies League for over ten years. So I think you can safely say that I'm an expert on educational matters. It makes no sense to experiment with Audubon. It's a model of what a school should be. It has the best principal and teachers of all the elementary sites. It has the parents' support. Why just last year the PTA raised over ten thousand dollars at its Walk-A-Thon Spring Fair."

"You mean they're selfish," Pam Sidel could not keep quiet. "You and your neighbors are hogging more than their fair share. And I have heard that you are segregationists too."

"We're what?" the flustered Mrs. Wolfe, now surrounded by Shirley MacGregor, Edie Conglin, and Jessica Flowers, asked.

"Segregationist, that's spelled R-A-C-I-S-T."

"I beg your pardon, Audubon is integrated. I don't have the figures with me now, but I could . . ."

"Point of clarification," Bernice Dever interrupted. "Was it not the Ladies League that recommended experimental relocation in the first place?"

Barbara Wolfe turned red. "Yes, it did, but we didn't think anyone could think of Audubon."

"You mean the League agrees with the principle as long as it's not them?" Adjustor Dever asked. McPhail, fearing further acrimony, banged his gavel and gestured in the direction of a large woman in army fatigues. Introducing herself as Suki Shamus, head of New El Salvador Tomorrow, she pulled several large photos of dead, wounded, and starving children out of an expensive-looking bush jacket.

"How can you be so bourgeois," she asked in a voice that might have peeled paint, "as to think about your schools when children are starving and dying in Central America? You're nothing but a bunch of selfish, middle-class honkies. You're not part of the solution, you're part of the problem," she railed. Then, modulating her tone somewhat, she urged everyone to make a donation at the table she had set up in the rear.

"I'm afraid the time for debate is over," McPhail announced. "Let's move on, then, to item D, application of the Truscott Corporation to build on census tract 55423. We have many requests to address the Board, so keep your remarks to the customary three minutes. Once the green light has become yellow, you have 30 seconds, and when it becomes red, you must stop. Our first speaker is Mr. Dave Porter." McPhail held in his hand for all to see a stack of small green cards.

"Ladies and gentlemen, I am here tonight to remind the Board of Adjustments of the unique opportunity that faces the City of Beacon in the chance to create the Truscott office and recreation center. According to the plans submitted, the site of the abandoned Blackstone Hotel will be transformed into an economically viable commercial center that will enrich the entire region. It will provide much needed office space as well as space for shops and stores. But above all it will provide jobs and taxes for the city. Life in Beacon will be enhanced by this proposal."

"Bullshit, don't believe the corporate flunky," someone yelled from the back of the room. "Just look how he's dressed."

"It's true, it's bullshit," another voice shouted.

"Please," McPhail banged. "Please continue, Mr. Porter. I will remove this outburst from your alloted time."

"How many jobs?" the executive asked rhetorically. "We are talking about five to six hundred entry level jobs targeted for Beacon residents and especially its poorest population." On cue the group surrounding Greer waved their signs and cheered. "And I don't mean dead end jobs either. These are jobs that will lead somewhere. Our figures show that the greatest future growth will be in office jobs. The Truscott Corporation wants to help Beacon become part of that future."

"It's futureschlock," yet another objector yelled as Porter sat down.

"Next, Ellie Pearl," McPhail read from a card.

Blessings gave her ex-lawyer a little shove. "Good luck," she said with a wink.

"We have all heard a great deal about jobs and taxes," the smartly dressed Ellie Pearl began, "but let's think too about the irreplaceable character of the surrounding neighborhood. This is not a neighborhood of big landlords but of small homeowners like yourself, who will be crushed by corporate blight."

"This one's a segregationist too," someone shouted.

"This has nothing to do with segregation," Ellie Pearl continued, "we were all part of the civil rights movement in the sixties and care deeply about integration. But we must stop development now before we make an irreversible mistake that will destroy forever the character of our city and the quality of our lives." The red light flashed.

Tucker, listening to the proceedings in the TV room, was joined by Bernice Dever, who dropped in for a quick sip of herb tea.

"Did you ever see such a bunch of selfish yuppies in your life?" Tucker asked.

Bernice felt better immediately and returned to her seat in time to listen to Blessings Winter's desperate plea for the Board to consider traffic and pollution. The Truscott Corporation, she announced with horror, had not done an environmental impact report as required by law. McPhail looked inquisitively at Dave Porter, who explained at some length that such a study was not applicable in this case since the Blackstone was already abandoned and since the direct environmental impact of any development on people would be minimal. Blessings's jaw dropped, and she sputtered as the red light began to flash. "I've got a right to my three minutes," she shouted.

"Your three minutes are up," McPhail replied.

"But, but, you counted what Mr. Portnoy said as part . . ."

"I'm sorry," McPhail said brusquely, "we must keep things moving. Mr. Harvey Pincus, representing the Helen Keller Center for Special Living."

Harvey Pincus's trip to the front of the room was accompanied by a silence so complete that the only sound that could be heard was the whirring of the electric motor of his specially designed wheelchair. He controlled no muscle in his body except that of his neck. From his head there protruded a long pencillike device whose other end was inserted precariously into a little electronic box on one armrest by which he maneuvered the entire apparatus the length of the cleared aisle. The unevenness of the floor made his head bob up and down such that the progress of the chair was halting and technically he had used his alloted time before he had even begun to speak.

"I-ung-mag-frens-leeve-live-ind-in-do-o-o-pen-eh-eh-ng-mar-ar-teen-wan-ta-us-ta-ta-ta-say-how-ha-ha-ha-pee-uh-wee-wee-are-ree-re-re-ah-bout-pro-pro-pro-pro-pro-pro-so-all-foo-foo-bla-bla-stow-my-moth-moth-er-er-farth-farth-er-pre-pre-shi-shi-ate-ind-dee-pen-ent-me-me-fee-eels-ug-good-rye-rye-now-so-so-ha-ha-pee-pee."

"What's this?" Carroll asked Zimmer. "I can't understand a word. I mean this goes way beyond Dam Dass."

"He's the Party geek." Zimmer said. "They trot him out whenever they want to pretend they've consulted the handicapped. They like him because nobody can tell what the fuck he's saying."

Joel Steinhammer, not to be outdone by Bernice Dever, had just wheeled his own chair from the back room where he had visited Tucker. He asked Harvey Pincus to say a few words about his work at the Center for Special Living, which set off another round of incomprehensible stammering.

"So, just to make things perfectly clear," Adjustor Steinhammer said, "you are in favor of the Truscott proposal as long as they provide appropriate facilities and jobs for the other-abled, is that right?"

The other-abled man shook his head up and down so resolutely that his stick accidentally tapped the control box, which sent the chair lurching toward the adjustor's high bench. McPhail, who had seemed on edge since the beginning of the meeting, shielded his face and ducked. Luckily, however, the force of the sudden forward motion pulled Harvey Pincus's head backward in time to prevent actually colliding with the Adjustors' dias. Several of the women in lumberjack coats rushed to his aid. One placed her hands around his head, which was still bouncing uncontrollably, stick flailing, and held it against her braless bosom. Such gentle nurture calmed the bobbing, as Harvey Pincus became a captive unicorn in the lap of a husky maiden.

Joel Steinhammer diffused the tension that had been building. "If I may be permitted to speak for a second directly to this courageous man, I would just like to say thank you Harvey Pincus for making the tremendous effort of coming down here tonight to share your concerns with us. I can assure you we will take them into account."

Wasserman smiled at Greer as Pincus again whirred down the aisle and took his place at the end of a line of men and women in wheelchairs waiting to make the long trip to the front.

It was not until Ovella Capps was halfway to the speaker's platform that Blessings Winter recognized her ex-mother-in-law.

"We're saved," she whispered to her ex-lawyer. "That's Moses's mother. We've got one of our own."

"Oh," Ellie Pearl replied. Blessings, meanwhile, was gesticulating wildly, convinced that if she could just attract Ovella's attention, the situation would be righted.

Ovella's testimony disappointed all concerned. She spoke for not more than thirty seconds about how good the city had been to the residents of the Keller. She said, without conviction, that she hoped such support would continue.

McPhail announced that the evening's next speaker was a Mr. Tyrone Powell.

One of Greer's men rose from his seat and strutted to the microphone. "Uh, yes, uh, I'm not much at givin' speeches, and I'm not real familiar with the details of what's been comin' down here tonight. What I do know for sure is that I'm out of a job. I haven't had steady work for some time. My mother, my sister, and I live on three hundred and seventy dollars a month in assistance plus food stamps, and I ain't no different from none of the brothers. Just look 'round." He pointed to the dozen or so youths surrounding Greer. "What do the brothers do when they can't work? They turn to drink, dealin', and pimpin'. Now I don't think it's right that we're stuck down on the bottom o' the heap just so some white bitch in a pretty suit can get up here and whine about the quality of her life." These last words were said mockingly in the direction of Ellie Pearl. The lumberjack women, apparently objecting to the speaker's choice of vocabulary, made loud "tsk, tsk" noises with their tongues.

"What you all cluckin' at?" he asked, and, without waiting for an answer, said, "that's right, *bitch* is what I said cause that's what she is. I say let any one of you come on down to the south side of town and hang around. Then we can talk some quality of life shit, cause folks down there're fightin' jest to stay alive. So, you sittin' up there," he looked at the Board, "can choose between leavin' us sellin' five-dollar bags and helpin' us get five-dollar jobs."

"I'm terribly sorry, Mr. Powell, but your time is up," McPhail interrupted. Then in succession each of Howard Greer's men approached the microphone. Some seemed angrier than others, some had more energy and style, but they all told the same tale of poverty and woe.

"The hour is advancing," said McPhail when the last had finished, "and we still have a few more speakers." Scanning the list of names before him, McPhail came to that of Leon Zimmer. The leader of the Urban Awareness Alliance, a frayed drawstring still dangling out the front of his sweat suit, waddled slowly to the mike as if he imagined himself a star baseball player stepping up to bat in the World Series.

"I want you, our Adjustors, to know that I marched with you in the civil rights movement, I spoke with you in the free speech movement, I helped you keep people from speaking to the FBI, I was with you on lettuce and grapes, I boycotted Safeway and didn't drink Coors, I was with you at the induction centers, and I was the one who organized the blockade of the troop trains so that the war machine couldn't pass through Beacon."

"That's funny," McPhail interrupted, "I was one of the organizers of the train blockade, and I don't remember seeing you." The President of the Board smirked.

Zimmer was furious. "I just want to make one thing absolutely clear," he continued. "This is not the United States. This is not even Beacon Land. This is Beacon. And we don't have to act like the rest of the country or the rest of the state. If the rest of the world is out to make a fat profit, let 'em. If they want to turn everything into one big industrial dungheap and everybody into corporate zombies, let 'em. If they want to screw up the environment, let 'em. There's not much we can do about it, is there?" His supporters clapped as he turned for an instant to face them. "What we *can* do," Zimmer went on, "is to make our city as much like we would like it as possible. This means stopping the rip-offs here at home. It means holding on to our neighborhoods, making them into places where people can work, feel safe, send their children to school or out to play, walk their dog—in short, where we can live."

"You mean where they can gouge the poor with big rents." Larry Newton screamed.

"I should say too, while I'm at it, that Beacon is not the urban wasteland we heard about tonight. There are a few bad blocks, there is unemployment, but this ain't the South Bronx, it ain't Philly, it ain't downtown Detroit."

"Racist bastard!"

"Look," Zimmer shouted, "I don't know where all the faces in this room came from, but I've been to a lot of meetings, and I've never seen most of them before." He glared at the row of seats where Greer and his men had been and which was now empty. "I'd like to know who's paying. I'll tell you who – a bunch of whores selling out to one of America's biggest, smoothest, and most corrupt corporations. I'll tell you something else. They're not even cutting a decent deal for the City." The red light had been on for some time now. Zimmer turned on his heels, looked at the Board angrily, and, as if he had just hit a winning home run, walked back to his seat to the cheers of the members of the Urban Awareness Alliance who were now convinced things had turned around.

"Irving Caplow, then Larry Newton."

Caplow, who owned and ran the Año Nuevo Bookstore and Revolutionary Information Center, spoke in the sad but indignant tone characteristic of many of Beacon's most progressive citizens. "Ladies and gentlemen, I'm appalled, just appalled, at some of tonight's speakers who should really be ashamed of themselves. How can we compare, I ask you, what we just heard? On the one hand we have a group of comfortable property owners worried about giving up just the least little piece of their precious lifestyle. On the other, the dispossessed, worried about where the next meal will come from. And what's really disgusting, the lifestylers are masquerading as progressives. We must lift the mask off pseudoprogressives and expose them for what they really are – nothing more than liberals all worried about how much their house is worth when other people don't even have a roof over their heads."

"Real estate is cheap," Zimmer muttered, "when you're giving away someone else's house. That schmuck has been holding on by a shoestring to the little commie newsstand he runs, and now he's telling us how to manage our lives. Fuck 'em. I say put his balls in one of those South American torture machines he's always talking about and turn on the juice."

In rapid succession each of the members of the Capital Exchange denounced the selfishness of Zimmer's neighbors, who finally huddled to discuss whether the most effective tactic might be to leave en masse.

"What is the recommendation of the City Manager?" McPhail asked.

"Mr. President, Adjustors, our office has studied the question thoroughly. We have run it by all the appropriate committees – rent control, traffic, environment, human services, budget. Zoning has also seen it. From what we can tell all systems are go, and the benefits to Beacon should be significant."

"Thank you, Manager O'Reilly. Well, Adjustors, what is your wisdom?"

The approach of a decision was more than Bernice Dever could bear. "I want everybody to know that I personally have been not only outraged but saddened by the childish behavior I've seen here tonight," she said. "And frankly, I'm disgusted by the display of greed exhibited by a big corporation like Truscott. I'm too drained emotionally to rush into anything, and for that reason I move that we table the application. It would do us all good to cool off a bit."

"Second," Joel Steinhammer added.

"All in favor?"

"Aye," the Board replied, and the permit to build on the site of the Blackstone was deferred for at least two weeks. The neighbors felt like condemned criminals granted an eleventh-hour reprieve. Some hugged and giggled nervously. Blessings sat transfixed in her chair weeping. Confused, the Urban Awareness Alliance turned toward its leader.

"Doesn't matter," Zimmer said. "The fuckers have declared war on us, total all-out war. If that's what they want, that's what they'll get."

"Calm down, calm down," Ellie Pearl urged. "They haven't done it yet. I'm sure there's a way to resolve the situation peacefully. Menaces will only make things worse."

"Oh yeah, what the fuck do you propose?"

"I'll talk to Bernice Dever. As a woman I may get her to change her mind. Now, do we have any disabled who might talk to Joel Steinhammer?"

"How about my ex-mother-in-law?" Blessings offered. "She's in a wheelchair and everything."

"That's a rich one." Zimmer burst out laughing.

"Okay," said Ellie Pearl, "let's not panic. We'll find someone. How about McPhail?"

"That cocksucker!"

"Cut it out, Leon," Blessings said. "Go smoke your dope if you can't act grown up."

"She's right," Ellie Pearl added. "The tantrums will do more harm than good. We'll meet in a day or two. Then we can decide where we go from here."

Ovella Capps had just finished washing the breakfast dishes in the low-slung sink specially built for the residents of the Keller when she heard a knock. She turned her wheelchair toward the door.

It was Blessings.

"Well, well, well," said Ovella, "let me get a good look at you. My, my, you look thin. I can tell you ain't been eatin' right, child. Now, how's about we fix ourselves something nice and hot to drink?" She started to roll toward the efficiency kitchen.

"No caffeine or sugar, please," Blessings reminded her. "You shouldn't have any either."

The two women sat down together for the first time really since the Winter-Reed divorce. They chatted amicably about the older woman's health and about Ocean. But Blessings could not resist for long asking the question that had kept her awake much of the night. "Look, I hope I'm not prying into something I shouldn't. You know I can be a little indiscreet, but I'm not dishonest, so I came by to see what you were doing at that meeting. I don't want to be nosy, but I just have to know."

Ovella pretended to be so busy at the stove that she did not hear Blessings's question, which she repeated as soon as tea was ready.

"Honey," Ovella replied, "it's part of living."

"Part of living? I don't get it. Do you have any idea who those people are? Do you have any idea what they want to do?"

"Honey, to tell you the truth, I don't know, and I don't care."

"So why were you there?"

"Like I say, it's part of living."

"You mean part of living here?"

"That's right, now let's us talk about something more interesting."

"Wait a minute. We can't let things drop just like that. Like who brought you? Who arranged the transportation?"

"You know the man who takes care of the Project, the one who's always poking his nose in other people's business?"

"No, what man?"

"His name is Wasserman, and he's always stopping by when you don't need him. Folks around here are afraid cause he's got some connection to the man downtown."

"I can't believe it."

"Can't believe what?"

"I just can't believe how they use you and the others this way."

"Child, when you been 'round as long as I have, and seen half what I seen, you'd believe a lot more than that. Now let's you and me talk about somethin' else," the older woman repeated. "How is it not to have everybody else's children to take care of?" The two women spoke for a few minutes about children and gardening, but Blessings was anxious to go. Before leaving she asked Ovella to promise not to allow Wasserman in her house. That failing, she begged her to call the next time he came around.

Blessings called Reed, who did not answer. She decided to visit the Traymor to see if any of his neighbors might know where he was working. A couple whispered and made muffled noises before addressing her from behind the chained door. Neither had any idea where Reed was, but asked if she would like to come in for a smoke.

"No thanks," Blessings said. "If you see Reed before I can get to him, tell him his ex-wife stopped by and they're out to get his mother. Shall I repeat?" Before the man could finish shaking his head, Blessings was down the front stairs and back in her car on the way to tell Zimmer what she had learned.

There too she could smell the stale remains of marijuana and incense. Zimmer, who was dressed only in a robe, tried to embrace her but desisted as soon as she informed him she had something to report.

"You won't believe this, but you remember my ex-mother-in-law, the one in the wheelchair. Well, I hadn't seen her in a long time, so I went by this morning to see what was happening. Listen, you've got to keep this a secret. Okay? No, don't just shake your head. I mean really, okay? Okay, well she said a guy by the name of Wallerstein got the people in the Keller to come. Can you believe it?"

"Yeah. Must mean Wasserman, that it?"

"That's the name. What do you think? We've got 'em, haven't we?"

"Wasserman, huh. I told you it was a put-up job. He works for the PAP. A little putz with curly hair who was there last night."

"Well, thought you'd like to know. Gotta run. Listen, before I go, I want to give you this." She pulled a few ruffled photocopied sheets from the bag. "Sorry I didn't get a chance to staple it. I thought you'd want the first copy of the Urban Awareness Alliance Newsletter. Surprise! Call me if you find anything out. Bye."

Zimmer, sitting behind the statue of Ho Chi Minh later that morning, made a sighting that he considered important. He spent the better part of the afternoon trying to locate Blessings. She had said something about a tai chi workout. He looked in the Yellow Pages under *Sports, Martial Arts, Meditation, Eastern Exercise,* even *Religious Education,* but could find nothing. He knew that she would not miss the antiapartheid rally on University Plaza, and sure enough, she was there distributing the newsletter to passersby.

"Listen," Zimmer took her aside, "things are really popping. The two executive types from last night had a little meeting with the

Chief. We got them there. I've been looking for you all over because I'd like you to introduce me to Reed."

"You men are on such a power trip," Blessings teased. "First you want to take my clothes off, then you want to meet my ex-husband. What about me? Am I the monkey in the middle?" Zimmer did not respond. Instead, he arranged to meet Blessings in front of the Traymor at half past seven.

Reed was understandably irritated at the idea of his mother being disturbed by Wasserman. The community activist did all he could to maximize the exterminator's alarm. "You don't know these people," he warned, "they're real nasty, and they're not interested in using people just once. They got one of their goons controlling your mother. The fact she gave into them this time means they'll be back harassing her to death. Matter of fact, they stop at nothing."

"What can I do?" Reed asked.

"You can help us fight them," Blessings jumped in. "They're using Ovella to support the big developers who've got investments in South America and everything."

"I don't get it. You mean to tell me my mother, who doesn't even have a place of her own, is involved in some kind of big real estate deal? It doesn't make sense."

Zimmer feared all would be lost if Blessings were allowed to continue her farfetched associations, no matter how true.

"Look, I can understand this may be an awful lot to take in all at once. But the fact is they're making your mother show up at public meetings against her will and who knows what else. If you could just come down to the Board for the next hearing, I think it would really make a difference. Blessings tells me you're in the construction business. You could be like a building expert."

"I do termite and a little foundation work. But I don't know the first thing about what's going on downtown."

"It doesn't matter," Blessings interrupted, "all you have to know is in this newsletter. Read it. Ellie Pearl wrote it, but I photocopied it myself." She handed him one of her stapled sheets.

Moses Reed was genuinely perplexed by Blessings's visit. But fearing traces of the very kind of madness that he knew were connected somehow to the end of the marriage, he decided to give it no more thought. No more, that is, until two chance events made him think she might not be so crazy after all.

When Reed stopped to pick up Ocean from his mother the following Saturday, he could see the fuzzy outline of a man's head through Ovella's half-cocked screen door. "I'm sorry, I realize I'm a little early. I didn't mean to butt in if you've got business," he said.

"No, come on in, we was just talking," Ovella replied. "I'd like you to meet my son, Moses Reed. Moses, this is Martin Wasserman."

"It's me who's intruding," said Wasserman. "Perhaps I should stop back." Wasserman stood up. Reed could tell the two had been having words.

"Momma, who was that?" Reed asked as soon as Wasserman had gone.

"Nobody at all, he works around the Project, that's all."

"Is he the one Blessings told me about?"

"What one you talkin' about?"

"The one who comes meddlin' 'round." Ovella was silent. Reed tried again. "The one who's got something to do with City Hall?" Ovella shook her head as if to say "yes."

"What's he want now?"

"Not much, 'nother meeting, that's all."

"And you don't want to go?"

"I sure don't. But it don't look like I got much choice since he's the man that runs this place, and I ain't got nowhere else to go."

Reed was embarrassed for his mother, but said no more. He gathered Ocean from under the kitchen table and took him to the Beacon pier, which was, it seemed, the only place where the troubled child could be drawn out of his shell. Ocean approached almost willingly the fishermen and crabbers who lined the edges of the long wooden structure. He would watch as the teenagers, the couples, or the other fathers and sons sliced bloodworms or grass shrimp before baiting the hook and casting into the surf. He was curious to see whatever they reeled in, and he peered into the sacks and buckets of fish for what many would have considered a disturbingly long time.

That evening after the child had gone to bed, Reed fell upon Blessings's newsletter while sifting through a pile of old magazines. If it had not been for having met Wasserman at his mother's, he might have thrown into the trash the poorly typed sheets full of spelling mistakes. Instead, he began to read it before falling asleep. Not even Blessings, who had lived with him for almost five years, could have imagined Reed's astonishment at the following sentence at the end of a column signed L. Zimmer, Community Activist: "In short, the developers are out to get all they can, the City can't even cut a decent deal for itself, and the Chief's in bed with the Board of Adjustments."

Either the guy is in on the business between Tucker and Martinez, or he was psychic, Reed thought, and he wasn't sure which was worse.

The following night, after dropping off Ocean at his mother's, Reed phoned Zimmer, who insisted on coming over at once.

"I read your speech in the Urban Awareness Alliance Newsletter Blessings gave me, and I wondered what you meant by the last line."

Zimmer, afraid that Reed had been offended by his choice of words, replied, "Nothing, nothing really, I tend to get a little carried away sometimes, that's all."

"You mean you were just talking, you don't know anything more?"

"No, I'm sorry if it turned you off because we could sure use your help."

"I don't know you, and I know even less about what's happening between you and the City, but I don't like what's going on where my mother lives. I might be able to help," Reed confided, "but maybe not exactly the way you think. You see, the Chief of Beacon is for real in bed with the Board, or at least their aides are in bed with each other."

"What are you talking about?" Zimmer asked. Reed, anxious to unburden to someone the secret which had begun to fester like a sore infected by anger at Wasserman, told the story of having heard Gloria Martinez and Tucker through the heating vent of the house on Lincoln Street. Zimmer, who had spent the last few months following the Adjustors around with not so much as a trace of scandal to show for all his effort, almost fell off his seat.

"Holy shit," he gasped. "Listen, you're not making this up are you?" Zimmer had often thought that anyone who could live with Blessings for more than a week must be, if not insane, at least capable of some great measure of self-delusion.

"No, I swear it. It's happened a couple of times."

"Jesus," the baby-faced man in a sweatshirt repeated, "that's it. They'll never build as long as Tucker's sucking Gloria Martinez's tits." Zimmer slid off the stool and began to do a little dance, moving his hands back and forth at waist level and rotating his hips as if he were drying his jiggling buttocks with a towel. His clogs made dull clicks through the thin rug on Reed's concrete floor.

"Okay," Zimmer said as soon as he had recovered, "now not a word of this, not even to Blessings. Especially not to Blessings. The time'll come when we can use it, but not yet. I used to be in real estate, and I know all about timing. Remember now, not a word to anyone. Believe me, we'll fix their nuts so they never come near your mother again.

In the days which followed Zimmer tried to contact Gloria Martinez. Each time he fell upon a recording: "Gloria Martinez, aide to the President of the Board of Adjustments, is busy right now caring for the citizens of Beacon . . ." On one such occasion the frustrated community activist left his own message: "Tell Gloria Martinez that Leon Zimmer, President of the Urban Awareness Alliance, has got some new information that might be of particular interest to the aide of the President of the Board." But Gloria, who heard the phrase "important new information" at least once a day, did not return his call.

When Zimmer had failed to make contact for almost a week after Reed's revelation, he became more bold. "Gloria," he dared into the tape recorder, "I've learned something that might interest you and the Chief, but it's private, and I wouldn't want to share it with anyone."

She phoned later that afternoon, and, apologizing for taking so long to get back to him, asked him what he meant by such a mysterious message.

"Are you crazy?" Zimmer asked, "You think with all the shit going on around town I'd talk about affairs like this over the phone?" Gloria was even more intrigued than before and wanted to get together the following day. Zimmer, however, delayed their meeting until Friday which would, he thought, give him time to set into motion a plan which had only occurred to him as a result of his recent experience of dealing so often with the recorded phone messages of Beacon's Adjustors and their aides. He headed for the Daedalus Pub.

Zimmer had frequented the Daedalus often at the end of a tense day of trying to close escrow. This was the period of Karen's intensive herbal training, before they had children, and he felt uncomfortable at the thought of returning to an empty home.

Wharfield greeted him like an old friend. "To what do we owe the honor?" asked the barman, who was wearing a T-shirt with the phrase *Life's Too Short to Drink Bad Wine.*

"I want to ask a little favor," Zimmer said. "You told me once you record music for the bar."

"I do it all."

Zimmer leaned forward. "I'm talking more than jukeboxes, my friend. You mentioned something about a sound studio."

"That's where I do all the music you hear."

"You have mikes and everything?" Zimmer asked.

"Sure do. What's on your mind?"

"I'd like you to set me up to record some, uh, uh, music, and maybe a conversation or two."

"Don't tell me, let me guess. Are we having a few problems at home?" The barman was accustomed to the myriad of suspicious confidences that passed over the broad mahogany counter. Many contained the fantasy in one form or another of spying on an unfaithful spouse.

"No, it's not that. You know I'm no longer a real estate agent. You may have seen my name in the papers. I'm a community activist." Wharfield shook his head both because he had not seen Zimmer's name and because, in all his years of serving people drinks after work, he had never heard of a profession called community activist.

"I'm afraid that's not my thing. I make tapes for the bar, that's it. But there is a guy who comes in you might want to talk to. He's a real techy."

"A what?"

"A techy, technician, you know, good with his hands and into little circuits and wires. Works for some kind of computer firm during the day, plays with gadgets at night. Here, let me write his name down. Or, if you can wait until tomorrow, I'll take you by myself." Zimmer, overcoming his suspicion that Wharfield might be collecting some kind of hidden commission, agreed.

Wharfield and Zimmer descended together upon Trenton's garage workshop, which was like a giant warehouse in which each piece of merchandise had been removed from the box and scattered. Wires hung from every conceivable corner, nail, nook, and cranny. Small discs, screens, miniature canisters and cartridges, batteries, lights, printed circuits, keyboards, electrical receptacles, and balls of solder lay on the benches which lined all four walls except for the narrow opening by which they entered. An assortment of fine tools was dispersed amongst the debris. Three-dimensional metal frames, skeletons from which some larger piece of gear had been extracted, covered the floor which in places was completely blocked. Nothing bespoke any human intention to impose order upon Trenton's computerized chaos.

"Hel-lo," Wharfield said in a tone that made it clear such visits were not infrequent.

"Jack Trenton, I'd like you to meet Leon Zimmer."

Trenton, who was bent over a minute bit of solder, wiped the dirty resin from his hands and raised the rectangular magnifying glasses from his forehead. "What can I do for you?" he asked.

"Well, uh, Alfred tells me you might be able to help me out. I'd kinda like to record someone's conversation without being heard." Zimmer was visibly ill at ease.

"You've come to the right place, headquarters of the PIA."

"I'm afraid I don't understand."

"You've heard of the CIA, haven't you?"

Zimmer nodded.

"Well the PIA is the Peoples Intelligence Agency. We can do just about anything they can, only they are supposed to operate abroad, and we're set up and ready to go right here in Beacon."

"You do phone taps?" Zimmer asked.

"No problem."

"What's something like that cost?"

"Depends on how sophisticated you want to get. Could cost you anywhere from a hundred and forty to over four hundred dollars for a voice-activated remote setup. Scrambling costs extra, and that could run you into money. Let me ask you, if it's not too indiscreet, to describe the theater?"

"The what?"

"The theater of operations. Where you plan to do your dirty work. Some places, like big corporations, tend to be a little paranoid. They've actually gotten quite sophisticated, if you will, about detecting surveillance gear."

"It's nothing like that," Zimmer said, "just a casual meeting of friends."

"You want to go body or portable?" Trenton asked.

"I'm sorry, I guess I'm new at this."

"I mean do you want to wear a device or carry it, say, in a briefcase?"

"It never occurred to me. Let's see, how about something I can wear. If they saw a slob like me with a briefcase, they'd know something's up. I don't need anything very kinky. You see, uh . . . you're going to laugh at this."

"Hey, if you knew some of the stories my machines could tell, you wouldn't be so uptight. Go ahead."

"Have you ever recorded sound, I mean intimate sounds, coming from a heating duct?" Zimmer asked.

"Let's see now, a basic domestic surveillance type situation. Heating ducts, that means you've got amplification. Why, hell, you're already halfway there. You want big or small?"

"What?"

"Do you have a place to put a big-reel recorder? You know, like in the cops-and-robbers movies with plainclothesmen in headphones waiting to hear stuff down in the basement with the sewer pipes."

"No, no, small. We got to get it in a small space and can't risk carrying anything too big." Trenton, who had picked up a pad, took a note.

"How about power? You got power or do we need batteries?"

"Hadn't thought of that. It's under a house so there has to be power. But batteries would probably be easier, right?"

"Right. Now, how about voice activation? You got somebody who can change the tapes?"

"Not really, like I mean there'll be someone there during the day."

"So we're not talking remote?" Trenton asked.

"Remote?"

"You know, like the two guys waiting in a van with painted windows across the street. They take a look through binoculars once in a while."

"I guess not," Zimmer said. "What's all this gonna run me?"

"I can get you out of here for under two hundred if you choose to purchase. Let's see, the same setup would cost you about twenty dollars a month if you prefer to rent. We do, of course, have our Listen Now Pay Later Plan if you would care to invest in something more elaborate."

"Later maybe, but this should do for now," Zimmer said. "When can I pick it up?"

"Stop by tomorrow about this time, and, oh, no plastic money or checks."

Zimmer settled into the contours of a smooth designer chair while Gloria Martinez made cappuccino in the kitchen. He didn't really want anything to drink, but used her absence to look around the plushly furnished study. Zimmer had never seen so much oak and leather in one room. It looked more like a furniture showroom than a place where people might live.

The brief respite also gave him time to review the homework he had done on Gloria—the study of her entangled pattern of involvement with men and politics of which, he had concluded, the affair with Tucker was merely the latest chapter. An unflagging commitment to overthrow whatever government was in place at the time seemed to be the common thread. During the Kennedy years the then Gloria Minsky from Long Island married a painter who was as outraged as she was by the attempt to overthrow Castro at the Bay of Pigs. Their opposition to the Vietnam War would have sustained them through the Johnson years had Gloria not fallen in love with Hector Martinez, the enterprising son of a migrant farm worker. Together they spearheaded the local anti-Nixon subcommittee of the Peaceful Freedom Party. Unfortunately, once Nixon resigned, Hector and Gloria Martinez discovered they had nothing more to say to each other. They divorced shortly after Gerald Ford became the thirty-eighth President of the United States. Gloria, who entered psychotherapy with Kate Yamato-Gelber a month before Carter's inauguration, discovered that she was tired of playing second fiddle to the men in her life; and so, when she married the lovable Alan Modell, whom she had met while doing legal aid for Amnesty International, she courageously kept her own, or at least her most recent, last name.

Moses Reed, who had heard Zimmer enter and followed his footsteps through the entry hall into the study, unwound the coils attached at one end to the recorder, which he hid in a tool box under a tarp. At the other end he attached the microphone to a wide overhead beam by means of hand screws like those used in kitchen cabinets to hang coffee cups. Crawling quietly on all fours through the dirt, he pressed the red button marked *Record*.

The exterminator wasn't exactly sure how he had allowed Zimmer to talk him into this, but he watched the needle jump and recline as Gloria shuffled in the kitchen. A dozen or so sharp jolts traced her footsteps back to the study. Shifting once again toward the rear of the house where the occasional noise of file and saw made it clear that he was hard at work, Reed thought to himself, "At least this time they won't be flushing their shit right on top of me."

"Sugar?" Gloria asked.

"No thanks," Zimmer replied, taking the cup. "Nice digs here, not bad for a revolutionary."

"Oh, it's not me," Gloria protested, "my husband's a lawyer, and you know how they are–into things. Now what's on your mind?"

"Well, some information has surfaced lately of, shall we say, a sensitive nature. I thought you might be interested and that I might get you to persuade McPhail to change his mind about the Blackstone."

"I'm only his aide, you know, and the job of an aide is to advise. What kind of information?"

"The members of the Urban Awareness Alliance had always suspected something funny was coming down between the Board of Adjustments and City Hall. Now we've reason to suspect that there are more intimate relations between the Board and people in high places." Zimmer, convinced he had won the day and that Gloria Martinez would break down and confess all or at least begin to cry, was surprised when she merely sucked the cinnamon foam off her cappuccino.

"I've no idea what you're talking about."

"I'm talking about corruption, selling building permits in some kind of sleazy deal. But I'm also talking immorality. We've run a little check on Tucker," Zimmer said, "and it turns out he has an unnatural weakness for married women. Now, we wouldn't want a little thing like that to embarrass the good citizens of Beacon, would we?"

"Is this something you've invented following us around?"

"Never mind how we know, the point is we do."

"No, I mean it's really important for me to understand, since the Board of Adjustments is supposed to investigate allegations of public corruption."

"Oh yeah, is it supposed to investigate itself? It's not important how we know. We got ways. The fact is that selling the city to the rich developers is nothing next to the scandal that's about to go public, unless . . . I hear you've got an in with City Hall. Maybe you could get that message to the Chief."

Gloria Martinez showed no sign of crumbling beneath the weight of Zimmer's veiled threats. Instead, she picked up his empty cup and announced that the demands of a busy schedule prevented their meeting from continuing any longer.

Listening to the tape that evening while smoking marijuana, Zimmer became giddy. "Like I told you," he assured Reed, "timing is everything."

"You sure did take your time" the skeptical bug man reminded him. "I was down there sawing away, but I didn't hear a thing . . ."

"No, no, you don't understand," Zimmer said. "Wait, you'll see. The bitch is stonewalling. It's only a matter of time before word gets to the top and the bullshit stops."

"Still didn't hear a damn thing that'll do anybody any good."

"Did you hear that place where Gloria gets real quiet? It's just like the gap on the Watergate tapes. You should have seen her face. These people can't take the heat. I could tell Gloria couldn't wait to get out of there and tell Tucker that we know he's humping her. Besides, look at it this way. We had a chance to test our recording system, and now we know it works."

"It may work, but there's not a thing on that tape but you talking in circles."

"She didn't deny it, did she? Look, it's a gamble, but I'm a gambler, remember. I know when to get in and when to get out. Let me handle this. It may seem like nothing to you right now, but the tape is rolling. Believe me, we're gonna wrap 'em up in it." Zimmer inhaled a large quantity of smoke and held his breath.

"Maybe you should go in with videotape next time. Just don't let on about me under the house, you hear? And I still say we got nothing."

7

FULL MOON

In each school zone affected by the Board's decision notices began to appear at regular intervals. Buried among the myriad of posters promising salvation on every corner—*A Firmer Body Through Inner Calisthenics, Partner Effectiveness Training, Rolfing the Whole Being, Creative Breathing, Tools for the Transcendence of Depression*—was the little notice: "Parents of school-age children residing in the Audubon district (census tract 52461) will report on or before June 15th to the Office of the Superintendent with their children's scholastic record and identity card. This is necessary in order to register for the fall term." Since few had attended the meeting of the Board and even fewer understood what had gone on, those who saw the announcement rushed to the district office which had been set up to receive them. There they filled out a form and were told that they would be notified by mail of each child's individual program. The notices arrived, but were difficult to decipher.

"What the hell's this?" Norman Elson guffawed.

"What's what?" asked Linda, on whom such tasks as registering the children usually fell.

"A letter here says that Dylan and Rachel should report to school on September first with bedclothes and underwear."

"It's probably a field trip of some kind. They're always going someplace. You wouldn't believe it. While you were away they visiteda restaurant and called it a museum." Linda thoughtit best to say nothing about her conversation with Alan Modell.

"What's this about uniforms?"

"It's very big in parochial schools. I'm sure Beacon is just imitating other places."

"A field trip, huh." Elson withdrew a calendar from his shirt, "September first is a Sunday. I told you, something's up." Elson's suspicions erupted like a diver whose oxygen had been cut surging to the surface.

"I'm sure everything's just like it is every year. If it'll make you feel any better, I'll call."

"As long as you take care of it," Elson insisted, and retired to his study.

Linda phoned district headquarters and was referred to the Bureau of Special Services."

"Mrs. Elson, your children, let me call them to the screen—oh yes, Dylan, age twelve, and Rachel ten—are fortunate to be among the very first students selected to participate in a unique educational experiment beginning next fall."

"What kind of experiment?"

"Mrs. Elson, they will have the opportunity, before now reserved only for the very rich, of attending boarding school."

"What do you mean boarding school?"

"They will actually be housed in the Dred Scott Elementary, where they will receive the very best education and around-the-clock attention."

"Is this some kind of voluntary thing?"

"I'm afraid it's not voluntary, Mrs. Elson, but I can assure you of the excellence of our staff." Linda thanked the man and decided to say nothing until Norman asked about it, which he did right after dinner.

"It's something like boarding school. You know, Andover, Deerfield, Choate." She tried to make him laugh. "Anyway, I'm sure there's nothing to worry about."

But Elson loved to worry. The next morning he too called and was told that the decision to give the students at Audubon and East Rock such an invaluable educational opportunity had been made by the Board of Adjustments.

"If you want to know more," Linda urged, "why don't you call Gloria Martinez. She is now aide to President McPhail."

"Gloria Martinez involved in politics? She's a housewife. What does she know about schools? They don't even have any kids."

"That's not true. She's done a lot of things, and keeping a house is doing something, Mr. Macho. Why don't you give her a call? I'm sure they can use people involved in education."

Elson phoned Gloria and, after listening to her recording, left a message. She eventually called back and was congenial but somewhat vague.

"My impression has been," said Elson, trying to draw her out, "that things were fine in the schools, enrollment up, integration working."

"That may be true in some places," Gloria assured him. "I'm sorry, I don't have the figures on the tip of my tongue. But the Board felt that it was a good idea to insure that the boarding school experience would be available to children of all social strata. It's only fair. Of course, the experience should be especially valuable in certain neighborhoods where the parents haven't been as cooperative as they could."

"Not cooperative? There was lots of parent participation at Audubon. I don't know whether you know it or not, but I was one of the organizers. I visited my kids' classrooms regularly to tutor."

"That's part of the problem," Gloria confided.

"What's part of the problem?"

"The parents' cooperation. It wasn't the right kind of cooperation."

"I don't understand. I thought you said . . ."

"I did. But that's not the whole picture. Truth is, the parents in some parts of town were getting too independent. President McPhail informs me Beacon was developing a two-tiered system. Certain schools were getting too good. They made the others look bad. They were not progressive."

"Weren't what?"

"Progressive. It's a question of attitude. It's the Board's job to be sure there's equal opportunity for everyone. The community was consulted. As a matter of fact, why don't you come down and speak? Every citizen has the right to address the Board at the open mike. Now, if you will excuse me, I'm off to a meeting of the Peace and Justice Commission."

In each of the menaced zones parents began to organize self-defense groups, and on almost any given night that summer they met in private homes. Thus among the usual posters appeared notices of the gatherings that gradually came to define the social life of parents who until then had been content with TV and twice yearly visits to the PTA.

Anxious housewives rushed outside as soon as new official announcements were posted. They remained in little groups around a telephone pole or bulletin board for as long as it took to assimilate the latest information. Then they would disband until that evening's session. Elson attended one such meeting in the home of Jessica Flowers.

"Let us begin," Barbara Wolfe said, clapping her hands, "by singing the Audubon anthem." The parents closed their eyes and launched into an incredibly discordant version of a high school cheer adapted to a bland Sunday school hymn.

"Now we are here tonight," Mrs. Wolfe continued in what Elson realized must be part of some weekly warm-up ritual, "as part of our continued struggle to send a message to Beacon's Adjustors.

This neighborhood intends to fight the Board's mistake all the way. There is just no reason in the world why our children should be taken away when the Meadow parents still have theirs. But there is reason for hope because we've organized. We have a steering committee, and eight, yes, that's eight subcommittees to help us win our children back. Tonight we will hear a report from our legal team. Eleanor . . ."

"Well, actually no one from our legal team could make it tonight," Eleanor Peavy said. Her husband was one of the lawyers who had volunteered to defend the cause. "This doesn't mean that they are not working very hard. Steve is sure the Board is in the wrong, and he thinks we're likely to get Judge McWilliams, who used to live in the neighborhood, to grant a temporary restraining order." The gathering sighed, and a few even began to clap weakly. "I should warn you, however, everyone agrees this could take a long time."

A suntanned man in a golf shirt, who identified himself as Dr. Lawrence Fulton, flexed his obviously cultivated biceps. "Our kids will be in college by then," he said. "If you want my opinion, we should cut the mamby-pamby stuff which'll get us nowhere slowly and do something that'll make an impression."

"Like what?" Eleanor Peavy asked.

"We could occupy the administration building, for example. Think of it. Fifty housewives trying to protect their kids by sitting on the Superintendent's floor. It'd be just like the sixties again."

"What a great idea," a long-haired woman in a pale purple leisure suit said warmly. "Just think of all the press coverage we'd get. That's my subcommittee, the media."

"Not so fast," Eleanor Peavy cautioned. "A sit-in is illegal, and might hurt us more than it would help. It certainly wouldn't do our legal case any good, and it might turn public opinion against us. I've got another idea. Steve and the others think there may be a potential split between the administration and the Board. Maybe we ought to try to drive a wedge between the two. But that's privileged information, and we can't make it too obvious."

"Just like we thought we could get the Adjustors to fight with each other," the doctor snapped. "Remember when we thought we could deal with them civilly, that they'd listen to reason. People would call up McPhail because he seemed reasonable, and he'd dance around us with his silly-putty words. We knew that Gloria Martinez always agrees with the last person she's talked to, so we followed her around trying to get the word to McPhail. Only someone over at Meadow got to her first. Then there were all the rumors that Bernice Dever or Joel Steinhammer might change their votes, or, better yet, resign. But they didn't. It's all false hope. The only thing the Board will understand is people getting angry enough to do something. Personally, I'm sick of all the legal promises. I'm ready for a little action."

"Who's going to take care of your medical practice while you're sitting on Stafford's floor?" someone asked the doctor.

"Well, I hadn't planned on actually sitting in myself. I thought Sylvia, that's my wife, would represent us both. And I would bring in food when I get off."

"I think an element of sexism has crept in the room," the woman with long hair objected. "If that's the game, then count me out."

"Okay, then," Dr. Fulton became suddenly aggressive, "what about trying to recall them? That's at least a political solution. After all, this is an educated community. Maybe the Board would wake up if we threatened. The Audubon parents could circulate petitions."

"Recall, recall," several of the frustrated neighbors cheered. Their enthusiasm was broken, however, by Elson, who had said nothing until then and who surprised even himself. He had always felt uncomfortable with any group lining up too resolutely behind this or that cause. And though he had participated in the mandatory campaigns of his age, he had always backed off at the moment he sensed his own fragile sense of self about to be swallowed by something too suspiciously whole. He had travelled as a teenager all the way to Washington to march for civil rights. What remained in his mind was the older black women drinking in the back of the bus, spilling gin on their blouses, taking them off. "Speeches by Joan Baez and Martin Luther King more powerful on TV, better read in newspapers. Impossibility of witnessing," Elson had noted on a 3×5 card. "We're taught to rely upon experience when in fact nothing could be more partial than the experience of great events. The participant always recreates a sum that is greater than its parts and in the telling becomes trapped in the power structures he contests."

"I think we ought to be cautious," Elson warned. "From the little I've seen nothing makes me think that reason will have any purchase upon our problems. We are just a small group that cares about our children, and we must remember that nobody cares about us."

"Just what do you mean?" Dr. Fulton asked.

"I mean that people basically care about themselves, and unless they are threatened, they don't notice or they keep quiet. Look around you. People don't make the effort unless they're up against the wall." Elson thought this last phrase, which he would never use in class, was particularly daring and would signal to his neighbors how practical and how familiar he was with the rhetoric of the sixties.

"Do you think you could go down to the Board and explain it to them?" Barbara Wolfe asked. "You're involved in education. Maybe they'd listen to you."

"I'd be glad to try," Elson said, finishing the last herbal cheese cracker on the enormous wicker platter.

Throughout the gathering Elson had been watching the man sitting next to him. His red beard and hair gave him the appearance of a Teutonic knight. The T-shirt, which said *Life is a Bitch and Then You Die,* barely covered his pot belly. Elson glanced from time to time at the notes he scribbled furiously in a dog-eared spiral notebook. The handwriting itself was oversize and less legible than that of many schoolchildren. The man had not opened his mouth once during the meeting, but descending the Flowers' stairs as things broke up he turned and said to Elson, "You know, we're never going to get anywhere with this goofy lawsuit or this recall petition. What we've got to do is contact people on the other side of town. My name's Alfred Wharfield."

"Norman Elson." The two men started walking toward the parking lot across the street.

"Listen," Wharfield said, "I've got some names. We've got to stop talking to ourselves." He handed Elson a piece of torn paper with four numbers scrawled in the space that might have held seven or eight.

Elson did make several calls, one to Ellie Pearl and another to Zimmer, who agreed to allow him to address the Urban Awareness Alliance. He and Wharfield went together to meet the members of the group they had only read about in the newspapers as being one of Beacon's "newest progressive alternatives."

The meeting at Zimmer's turned out to be as inconclusive as all the others. Eliot Friedman, who introduced himself as head of the Free Rent Coalition and was himself wearing a T-shirt that read *If You Think the System is Working, Ask Someone Who Isn't,* began on a belligerent note by recounting violations of Beacon's rent control law in the Audubon neighborhood.

"I'm afraid I don't know much about housing," Elson apologized. "I can assure you that neither of us is a landlord."

"Well then, you might want to purchase my book on meditation and real estate," Bobo Dam Dass said, rising from his lotus position to fetch two copies from his car.

Walter Carroll questioned Elson and Wharfield about their views on Central America. And when Elson denied being able to see the connection between foreign policy and relocating children, Carroll began to lecture about Truscott, copper mining in Chile, and the city's building code. Blessings added immediately that the whole situation had been gravely worsened by the advent in Beacon of fast foods, which had destroyed people's minds to such an extent that they were now allowing outsiders to come in and build skyscrapers. Wharfield sat quietly taking notes.

"Look," Zimmer broke in and said directly to Elson, "You Audubon folks haven't been around the Beacon political scene as long as some of us. And you've been ripped off by the City because you're naive. But we've been ripped off too, and I think we could come to some kind of agreement, which is why I'm proposing that if you support us against Truscott, we'll come in with you against the Audubon agenda."

"I thought the Truscott project had already been decided," Elson said.

"The Board gave the developers a permit," Zimmer replied, "but we've been working secretly behind the scenes to repeal it. The corporate bastards haven't won until the building goes up. And Bobo over there even has plans to make it fall down by humming a special mantra. We thought maybe the people in your neighborhood could provide the funds to help us fight it in the courts. We hear you've got lots of volunteer lawyers."

"But you're in with us already," Elson pointed out. "Your kids are menaced too."

"Doesn't matter," Blessings said. "You don't understand, it's all part of the same thing, it's the same people. They want to do away with the middle, to get us out of town. They don't like you because they think you're rich, and they don't like us because we offer an alternative."

"We'll have to give it some thought," Elson replied.

When Elson had left, the members of the Urban Awareness Alliance turned to Ellie Pearl.

"You're right," she said, "they are naive, and I'm a little suspicious. They may be politically incorrect as well. Getting too close could harm our cause with the people downtown."

Elson read to the Board a list of questions drafted by the Audubon parents. The Adjustors were prepared. McPhail deferred to Stafford who repeated that the assessment he had done, after consulting with experts in the community, proved that things would be better for the specific children involved if they might board at school.

Portions of Elson's speech appeared in the *Tribunal* along with Stafford's response. "We're an understaffed district," the paper reported the Superintendent as saying. "We have neither the time, nor the resources to answer the kinds of questions that a small group of angry parents ask week after week. Large public meetings are not meant for this type of communication."

"Did you see this?" Elson shouted.

"See what?" Linda shouted back. "I'm up here changing a monumental bowel movement and you're yelling up the stairs. I can't hear a thing. And you," she turned toward Rachel and Dylan, "you've got to stop feeding Alex so many raisins. It turns his poopy to beaded mush." The older children laughed.

"How do you like this?" Elson asked coming up the steps, "Jesus, what stinks?"

"If you had been listening, you would have heard me say I was changing a load. Honestly, you are so distracted," Linda replied.

Elson was distracted, and excited. The idea that a public official would actually say to the press something as blatantly indicting as Stafford's refusal to communicate with the public seemed like just the kind of fatal mistake the Audubon parents had been waiting for. All they had to do was to inform the higher authorities, and the foolishness would cease. Elson decided to go right to the top, and, sitting at the typewriter, he composed a letter to the governor of the state.

Elson mailed his letter in the course of one of his late-night jogs with Wharfield. Before the fight for Audubon he never gave much thought to exercise. Now, however, at the barman's suggestion, he would change into athletic shoes and shorts and leash up Nietzsche for a run before bed. Elson would invariably find Wharfield seated before a glass of wine, which he voraciously gulped, as the professor carefully did his stretches against the frame of the living room door.

As much as anything they did during the day, this race through the night contributed to the struggle. "If we're going to beat them, we've got to stay in shape," Wharfield had admonished. "Besides, it gets the asteroids out of the blood."

"The what?" Elson asked.

"The anger that builds up during the day. Running is good cover. We can use it as a way of familiarizing ourselves with the city."

Elson and Wharfield would trot to inspect some hitherto unknown school site or public building. Or, having obtained from the City Clerk the list of contributors to each Adjustor's electoral campaign, they headed for this or that supporter's business or house.

On evenings like tonight, when they had no specific strategic goal, they plotted a ritualistic course around several of the Board members' houses as if, as Wharfield would say, "to bring them in with magic."

"What's this magic?" Elson asked.

"You don't understand anything. Tonight's the beginning of a new moon. We're entering an enhanced energy field, and the force will start to turn with us."

Elson glanced at the little silver sliver against the dark sky. He often thought that if Wharfield were one of his students, he would have had the obligation to set him on a more reasonable track. As it was, he tried. "We must be careful about our terms," he corrected Wharfield as they puffed up the hill closing in on Gloria Martinez.

"I'm sorry. Did I make a grammatical mistake?"

"Not exactly, but the term 'magic' is prerational. It implies a hidden cause behind visible phenomena. Rational people have tended to use a more objective term since the advent of scientific psychology. Freud, for example, showed in his writings on religion how closely the belief in magic is linked to the experience of paranoia."

"What's that got to do with saving our kids?"

"I've been thinking about this a lot lately," Elson said as they descended and the stride grew easier. "I've come to the conclusion that there's a necessary link between paranoia and political action. It works like this. The more direct one is, the more limited his vision. This means that when you jump right into some great cause . . ."

"You mean like commit yourself?" Wharfield asked.

"Yes. When you commit yourself too strongly to anything you lose perspective. The more perspective you lose, the less you see of the whole picture and the more you're forced to invent explanations for what you don't see. Pretty soon the whole exceeds the sum of its parts. That's a textbook definition of paranoia. I'm convinced on the basis of considerable reading in the field . . ."

"What field?" Wharfield interrupted.

"It doesn't really have a name yet. I'm thinking of calling it something like Applied Literary Theory. What do you think?"

"A little long in the mouth."

"Then let me finish. Where was I? Oh, yes, recourse to abstract explanations for what one does not actually experience has two important practical consequences. First, if we are to avoid becoming paranoid ourselves, we've got to become less direct. That means working behind the scenes. Second, and this is really just a corollary, such indirection is the essence of power."

"Hold on, you lost me again."

"You see, the more directly one desires a thing, the weaker one appears; and the weaker one appears the less chance one has of obtaining it. To be strong, therefore, is to be devious. That's where the literary comes in. Every great novel is about just this—the hidden nature of desire."

"You can call it anything you want. I still say we're casting a spell." Unable to disabuse Wharfield of his primitive thoughts, Elson came gradually to revel in the vein of irresistable superstition that the barman radiated. And he did enjoy the late-night jogs that made his body feel better. Beacon's nighttime sports life intrigued him—the soccer and softball games on astroturf made chartreuse by halogen lights, riders on flashy silver bikes, hordes of joggers in fluorescent shorts and tops.

No more than three days after sending his letter to the governor, in fact at the beginning of a new lunar cycle, the chaos of dinner at the Elsons was interrupted by a phone call.

"Herb Stafford here," an unfamiliar voice identified itself. "Say, I just had a call from my old friend Barney Roberts, you know, the governor's man on education. Now what seems to be the problem?"

"I was shocked," Elson said, "by the district's reluctance to be forthcoming with what is, after all, public information."

"I can explain all that," Stafford offered, "but I'd like to arrange for you to come on down so that we could chat in person."

"When?"

"At your convenience, really, anytime you like. Late afternoon, say, any day. Saturday, even Sunday."

Elson visited Wharfield at work. "It's not over yet," he confided, over the bar, "but at least we've got a foot in the door." Elson also talked to Zimmer, who advised them to try to catch the administrators off guard with the question about documentation.

But the meeting with Stafford was another of those orchestrated performances to which the staff had become accustomed and which improved with each rehearsal. Elson learned little about the protocol of the decision that had come to haunt him and which more than anything else he sought to understand in order that the world, even if in some distorted way, might still make sense.

And so, when Glen Chiang, as with Blessings and the League ladies, again denied there was anything unusual in writing nothing down, and Frank Hines offered to discuss the district's recycling program, Elson realized that he had been had.

The annual Audubon Spring Fair and picnic might have been a gloomy affair were it not for a piece of good news. The lawyers had just the day before managed to obtain a temporary restraining order. As Eleanor Peavy went from cluster to cluster of picnicking families to recount personally her husband's skillful maneuver, she cautioned that it was just a first little step. The neighbors were nonetheless cheered.

The cautiously gleeful mood of the picnic was short lived, however. The parents' hope was dealt a severe blow the very next day by a flurry of activity. Eleanor Peavy, who lived directly across the street from Audubon, noticed that four men were loading furniture into moving vans. She immediately phoned Barbara Wolfe who consulted Jessica Flowers who activated the elaborate telephone tree they had devised for just such an emergency. Within half an hour a crowd had gathered on the lawn of the school.

"What shall we do?" a thin woman clutching a half-dressed infant asked Eleanor Peavy, who was trying to conduct the semblance of a meeting.

"Someone has called Stafford to ask why they're moving out on the weekend," Eleanor said, "but other than that I'm open to suggestions."

"I say we try to explain the situation to the drivers," the thin woman suggested.

"Bullshit," Dr. Fulton said, "we should lie down in the driveway in front of the trucks."

"I was just suggesting we try to reason with them first," the woman insisted. "We should let them know they're ripping off the children. Maybe they have kids too."

"Has anyone called the police?"

"What for?" said the man who had just reached Stafford at home. "There's no crime. It's all perfectly legal. I'm only surprised they didn't do it at night."

"What about the restraining order?" Dr. Fulton wanted to know.

"What do you want us to do," Eleanor Peavy replied, "call the judge on a Sunday? If the temporary order becomes permanent, then we can get them to put everything back."

The loading of the furniture preceded by only a couple of days the unfortunate outcome of the legal case. The judge, anxious to avoid hearing it at all, declared the plea of the Audubon parents inadmissible in his court. His ruling initiated a shift in the tactics of the neighbors away from a quick legal solution and toward increased efforts to sway public opinion.

Thus began the reign of letters. Outraged parents wrote the newspaper to protest the relocation of their children. The newspaper loved the controversy which increased circulation. In any given copy of the *Tribunal* one could read two or three diatribes against the Board. Typically, the author would accuse the Adjustors of acting illegally, of not thinking of education, of playing politics with children. Just as regularly, letters, written for the most part by Tucker, though signed by other loyal PAP members, appeared in response.

"We the citizens of Beacon should be appalled," one such letter signed by James Meyer began, "that a handful of angry parents should think of themselves before thinking of the good of all our children." Others focused upon what was perceived to be the privilege of a few. "One segment of this town has for years hogged more than its share of the city's wealth, and now once again with its team of lawyer daddies it is trying to buy the biggest slice of the pie."

In order to make headway with what they assumed to be their natural allies, the parents began a phone campaign to convince the residents of other hill neighborhoods that if they allowed Audubon to be attacked, they might be next. Such warnings fell on deaf ears, since the others were convinced of just the opposite. The more Audubon was besieged, the less the others had to fear. Some even secretly felt, though they dared say nothing, that their own property values would rise.

The Audubon mothers met one morning a week for coffee and to telephone. Most of the calls were greeted with a friendly but patronizing, "I personally believe that it was wrong to single out Audubon, but if they had to try it somewhere . . ." There was never any follow-up as the mothers had planned at the outset. After several weeks they became discouraged. Fewer and fewer attended the public relations meetings which rapidly turned into seminars in self-criticism.

The Audubon parents still tried to convince the Board of its mistake. Long after the Adjustors would no longer return their calls, they continued to show up at the weekly meetings to plead and cajole. Each time McPhail used the occasion to remind the radio audience that it was the same small band. Someone from the Capital Exchange was usually there to cluck his or her tongue.

The only thing that gave the Audubon neighbors the faintest glimmer of hope as summer began to fade was a meeting they managed to obtain with State Assemblyman Peterson. The parents carefully discussed who should come along and what they would say. They agreed that it might be best if Barbara Wolfe, given her early stand in favor of Stafford's plan, stayed behind. From that moment on she lost interest in the struggle. Wharfield, Eleanor Peavy, and Elson made the trip to Assemblyman Peterson's office. Elson was struck by the plushness of his chambers. The thick carpet on the floor matched the drapes. Both were coordinated with the carefully selected modern furniture and meticulously painted walls on which were hung various diplomas and awards. The long credenza under the bank of redwood windows held several rows of the kinds of photographs almost obligatory for those elected to public office—pictures of family, of handshakes with various more important officials, of ground breakings and testimonial dinners.

Jim Peterson was one of those local political figures so used to pleasing others that his face had lost any trace of distinctness, any line or mark that might somehow indicate the possibility of a thought other than that he imagined to be capable of garnering the greatest number of votes. Such flaccidness was compounded, Elson later learned, by a drinking problem that denied to the darker areas just beneath the eyes even the distinction of wisdom or age. The Audubon parents pleaded for him to intercede on their behalf. They recounted the arguments they had grown so accustomed to presenting either in the paper or before the Board. All to little avail. Assemblyman Peterson was evasive, saying simply that he had always fought, and would continue to fight, for educational reform. The skillful politician offered sympathy and moral support but nothing more.

At the end of the summer Elson went fishing with his older son. They left early enough in the morning to make the evening hatch on Silver Creek. As he was tying on a very small fly, struggling against the fading light, Elson laughed. He had caught himself in one of the moments of self-perception that had occupied such a large place in his seminar on laughter that spring. "Of course Peterson promised nothing," he thought, "he's in their pocket too. How naive can we be?" Elson reached into his fishing vest and made a note on the back of an empty leader package. Just then, Dylan, who had been fishing the hole just beyond a clump of duckweed, let out a shriek of the kind that at first allows no distinction between terror and joy. Elson managed to pull his waders from the muck, and, climbing on the bank, admired the boy, waist-high in the swift current, landing a large rainbow trout. As they held the mouth of the sparkling fish, silver on top, pinkish on the side, against the current before releasing it, Elson smiled. The struggle in Beacon was like fishing, he thought. It was time for lighter tackle and finer flies.

The next day they moved to the Henry's Fork and then to the Madison. When the fishing slackened in midafternoon he and Dylan lay down on a bluff where they watched a woman dressed in hip boots and a cowboy hat. Despite the slowing of the river's action, she continued to pull fish after fish from the raging stream, using a technique that Elson had read about but never practiced—nymphing. Dylan went down to watch her, and she gave several of the little shaggy lures to the fascinated twelve-year-old, who immediately caught two big browns. That night in the motel room father and son worked until midnight, tying enough nymphs to get them through the next couple of days.

The change of light and air, the high mountain scenery, helped Elson to forget his obsession with McPhail and the Board. Rather, he began to think one afternoon while fishing next to a steamy geyser on the Firehole about the way obsessions displace each other.

He wrote on the reverse side of a leader packet, "The object of fixation doesn't matter. It could be children, fishing, or Proust. Come to think of it, that's what Proust calls falling in love." Elson's mind began to turn in circles. "If the object of fixation doesn't matter, what prevents my discovery about fixation from becoming just another obsession? Then there really would be no outside. Fascination and the esthetic are connected. If I could shift obsessions a bit, I could transform what I used to think was paranoia into a work of art."

"Do you remember the eighteen-incher on the number sixteen Adams?" Dylan asked over dinner. Elson, who was daydreaming, did not respond.

"God, for the first time in months you seemed to be there," the boy said, "and now, you've gone away again."

"I'm sorry, could you repeat the question? I was thinking about something."

"Honestly, you're so distracted. It's as if you're not in the room. What were you thinking about anyway? Same old stuff? Saving Beacon?"

"No, actually, I was thinking about writing."

"Writing what? Another letter to the editor about how corrupt everything is?"

"I was thinking about writing a work of fiction, maybe nothing as ambitious as a novel. A short story, perhaps."

"What about?"

"Well, I'm not really sure what I could write about. I've read a lot of what you would call critical books, that's like philosophy, but they wouldn't make a very good tale. Fishing is about the only thing I know, I mean firsthand."

"Why don't you write about fishing then?"

"Oh, it's just a fantasy. I wouldn't know where to start."

But Elson did start in a modest way. Later that evening he noted, "Fishing as metaphor and the metaphor of fish in Western art. Proust compares making unexpected links between unconnected things to bringing a fish to the surface of water in whose depths it was invisible."

On the banks of the Firehole River, with grasshoppers jumping all along the chalky, sulphurous undercut edge, Elson watched Dylan cast a number fourteen caddis to a rising rainbow and understood something which, at least for the rest of their trip, seemed an enduring truth. That is, the extent to which his own children had surpassed him in almost every respect. At Dylan's age he didn't know how to tie flies, much less to fish like that. And as he watched an elk that had come to drink in the evening at the edge of the alternately chilly and boiling stream, standing no farther from Dylan than the length of the child's controlled casts, Elson laughed, realizing that his mother would never have let him near dangerous water like that.

The lull in Elson's obsession did not last long. Several things happened in the days following his return to Beacon that upset him as much the prospect of losing the battle over the children. He began receiving pieces of anonymous mail at his office. One contained letters carefully cut from newspaper headlines. It read *This One's for Writing to the Gov.* The second was a mawkish sweet sixteen card on which was written an invitation to call the following telephone number. Elson dialed, listened just long enough to realize that the recorded anti-Semitic message must be that of some ultra right-wing group, and hung up. At least it had not been a local number.

Shortly after dinner two days later an older neighborhood couple knocked on his door and asked to come in. They explained in a distinctly patronizing tone that Audubon had always been a quiet neighborhood and that they preferred to keep it that way.

"My own stance has been to maintain a low profile," said the old man, "so that our homes don't start to look like the slums of New York."

"I beg your pardon," Elson said.

"We think that all your protest is drawing too much attention," the man's wife added, "which is why they want to take the children."

"But we only protested after they said they were . . ."

"It doesn't matter," the man replied, "now they're going to use it to attract the wrong element to the neighborhood, and some people are saying it's your fault."

A strange sensation came over Elson. For a moment he was rooting for the opposition – he would have liked to see the City appropriate the old couple's house and turn it into a brothel.

Several days later, while Elson was at his office counseling the fall semester's new students, someone threw a rock through his front window. He never knew whether it came from his enemies on the Board or from an irate neighbor.

8

THE AUDUBON BRIGADE

■ Gradually, the Audubon parents realized one by one that all the visits downtown and upstate were symptoms of defeat. By a slow process of attrition, those who could not leave Beacon or send their offspring to relatives nearby came to accept, as they phrased it to themselves, that "the children would no longer be living at home." To explain the situation to the children, who suspected something was wrong without knowing exactly what, Norman and Linda Elson consulted Luftman.

"Experience shows," the therapist said, "that consistency is the rule. If there's no alternative, then give the children your support, and try not to intensify what must already be a tremendous sense of anxiety for them."

"Intensify anxiety?" Elson gasped. "We're talking about relocation."

"I know, and you know, but we must be sure that they don't know. So let's try to use a less aggressive term. I've worked with many of the parents preparing for the move to Dred, and there is not necessarily any reason to fear long-term psychic effects."

"Long-term effects on whom?" Elson asked.

"If you're thinking about yours and Linda's relationship, I'd be glad to help in any way I can. Would you like to come in, say, twice a week?"

"No thanks. I don't need more support groups to help me get over the goddamn fact they're carting off our kids."

"I know how you must feel," Luftman assured the Elsons, "but it wouldn't be fair to let your own fears spill over onto Dylan and Rachel. You must give them the psychic space to make their own choices."

"What choices?" Norman asked. "They didn't give us any choice."

"I think I detect a generational rivalry thing creeping in here," the therapist warned. "Let's not deny our children what we think we didn't have. Parental pressure will only harm their already fragile sense of self."

"What would you do if you were us?"

"We must try not to personalize the therapeutic setting. Now, if I can be of any assistance during this difficult transition period, please don't hesitate to call."

No less anxious after the visit with Luftman, Linda and Norman found themselves obliged to identify with the enemy to the extent of justifying some brave new social experiment from which the family would emerge stronger. Linda promised the children that they would be with their friends, that she and Norman would come to see them on visiting days, and that they would be taken care of.

"Some kids," she comforted them, "lose their parents at an early age."

"You mean we should feel thankful we're not orphans?" Rachel said.

"Not exactly, but don't forget that many children, and some of the most privileged, live away from home at boarding school and think nothing of it."

"That's not what I call privileged," Rachel said.

The children moped about the house. Rachel seemed more irritable than usual. Dylan complained of nightmares. Each time Elson became aware of what he imagined to be their suffering, he remembered something that Joel Steinhammer had said at the time of the Board's decision—that children were very adaptable and that change did them good. He wanted to believe the Adjustor, which only unleashed a new round of obsession.

Elson would shut himself in his study from early morning until dinner. Linda never knew whether he was working on some urgent literary project or just brooding since her loving attempts to draw him out were invariably thwarted by his refusal to speak. It was during this period that the 3×5 cards, which the professor had always produced at the regular rate of one or two a day, ten or twelve a week, multiplied, dominating his psychic life. He would write one after the other, arranging them on bookshelves and in files, changing their order, destroying the ones that, in as little as twenty-four hours, no longer made sense.

Nor was he unconscious of what was happening. A whole series of cards which ended up under the letter *C* detailed Elson's helplessness even to escape the vicious cycle of cards written about writing cards.

Late that summer was a time of ground breaking. The developers were as eager to begin as the Chief was anxious to bring the Blackstone project into being.

Tucker insisted that the Truscott Corporation sponsor an elaborate ceremony to mark its arrival in Beacon, and there was a picture in the *Tribunal* of Jerome Horton dressed in a hard hat picking up a shovelful of dirt. He was surrounded by a handful of smiling model citizens—two members of the Gray Panthers, Pam Sidel and Larry Newton, Assemblyman Peterson, Martin Wasserman and Howard Greer—plus vice-presidents Porter and Nelson.

Elson was phoned by Wharfield, who had talked to Zimmer, who had been awakened at some ungodly hour of the morning by Blessings, who somehow had managed to get the paper before it was distributed. They were not so much shocked as excited, perversely, by the publicity which would cause others to see that they had been right all along about the Blackstone and to wake up to what was about to happen with the schools.

When that did not happen, they became disheartened by the indifference that began to set in among the neighbors who abandoned the struggle one by one. Some admitted defeat, resigned in the face of what they saw to be the inexorable march of a new social destiny. Others claimed to be preoccupied. "I would love to help," the wife of one of Elson's colleagues confided, "but this is Willy's tenure year, and what with all the wee ones." Elson was particularly depressed when, making his way down the shrinking phone list of an organization they had formed called Save Our Children, Ellie Pearl refused either to contribute money or to attend any further meetings. "It makes no difference what we do," she reluctantly confessed. "Anyway, Sid and I are spending all our spare time working on nurturing ourselves."

Elson took what solace he could in the graduate seminar he was to teach that fall entitled "The Human Condition." The works discussed in class taught how readily those who are oppressed identify with their oppressors. Elson encouraged the few parents still working with him to read Camus's *The Plague* and Malraux's *Man's Fate* in order that they might not lose heart. The results were not always what he expected. Blessings refused right away on the grounds that she was too busy. Zimmer made fun of him for thinking that one could learn anything from a book. Wharfield, on the other hand, enjoyed the reading and asked for more. Elson passed him a copy of André Gide's *Counterfeiters*. "If we are going to understand anything about the present struggle," he assured the barman during one of their nocturnal jogs, "we must come to grips with the positive function of evil."

"That sounds like a contradiction."

"Not exactly. You know as well as I that we're never going to eliminate evil, which just changes form every time we try. What we can do is to use our intelligence, and the knowledge we have gained about the power of indirection, to make a better world."

"Isn't that elitist?"

"Perhaps. But sometimes it's possible for people with superior vision, artists for example, to transform what is mean and petty about the human condition into a greater good. We are artists in an artless world. Where the painter may use oils on canvas, or the writer pen on paper, we're using our lives as creative tools. There may, of course, be some sacrifices along the way."

As the number of interested neighbors dwindled, the small group of East Rock parents joined with their fellows of the Audubon to form the Audubon Brigade. They thought of themselves as freedom fighters, partisans in some brave resistance movement. They would talk on the phone at least once a day and would meet once a week. At first they gathered casually at the Daedalus at the end of Wharfield's shift. Then, because a certain tendency to overdramatize led them to imagine they were being watched even within the safety of the pub, they moved to Zimmer's house. There they acted like members of an underground, discussing what scant news appeared in the paper, verifying this or that rumor, plotting strategy, trying to interpret the little signs in their enemy's behavior that would yield some hint of what was in store, such as Tucker's mysterious exit from Wonderland Day Care one morning just as Elson arrived to drop off Alex.

Like a secret teenage boys club, they elected officers. Elson, because of his professional degree, was named Chair. Wharfield, who continued to take copious notes of all that was said, made a natural Secretary. Zimmer's experience in real estate earned him the title of Treasurer. They even had T-shirts made to order with the inscription *Obey Little, Resist a Lot.* The resisters would sometimes be joined by an outsider. Zimmer and Wharfield encouraged Reed to take a more active role. The bug man dropped by occasionally until he ran into Blessings, who appeared between other meetings to relate what she had gleaned from her circulation through Beacon's civic bodies. She would enter in a whirlwind of gossip, spouting accusations, offering the sketchy details of Horton's and Tucker's plot to take over the city.

"They want to divide us," she inevitably began, "because there's only a few of them and lots of us."

"There's not so many of us," Elson said.

"I mean in the whole town. They want to get us fighting with each other so they can step in. It's all part of the plan."

"What plan?" Elson asked.

"To get the Audubon parents to fight with the East Rock parents. Don't you see, that's the only way they can rule. But it's not them. It's people from outside."

"Who?"

"Come on, Norman, we've been over this a hundred times. Here, read this." She held out a copy of the seventh issue of the Urban Awareness Alliance Newsletter. "This tells all about Truscott's connections to one of the biggest Mafia people in the state. They want to bring in their friends and make this the first city."

"The first what?"

"The first communist city in America." Blessings pronounced these words with such a violent gesture that a small cloud of feathers puffed out of holes in both arms of her down parka.

"The Mafia in with the communists? That just doesn't compute," Elson replied. "A big corporation like Truscott may be connected to some kind of underworld, but I hardly think they're anxious to turn Beacon into some kind of brave new socialist world."

"Wait, you'll see. I attended a workshop lately on ways for socialists to make their capital work. From there it's only a step to what's going on in Beacon. The capitalists are using the local communists to make money, and the communists are using capital to further their social aims. It's clear as day with the children. They want us out, and they figure taking kids is the way to do it."

"Still doesn't make sense," Elson protested.

"They think schools are middle class, and if they could just get rid of the middle, then whatever they call it, something like crass warfare, will begin. It's all meant to polarize."

"I think it's actually class warfare," Elson corrected her. "Anyway, red-baiting will get us nowhere."

"I don't care if they're communists or socialists or anything else," Zimmer said. "All I know is they're cutting deals and fucking up my neighborhood."

"You mean there's a deal, and you're not in on it, is that it?" Blessings asked. "Honestly, you men are on such an ego trip you can't get together on anything. That's your problem."

"And your problem," Zimmer snarled, "is that you're so disconnected you connect everything, so that nobody can follow a fucking word you say. You take a piece of thirdhand cockamamy rumor and blow it all over the place until nobody will believe us on anything. Then you wonder why people think we're nuts."

"Oh, no, no you don't, you're not going to pin this one on me. No thanks. If nobody believes you, it's because you used to be in real estate and now you smoke too much dope. You hang out in your men's club instead of fighting like in the old days. Anyway, I can't waste any more time around here."

What depressed the small band of resisters most was that many residents of the threatened zones began to think about leaving. It was hard to tell at first if houses came on the market due to the recent decline in interest rates, some seasonal cycle, or a loss of faith in the future of Beacon. Zimmer seemed the most immediately alarmed. "Believe me, I was in the business. I can smell when people want to sell."

Houses may have been put up for sale, but they did not sell as quickly as they once did. Suddenly, a couple of incidents in the Audubon neighborhood gave pause to those who would never have imagined moving—including some who had lived in Beacon all their lives. Several suspicious fires were contained by less than swift action on the part of local firefighters. Rumor had it that the fire department had been instructed by some high official to respond only minimally to calls from certain areas of town. Then there was a rash of armed break-ins by a gang that followed citizens walking their dogs right up to the doors of their homes, which they would enter at gunpoint. The gang threatened and robbed their victims before tying them up and driving off in their cars. The police seemed as slow in responding as the fire department and on several occasions claimed not to have been able to find a particular street or house. This fanned the rumor that the police too had been instructed to exert as little effort as possible in combatting crime in the Audubon.

Elson, who until then had not been afraid for his physical safety, bought a larger dog. He and Linda unlisted their phone and argued about installing a burglar alarm. Their long-running dispute about whether to move took on an added dimension.

"The place is turning into a gulag, and it'll only get worse," Elson said, knowing as he did that such talk would eventually irk Linda into some kind of response which, though it might contest what he said, would nonetheless reassure him that things were not as bad as he claimed. Shawn Luftman had spotted the pattern and referred to it as Norman's "little child within thing."

"Oh, come on," Linda replied, "this is just a bad phase that will pass. We should be buying houses now instead of thinking about moving. Think of all the money we'd make when prices rise."

"The difference between us and those around us is that I study history. I can tell when it's time."

"You're beginning to sound like Zimmer. Why do we have to listen to him?"

When the actual day came for the children to leave their homes there were, of course, tearful embraces as clusters of parents hugged their offspring at the bus stops where in previous years the children waited alone. There was long and demonstrative waving and blowing of kisses as the heavy diesel pulled away. But the children stopped crying immediately upon the arrival at Dred Scott for which Tucker, in consultation with Martin Wasserman, had carefully planned.

As soon as the door of the bus opened a gaggle of women with long hair and peasant blouses descended, arms outstretched, hands full of tofutti popsicles and carob cookies. Led by Terri Kantor, they constituted Beacon's Maternal Nurture Corps, an elite crew hand-picked by Tucker to ease the children's transition between their families and their new home. Their task was, in fact, easier than anyone might have guessed, and precisely for the reason that caused Elson's unease. The Nurture Corps, full of warmth and interest, provided what the kids had most lacked at home, especially in recent months when their parents were so involved in the struggle to save the Blackstone or were simply alienated and depressed.

Over the main portal of Dred Scott could be read the motto that would become the watchword of the children's stay—*Progress Dwells in the Community That Thinks Globally and Acts Locally.* Once inside, they were greeted by yet another phalanx of Nurturers who had studied the photos submitted as part of registration and seemed magically to know each child's name. The younger ones were led to a room where there were stories, the older ones to a giant game parlor with as many free video games as they could play. Around lunchtime they were bathed and shown the long dormitory rooms on the third floor where every child found waiting on his or her bed not only the fresh underwear brought from home, but two attractive uniforms, a pair of jeans, and a new-age puzzle made of rope and hand-polished hardwood.

For the children, life at Dred Scott held the promise of summer camp all year long. They would rise in the morning, make their beds, and prepare for breakfast which was never the chaotic affair most were used to at home. The case of Dylan and Rachel Elson was not unusual. There were no anxious parents already enmeshed in newspapers by the time they came downstairs or rushing to get younger siblings to day care before rushing off to work. There were no interrogations over permission slips, or reproaches over spilled batter and messy rooms. Instead, the Nurture Corps arrived each morning with warm whole wheat croissants and jelly, and thoughts only of the children's welfare. Nor was the daily schedule ever uncertain. After breakfast and clean-up Terri Kantor read the list of activities. Then, voice filled with interest, she asked her captive young if there were any questions, which there never were.

From breakfast the children moved to classrooms where they attended courses not unlike those they had always known, except for the specially designed social studies curriculum that ended each morning. In these groups they discussed issues as varied as world peace, the environment, safe sex, and domestic violence.

After lunch they would nap or read books selected by Tucker in consultation with Glen Chiang. The older ones were permitted to write one letter a week to be deposited in an open envelope for posting. The occasional negative letter was mysteriously lost in the shuffle, but most were full of praise for their new home. This depressed Elson, since he had counted on the children's letters as tangible proof of the mistreatment of minors that would finally cause the outside world to listen.

The quiet period over, the children would again gather for classes, ending the afternoon with recess—aerobic exercise and games that encouraged cooperation not competition.

All through the day children were removed one by one from class or gym for a series of individual consultations which they were strictly forbidden to discuss with each other. During these meetings with an even more elite group, the intelligence services of the Maternal Nurture Corps, they were asked questions about their family—easy questions at first having to do with the layout of their former homes, what they ate, or where their mothers and fathers worked, then more difficult ones such as how their parents related or if they ever fought and what they fought about. Such was the prelude to a deeper probe into family secrets. Wasserman scrutinized the answers each night and drew up a list that determined the next day's line of inquiry. Information gleaned about families considered to be especially troublesome was entered into a computer run by a software package—called Socialnet—designed for input and output of positive communal thinking. Tucker read the printouts once a week. This was how he learned that Elson, up until the time of the children's departure, still engaged in writing letters to outside political groups and that he and Linda had seen a marriage counselor.

In the Audubon a kind of general panic set in slowly, almost imperciptibly, as the neighbors noticed that a deluge of *For Sale* signs appeared on front lawns. The Beacon Board of Realtors was at first excited by the prospect. But, as prices began to soften, then to slide, and, finally, to tumble, the realtors were less enthused. Soon it seemed as if every other house on certain blocks was offered for sale. The Audubon neighborhood, one of Beacon's oldest, suddenly took on the appearance of a new tract development ready to be disposed of by an ambitious developer all at once. But nobody was buying. Nobody, that is, except a few adventuresome citizens who had, it seemed, a limitless source of newfound capital.

All through the summer the Capital Exchange was engaged in feverish activity consummated by one final meeting at which Tucker announced that they would soon reap their reward.

"You have all been extremely good over the past few months," he told the group of loyal followers who had almost completely forgotten the reason why they had been called to attend public gatherings and write letters. "I have a couple of pieces of extremely good news. First, if you approve, we will be joined by a new member. I propose that we make Gloria Martinez a director of the Capital Exchange, since we can all learn from her experience as aide to the President of the Board of Adjustments. I have spoken to Gloria, and she agrees . . ."

"Wait," Pam Sidel interrupted, "isn't she the lawyer's wife, the one who drives an expensive foreign car?"

"Yes, she is," Tucker said, "but you must realize that sometimes buying a foreign car can be an important political statement. Gloria courageously refuses to support the U.S. military industrial complex. Now, if you would allow me to continue," he said, "Gloria has some extra room in her house, and instead of becoming a landlord, she has offered to let us use it as an office."

"Does that mean we have to pay rent?" James Meyer asked.

"Not exactly," Tucker assured him. "That brings me to the second piece of good news. None of us will have to pay rent ever again."

"How's that?" Irving Caplow said.

"The progressive movement has finally obtained the means to finance affordable housing not only for those in need, but for those who have struggled all along."

Caplow removed the cap from over his eyes.

"That's right," Tucker continued, "now here's how it works.

Together with a small group of right-thinking backers we have created a financial institution that will lend money to people in need at extremely moderate rates. This will permit those who are worthy to purchase affordable housing."

"What do you mean, worthy?" Caplow asked.

"Well the worthies could include a number of people."

"Like us?"

"Of course. That is, if you're interested." The directors were all sitting in an upright position and seemed wholly conscious for perhaps the first time since their incorporation. "I thought we might create a special category of extremely worthy to cover those who have worked hard over the years. Those who qualify would receive an interest-free loan, say, over a ninety-year period."

"Ninety years, we'll all be dead," Pam Sidel squealed, delighted to have found a chink in Tucker's flawless armor.

"That's the point," the aide responded. "It'd really be more like a permanent grant for noble service. Let's see, can we take a vote?" The directors raised their hands.

"Wait just a minute," Larry Newton interrupted. "Wouldn't we be landlords?"

"Not exactly," Tucker said. "We'd be earning sweat equity, and that's not the same as being a landlord since it's more equitable. At worse you'd be a property owner."

"We'd have to pay something, wouldn't we?" Newton asked weakly. "How would we pay even for an interest-free loan?"

"You do have some source of income, don't you?" Tucker asked. "Some of you might want to supplement that by working for the housing authority which would administer the loans. You wouldn't make much, but it should cover your monthly payments."

The Capital Exchange thus voted to reconstitute itself, including Gloria Martinez, as a branch of the Beacon Home Exchange Bank with headquarters on Lincoln Street and with a capital of a little over four million dollars. They had cards and stationery printed in addition to a little brochure which the directors distributed to friends like party invitations. "City-backed loans," the pamphlet promised. "Borrowers must be a first-time homeowner. Preference given to aged, other-abled, single parents, living groups with a strong ideological basis."

The Beacon Home Exchange Bank met more often in the following weeks than at any time before. They were obliged to decide whether to fund applications from non-Beacon residents and how to establish priorities among those who qualified under more than one category. When it came to the question of loans to their own family members, the directors debated long and hard, finally allowing each to offer five grants on a discretionary basis. Such decisions, not to mention the task of screening the applications, conducting interviews, and making the actual selection, took so much effort that the members of the Capital Exchange barely had time to seek their own future homes.

The directors came to constitute a small coterie whose members would speak only to each other, and only about the thing which concerned them the most—the purchase and fixing up of houses. They found a natural leader in Gloria Martinez, who was the only one to have owned property before. Gloria was like a mother hen, scout leader, and spiritual advisor all in one. The others would make no move without consulting her first. They called to seek approval of agents, to gossip about a particular house, to ask her advice about the cost of landscaping or remodeling. In turn, Gloria was pleased to find herself so needed by those less experienced than herself. None of the directors dared to purchase without inviting the others to look. In most instances they returned en masse several times, offering little suggestions as to how a living room might be made lighter, a kitchen more efficient, a bedroom more tranquil. They got to know the names of the most appropriate contractors and merchants—hardware and paint stores, experts in roofing, drainage, and sheet metal.

Moving day was always a festive event. The person changing houses rented a truck that the others would load and unload. Gloria, dressed in workman's gloves and designer overalls Alan had purchased at Neiman Marcus, would be there to orchestrate the delicate maneuvering of old sofas, cartons, posters, and plants from the underground grottos in which most of the members of the Capital Exchange had lived. The group would finish its day of labor with dinner arranged by Gloria and catered by one of the local gourmet shops. On one such occasion she unveiled at the end of a meal of smoked chicken on its bed of radiccio a Grand Marnier torte on which was inscribed *Power to the People.* Then there would be the letdown, that moment at which, all gathered in the living room of the new home, the owner would realize that he or she didn't have enough furniture to fill the empty echoing space.

"Don't worry," Gloria assured the group, "every house is like this when you first move in. As an aide to the President of the Board part of my job is to know the best thrift shops around. We'll have you fixed up in no time." Under her guidance the "exchangers" rushed off to the flea market and second-hand shops. They would appear faithfully at the garage sales that were such a regular part of Saturday mornings in Beacon, all the more since those lucky enough to leave the Audubon were anxious to dispose of accumulated household goods. For Gloria's little clan, moving represented a form of combined physical therapy and social life.

Toward the end of fall a bright orange-colored truck pulled up across the street from the Elson home. Norman watched as a band of middle-aged men with wire rimmed glasses, pony tails, Birkenstocks, and beards unloaded boxes of records and books, a few pieces of furniture, and a stereo set. "These must be the new neighbors," he thought and continued writing the article that had developed from the note he had scribbled on politics and paranoia. Later in the week he and Linda dropped by with a plate of cookies to meet the owner, who introduced himself as James Meyer. The dark wainscoting and beams of Meyer's new house gave it the feel of an aristocrat's hunting lodge. Despite the clutter of unpacked crates, the empty echoing space made it clear that this was a house too big for one. Indeed, a three-legged rustic milking stool was the only visible piece of furniture—on which, still dusty and dressed in overalls, sat none other than Moses Reed.

Meyer asked the Elsons if they would like something hot to drink. As soon as he turned toward the kitchen, Norman, who hadn't seen Reed since the bug man ran into his ex-wife at Zimmer's, put a finger to his lips to signal that it would be best for both to remain quiet. The Elsons found Meyer congenial enough, though Linda thought it curious that he never returned their plate.

Elson assumed that Reed's truck, parked regularly across the street, meant nothing more than a routine extermination. In fact, he thought no more about his new neighbor until one day, lifting his eyes from the book he was reading, he saw from his study Gloria Martinez enter James Meyer's infested lair. Yet more alarming, he saw her come back a second day, and a third.

"I don't know whether I should give you this right away," Gloria, dressed in a pink silk turban with matching culottes, teased. "It's something a little special to make a house a home." She extended a Saks Fifth Avenue shopping bag toward Meyer, who began to tear ferociously at the inner wrapping.

"It's beautiful," he exclaimed, holding up to the middle of the bare wall a gold-framed needlepoint sampler that read *Thank You for Not Smoking in Our Home.*

"Now," Gloria urged, "let's get down to work. I've given a good deal of thought lately to your layout, and I think it would be a good idea to break down the wall between the dining room and the kitchen."

"Break down the wall?" Meyer gasped. "That costs money."

"I know," she insisted, "but it's worth it. Walls create barriers between people. You wouldn't want the person cooking in the kitchen to feel excluded, would you? And while we're on the subject, I've also been thinking about nature. We must create a comfortable atmosphere for plants. That means skylights over here."

"Skylights?" Meyer muttered.

"Yes. We simply must bring in light to make things seem more outdoorsy. The difference between inside and outside is one more of those things that leads to differences between people. Now, I know just the skylight man. One hundred percent correct." Meyer acquiesced.

Elson, meanwhile, informed Zimmer of Gloria's repeated presence in the Audubon.

"The bitch is up to no good. You think she's fucking him?" he asked.

"He doesn't look the type," Elson replied.

But the community activist, unable to resist even the slimmest lead, dropped in on Reed. Having just finished a dinner of spoon bread and kale, the exterminator was drinking the still warm liquid from a bowl.

"Sure she comes over," Reed said.

"What do they talk about?"

"Mostly about fixing up the house. I hear them moving from room to room discussing curtains and paint. She sounds like an expert, spouting off about carpet and drapes, this color this, that color that. He'll ask what cleaning product to use, and she sounds like a TV commercial for Mr. Clean."

"How about Meyer?"

"The man's not where it's at."

"Let's do some recording anyway. You never can tell."

To Elson's surprise things were slightly easier once the children were gone. Not only were they no longer there to remind him of some unknown horror to come, but daily life was less chaotic with only Alex to care for. Gradually regret replaced fear. Elson realized how little he actually had communicated with Dylan and Rachel while they were living together. Oh, he had been what any outside observer would have considered a dutiful father, going through the motions of attention and respect, giving advice, correcting homework, and visiting their school, but they rarely had spoken about the things that mattered.

Elson acknowledged that he had very little sense of who his children were. It reminded him of another secret sadness, the feeling of not having known his own father even to the extent of not knowing whether his father felt the same way about his father or about him. Elson vowed to do something about this feeling when circumstances permitted, and he tried during the weekly visits at Dred to talk about it with Dylan and Rachel. That was difficult, however. Immediate relatives were allowed to see the children only on the large paved playground between the main building and the sheds aligned along one of Beacon's busiest streets. There was no privacy, and the children seemed more interested in telling about what they had been doing than in talking about communicating with their parents. Elson and Linda were to some degree even consoled that Dylan and Rachel seemed to be interested in something and not merely fearful and mopey as before their departure. The older children were, of course, always anxious to see and hold Alex.

A few parents were actually pleased at the internment. Those who had had a hard time caring for children, given difficult economic times and the former lack of adequate housing in Beacon, found that a load had been lifted from their shoulders. Reed, for example, was relieved not to have to ask his mother to babysit Ocean in the almost total absence of Blessings. He was able to work long hours in James Meyer's basement.

One day well into the job of reinforcing Meyer's foundation so that the workmen upstairs could remove a wall, the alert exterminator phoned Zimmer to report that Gloria Martinez had arrived that morning to help select wallpaper.

"They had expresso. Then they started to reminisce about old times and to argue about money."

"How much are we talking?" Zimmer asked.

"It was pretty hard to hear," Reed said, and the recording wasn't worth a damn. Not like the old days of heating ducts. I only hear what comes straight through the floor, and I had my head up against the post so long I got splinters in my earlobes. They did mention something called the Capital Exchange. One of them, I can't remember which, kept taking about a bank, or banking at night. In between all the lifting and shuffling of materials, about all I could make out was Meyer asking Gloria if she thought something was immoral."

"Oh, yeah, what'd she say?"

"She said not to worry, that even if whatever they were talking about was immoral, it wasn't illegal, and even if it was illegal, she would see to it they didn't get caught."

"I knew it," Zimmer said. "How about Meyer? Where'd he get the cash to buy in the Audubon?"

"Got me. All I do is get rid of the termites and clean out the rot."

With no news from Reed for some time and little hope of awakening the conscience of Beacon, Zimmer took once again to following the Adjustors around. "I know they'll do something stupid sooner or later," he told Karen over dinner, "then we'll nail the suckers."

In shadowing McPhail's circumnavigations throughout Beacon, Zimmer thought he had spotted just the break for which they had been waiting. He noticed that the President of the Board dropped by Dred Scott slightly too often for such visits to consist only of official business. He waited patiently for the one teacher he knew to leave the premises and managed to learn that McPhail always stopped by the classroom of a second grade instructor named Daisy Herring.

Zimmer decided to attempt something daring. That Sunday, changing his clogs for sneakers, he entered the playground of Dred Scott during the parents' regular visiting hours and actually managed to stay the night, hiding first in the stall of a bathroom, then in an apparently unused broom closet where he slept. The closet was just opposite Daisy Herring's classroom.

Early the next morning the children were brought from the cafeteria after breakfast. By merely opening and closing the door Zimmer could see who entered and left. A short man dressed in a gray Mao suit went into the orderly classroom. Zimmer watched him take attendance by marking names on a clipboard. It occurred to him that it was a lot like checking to see if your pet goldfish had escaped from the bowl. He saw the children leave for lunch and then recess. Zimmer waited, eating only the camping food he had brought in his pockets and drinking from the janitor's sink. Suddenly, toward late afternoon, as he had almost drifted into a doze, came the moment for which he had hoped. McPhail appeared and greeted Daisy Herring, who disappeared from view as she walked toward the seated students. The President of the Board of Adjustments then left the room holding by the hand not Daisy, but Ocean Reed. Zimmer watched as they rounded the corner.

Opening the closet door slowly so as to make no noise, and looking both ways to make sure the hallway was clear, Zimmer followed them through a basement corridor to an isolated part of the building where McPhail led Ocean into a large abandoned room that must once have been a cafeteria. McPhail withdrew a key from his pocket and opened a door marked *Staff Only,* which Zimmer imagined to be not unlike the broom closet where he had spent the night. No longer able to see them, he feared having lost the most promising trail yet. The community activist turned sleuth retreated on tiptoes the length of the cafeteria, reentered the corridor, and positioned himself next to an adjoining wall from which he could hear muffled sounds.

Zimmer was too disturbed to tell whether the queasiness which he felt invade his whole being came from having slept so little, from knowing Ocean's parents, or from the freeze-dried camping food that continued to swell in his stomach. Despite his physical distress, the ex-broker leaned close to the wall and listened, knowing that what he heard was likely to be something, finally, with which he could deal.

The year ended on a somber note. The children were given permission to spend the holidays with their parents, but many opted to remain at school. Of those who came home all were to some extent reserved. Few would talk about their experience while away, and many parents confessed to feeling that they were being eyed with suspicion.

Norman and Linda Elson tried to initiate a serious discussion with Dylan and Rachel over whether to leave Beacon for some new place where they would again be able to live together as a family. The children seemed at first not to understand, then very cautiously revealed that they had been instructed to report any such talk. The Elsons were torn between trying to reestablish contact with their children, thus alienating them from the environment to which they would return, and letting the matter drop. Norman protested what he openly referred to as their indoctrination, to which they replied almost in unison, "So what? You never seemed interested in anything we said when we lived here." In order to prove how attentive he could be Elson was forced into admitting he had almost never listened. The ten-day period was so painful for both parents that they were relieved when Dylan and Rachel were back at Dred.

After that things seemed a little better. For the first time since the Board of Adjustments had made boarding school available to all, Norman and Linda Elson spent a weekend away—with the Wharfields on the coast. There they slept late, read, played tennis and cards, cooked out, and ate too much. One night after a particularly copious serving of cracked crab they took a long walk in the sand. From the beach they could see into the homes where other families were eating together, playing games, or watching TV. Bonfires in the sand lit their way, creating the feeling of a warm summer night in the middle of winter. Had it been several months earlier, Norman and Linda Elson would have been indescribably sad. Now they could commiserate with the Wharfields. The two couples discovered together the feeling of having passed the most difficult stage of adjustment to their condition with the certainty that when things improved, as they no doubt would, they and they alone would know how to savor the moments that other families, congealed in their nightly routines, took for granted.

Zimmer finally received another call from Reed. "I don't know what it's worth," the termite man said, "but I'm just about through over at Meyer's and I thought I'd give you my new address."

"Where you off to next?" Zimmer asked.

"Believe it or not, I'm actually going to work for Eric Tucker. He's bought a big place over on Page and Dubois."

"Christ, you're lucky the radicals buy so many dumps."

"Wait a minute," Reed replied, "that's my bread and butter. If it wasn't for what you call dumps, I would have no business at all."

"Never mind, this time you've gone right to the top. Be sure to keep your ears open under Tucker's place, will you? I'll be around with more tapes as soon as I can."

Reed collected and delivered the materials he would need on Tucker's front lawn. He installed the jacks along the beetle-infested foundation. This was the most opportune time for eavesdropping since all the preparation—the placing of supports, the leveling of beams, the tightening of screws—made next to no noise, and he did not have to simulate the kind of activity—the sawing, hammering, and mixing of concrete—of the middle and final stages. Preparation also gave Reed the chance to check out the acoustics, to find the best places to hear the goings on upstairs when and if the situation warranted.

Reed was about to quit late one afternoon when he heard a voice that was familiar but that he could not place at first. It was not until he heard Tucker say, "Rory, you asshole, you've really blown it this time," that the exterminator realized that the feet standing just on the other side of the floorboards, not ten inches from his head, belonged to Rory McPhail. Then there was silence. The men walked toward the kitchen from which Reed could hear the noise of a kettle. They returned to the living room where they were joined by another voice which Reed recognized as that of Jerome Horton, who must have entered without knocking.

"Look, Rory," he heard Tucker say, "we've got a problem here. It seems you've been in the closet again. And not alone. Now that's not nice."

"Who told you that?"

"Does it matter?" There was a long silence during which Reed, had he been upstairs, would have seen McPhail simply bow his head.

"Naughty, naughty," Horton chastized.

"Come on, what do you have to say for yourself?" Tucker asked.

"It wasn't what you think. I only wanted to ask a few questions in private. It won't happen again, I promise." There was another long pause.

"From now on you leave the questions to us," Tucker insisted.

"I'm sorry. It was a mistake. What do you want me to do? Resign? Kill myself?"

"No," Tucker reassured him, "but we want you to know we've got spies in the field. Any more funny stuff and we're going to let the little wife know."

"Oh, no, wait, please, let's not bring her into this."

"You wait," Horton grew angry. "You're the little pervert who's gone and got yourself caught."

Tucker was consoling. "Rory, we've known each other a long time, and I would hate to see your fine family ruined by adverse publicity. I think you'll agree that the simplest thing for all concerned would be for you to be accommodating. Now, Jerome and I have been looking into the land along the waterfront. It seems . . ." There was a shuffling of feet that rendered the rest inaudible.

"Run along now," Tucker urged.

"You happy now," the aide said to the Chief, "killing two birds with one stone? We can up the stakes with Truscott and keep McPhail in tow."

Horton merely grunted.

That night Reed phoned to report what he had heard to Zimmer who made him repeat it several times. The community activist, disappointed that his bold anonymous telephone call to Tucker to denounce Adjustor McPhail had produced only the mildest rebuke, gathered Wharfield and Elson.

"McPhail's an abuser," he said straight out.

"Drugs are a new element," Elson replied, "but I'm not surprised. As the French say, that was the only thing missing."

"I don't give a fuck what the French would say. I ain't talking drugs. I'm talking child abuse."

"How do you know that?" Elson asked. Zimmer told him the story of hiding in the closet and following McPhail and Ocean down the hall.

"What are we going to do?" Wharfield asked.

"How about telling Lucille? Or just threatening?" Elson suggested. "We might be able to fix it so that we could influence McPhail."

"Are you kidding?" Zimmer said. "Tucker would only use it as an excuse to get rid of him. Then we'd have played the only card we got left. Come on, get serious."

"How about having Trenton wire Gloria's house again? We could . . ."

"Oh, yeah," Zimmer interrupted, "Trenton might as well wire his own dick. We could get stereo tapes of them pissing all over each other. We could make the cassettes into long-playing records. You know we tried all that with Tucker and Martinez and a lot of good it did. The problem is not getting the stuff, it's that nobody gives a damn."

"Christ," Elson blurted, "we've got to do something. It could be any one of our kids."

"I don't know how to break this to you," Zimmer said, "but it is."

"What do you mean?" Elson asked.

Zimmer was silent.

"Come on, cut the crap. You mean one of our kids?"

Still Zimmer said nothing.

"Leon, don't mess with us like that."

"You don't want to know," the ex-agent said.

"You saw it?" Elson asked.

"Not exactly. But I know another teacher," Zimmer lied. "So I asked her who McPhail takes out of her room. She mentioned three or four names." Elson grew quiet.

"Look," Zimmer added, "if it's any consolation, I stopped it."

"You what?"

"I stopped it. I mean I put the word out to the Chief that if he didn't get the President of his Board of Adjustments to stop molesting children, I'd blow it to the press that his early childhood development program was code for child abuse. My sources tell me McPhail hasn't been near Dred Scott since."

"It's a wonder," Wharfield said, "that nobody's gone in there with a bomb or at least a gun."

"Blowing 'em away wouldn't be worth it," Zimmer countered. "We'd be the ones who'd have to pay."

"Don't look now," Elson said, "at who's paying." He was holding his head between his hands.

"I mean like getting locked up in the fucking prison we've got now instead of a school."

"The trouble with you, Leon, is that you've relied on timing instead of brains, and now the clock is running out." Elson, who had regained composure, was as angry at Zimmer for being the bearer of bad news as he was at the news itself.

"Well, listen to the professor. Who, Mr. Brains, who, I ask, had the balls to confront Gloria Martinez? Who, huh? And who hid out in the barracks overnight and risked getting arrested to catch the President of the Board? If you're so smart, what do you suggest?"

"I don't know yet, but I do study novels, and the situation we're in has become fiction. Reading it is not all that different from reading a book. We've got to learn to read the social text."

"Jesus," Zimmer slumped in his chair, "why don't you save the lecture for class."

"Let him finish," Wharfield insisted.

"If I were writing the book, we'd try to get our kids out. We could count on the social text to do the rest."

"What the fuck's that?" Zimmer asked.

"The social text," Elson replied, "it means understanding the complex web of their interpersonal relations and identifying the one thing we could do to make things turn our way. It could be something simple. Wharfield over there calls it magic. Hegel compares it to finding the one place in a pyramid to insert a blade of grass that will make the whole thing crumble."

"Oh, yeah, Professor, just how're we gonna do that?"

"I said it, kidnapping our own kids."

"I think you're dreaming," Zimmer muttered.

"That may be," Elson responded, "but we're in a kind of dream turned nightmare, and it's time to wake up."

Elson told Linda the news as soon as he came home. They agreed to discuss the situation with Luftman.

"Look," the therapist said, "though this is upsetting, it's not what we specialists term a violent episode. I mean there was no real physical harm to add to our little traumatic incident. It's more on the level of a gentle abuse, especially if, as you say, it's ended. We have to keep in mind that children are abused hundreds of times each day and in a variety of imperceptible ways. Growing up is a gradual process of learning to cope with being abused."

It was Elson's conviction that he could never cope, combined perhaps with frustration at Zimmer's deedless bravado, that pushed the professor to what he had always considered the edge of his mental universe, that is, to the point of action. And so, without telling the others, he placed a call to the man they read about almost daily in the newspapers, Beacon's most prominent paramilitary leader, the head of the Popular Front for the Liberation of Beacon Land, Cinque X.

The PFL had always been eyed with suspicion by Tucker, who preferred slower, more bureaucratic means of securing first the City and then the State. Upon his aide's advice, Horton had tried several times to offer the uncompromising maverick figure an official job in his administration. Each time Cinque X had refused, once even telling him to his face that he preferred "the scrappiness of struggle on the front lines to the fat-cat, shuffle-butt life behind a desk."

The phrase had irritated the Chief not only because he knew Cinque X had a way with words that he could never match, but because he knew his opponent was right. Cinque X was too independent, unpredictable. You could never tell where he would show up or whose side he would be on. Tucker had on several occasions arranged for Beacon's special forces to make things difficult for Cinque X's private army by breaking into his headquarters while the group was out on maneuvers. Try as he might, however, Tucker could not eliminate the man whose reputation for defending the rights of those in need, regardless of ideological purity, offered an always vexing alternative to the still fragile regime.

Rumor had it that Cinque X and his men were always in need of cash because Tucker and the Chief had disqualified the Popular Front from receiving any of the block money that the PAP granted its supporters each year. Elson had also heard from a reliable source that the fearless progressive soldier of fortune occasionally undertook an operation for a price as a "favor to a friend."

Norman Elson knocked loudly on the metal grill surrounding the thick wooden door scarred with the evidence of repeated break-ins. He could hear heavy footsteps coming down the stairs. A pair of eyes peered through the oval slot. The professor was frisked and led upstairs. Were it not for such caution, no one might have guessed that it was in the humble two-story dwelling on Luxemburg Street that Cinque X directed both the overt and covert actions of the Popular Front.

Elson was overcome by the sight of Cinque X's war room. The rows of files and bank of computers made it seem like any downtown office. Yet the palm ferns and cane furniture transformed it into some secret headquarters deep in the jungle. The walls were filled with mementos of various campaigns, newspaper headlines, an oil painting of the freedom fighter's dead wife, photos, plaques of recognition from this or that grateful committee.

On one wall, surrounded by blankness, a poster blowup of Cinque X's mug shot, front view and profile side by side, number below, stared with determined hatred into the room. The red and yellow flag of the Popular Front for the Liberation of Beacon Land floated suspended from the ceiling, lending to the room the feeling of a tent. So taken was Elson by all he saw that he failed at first to notice the fearless leader sitting silently on his high African throne.

"Now, what exactly seems to be the problem?" asked the guerrilla leader dressed in crumpled army fatigues.

"It's a case of child abuse."

"Child abuse. Damn. Your child?"

Elson nodded. Cinque X motioned to the secretary, who until then had been reading messages, Elson assumed in secret code, on a computer screen. She picked up a steno's pad.

"Where?" Cinque X asked.

"Over at Dred Scott."

"One of the teachers?"

"Not exactly. I know this is going to be hard to believe, but it's someone high up."

"We can't beat around the bush," Cinque X replied. "If you want us to stop it, you've got to name names."

"Goes right to the top. Head Adjustor. Rory McPhail."

"I see. How do you know? Did your kids talk?"

"One of the people in the group I work with spent the night in a closet. He saw it the next morning."

"And may I inquire which group is that?"

"The Audubon Brigade. We're a group of parent advocates."

"And who is it you say snuck into Dred at night? How'd he do it?" Cinque X seemed to take a professional interest in any maneuver in Beacon that might rival his own.

"One of our people."

"We need names," the impatient leader insisted.

"It was Leon Zimmer, you may have heard of him, the community activist." Elson was aware for the first time that he was beginning to sound like Blessings. He made a mental note to fill out a 3×5 card, later found under the heading *I*—"Insanity and

Language. Madness is simply a way of speaking the truth of unapparent connections."

"Zimmer hid out and saw McPhail take a child, the son of another friend, out of class and down in the basement of Dred."

"So what about your kid?"

Zimmer says it happens to my son too."

"Bad, very bad," Cinque X sighed. "I'm afraid there's not much we can do about someone so well placed. I would have been more encouraged if it was a teacher. We've seen that before. But the President of the Board, that's unfortunate."

"So there's nothing you can do?"

"I didn't say that," the guerrilla replied sharply. "We should think creatively. But I must warn you, it might cost."

"We could pay," Elson reassured him despite the fact that the Audubon Brigade had long since exhausted its meager funds. "Actually, if I might make a suggestion, we were thinking along the lines of removing my children. I have two there. I don't know whether you're familiar with the program, but they live at school."

"I know all about it. But let's see if I understand. You say if a few of my men were to take them out of the unhealthy situation, that might be of interest?"

"It certainly would." The vision of somehow returning to the days before all the trouble had started suddenly flashed before Elson's eyes.

"I think it can be arranged, but like I say, it'd cost."

"How much?"

"I think we might be able to arrange removal to a safe spot of your choice, neutral territory, for, say, five thousand dollars."

"Both kids, safely out of Beacon?"

"No, I'm afraid it's five thousand apiece. You must realize, Mr. Elson, that operations like this are dangerous and risk raising some eyebrows downtown. Besides, I must cover my expenses with a little something left over for the cause. You think about it, and if further discussion is in order, the resources of the Popular Front for the Liberation of Beacon Land are at your command."

Elson promised to return as soon as he could raise the funds.

So impressed was Elson at Cinque X's not wholly negative response that he informed the others.

"Nice work, Professor," Zimmer snorted, "but I thought we agreed to work together, not to do anything without checking it out first."

"We did. I just couldn't resist. I wanted to make sure it could be done, and it worked, didn't it? Taking kids back is just the kind of action that we need right now to show them we're not dead. It's perfect, the beginning of a new social text."

"He's right, Leon," Wharfield said. "If they can kidnap, then so can we."

"Oh, yeah," Zimmer replied, "if it's so perfect, then how come it costs so much, and just where do you propose to get that kind of money?"

"Leon," Elson teased, "This is your domain. Couldn't you make a quick ten big ones in orange juice or pork belly futures?"

Zimmer shook his head.

"Then listen. You remember the Home Exchange Bank brochure you showed me with the application for home loans? Well, think hard, and tell me who's the biggest shoe-in of anybody you know, maybe of anybody in town? Come on, think hard. You want a hint?" They nodded again.

"Old, black, handicapped, single grandmother, never owned a home." Elson repeated each word with deliberation. "She's got everything going for her but ideology. On the scale from one to ten she's at least a nine."

"Of course," Zimmer rang like the opening bell of the New York Stock Exchange. "That's it, that's her, what's her name, Reed's mother. Only one thing, Professor, how do we get to her?"

"There's only one way, that's through Reed. We're gonna have to tell him."

"It'd blow his fucking mind, and that would be the end of that," Zimmer warned.

"Look at it this way. You told me, and I survived. In fact, it's what produced the only real action we've seen in weeks, months. The only thing that might upset him is that we didn't say anything right away. It's a gamble, but worth the risk."

"Okay," Zimmer granted, "but no more wild cards and no more lone wolves. We don't move till I say. Is that a deal?" Elson and Wharfield agreed.

The Audubon regulars told Reed, and, as they predicted, he was furious.

"Moses, Moses, look, what could you have done? We knew how upset you'd be, so we found a way to stop it," Zimmer consoled the exterminator, "I got them to stop pushing your mother around, didn't I? Didn't I? You know I did. And this time we found a way to keep McPhail from messing with your son. Look, what are you going to do? What are we all going to do? You know you're not alone, don't you? It's not only Ocean, but Norman's kid too." Reed looked at Elson who said nothing. "I can tell you, then," Zimmer continued, "we're going to get even."

"How's that?" Reed asked.

"One of these days we're gonna fix his little commie peter for good. But first we're gonna rekidnap two of the kids. You'll have to trust us. It's the best tactic for right now."

"Get Ocean out? I don't know. That'd mean going back to Blessings or my mother. I'd have to check it out."

"We intend to get Ocean out of there," Elson assured Reed, "but maybe not right away. It's complicated. First, you'd have to have some safe place outside of Beacon you could send him to live."

"Whoo, that's right, the only people I've got are in Beacon. Only trouble is one's disabled, the other's nuts. You say McPhail's stopped?"

"Leon promises. But let's get back to business. I think it'd be best if we got my children out of there first. You'll have to trust us. We've got a plan, but we need your help."

"How's that?"

"We need ten thousand dollars."

"You must be kidding. We didn't have that kind of money when Blessings was selling menstrual sponges. Now I can't even fix my truck."

Zimmer began to read aloud the requirements for borrowing from the Beacon Home Exchange Bank.

"Hey," said Wharfield who had been taking minutes, "how about my kids?"

"You've got three. That would be fifteen thousand," Elson reminded him. "I'm not sure we could raise that much."

"I don't get it," Reed said, "I'm not handicapped or old, and I owned a house, or at least half of one, once."

"We're thinking more along the lines of your mother. Think of it, her own home. She'd never have to worry about Wasserman again."

"Leave her out of this," Reed protested.

"She doesn't have to know a thing," Zimmer assured him, "except you need ten thousand dollars, which is what they allow the chosen few to borrow for extermination. Look at it this way, you've already had a piece of this money getting rid of the rot in Meyer's and Tucker's houses. All you're asking for is a little more."

"You're not into any Mafia stuff like in the movies?" Reed asked.

"No, nothing like that," Elson replied.

Reed agreed to convince Ovella Capps to ask for the loan, reminding her that this was the kind of opportunity that did not come along very often. Besides, it was a place where he and Ocean could live after she was gone and the children had returned.

The Directors of the Capital Exchange received Ovella with open arms. Her loan was approved almost before the forms were submitted, and Reed began looking for a house, which was simpler now that a whole neighborhood was for sale. The only requirements were that it be other-abled accessible and have a large amount of termite work. He looked at a stucco and a clapboard, but neither was sufficiently rotten. Finally, Reed found the perfect home, a one-story shingle on Washington Street with access, solar heat, termites, beetles, and bundles of dry rot. Within a matter of days from the exterminator's conversation with the regulars of the Audubon Brigade, Ovella Capps had purchased her son's dream home and given notice to Martin Wasserman that she was leaving the Helen Keller Center for Special Living. Reed drew up the contract for the structural work, and, as soon as escrow closed, received exactly ten thousand dollars.

"Let's go," Elson urged.

"Go where?" Zimmer asked.

"Why, with the social text. Our plan."

"Not yet," Zimmer insisted. "I'm the Treasurer, and the money goes to me for deposit. I know how anxious you are for a quick fix, but believe me, the time is just not right."

Nor was it right for a long time. For the resourceful ex-real estate broker, taking literally Elson's suggestion that he invest in commodities, had already placed the entire sum in bulk brown sugar futures, which, even in so brief a time as between their original decision and the actual receipt of the money, had taken a precipitous decline.

At least once a week either Elson or Wharfield dropped by to inquire what could possibly be holding things up, and each time their treasurer managed to stall. "Don't worry," he assured the others, "I'm working on something that'll more than make their cocks fall off." Meanwhile, the price of sugar had plummeted from almost a dollar to thirty-six cents. Elson, perplexed at Zimmer's obstinacy, threatened to expose the community activist.

"Go ahead," Zimmer replied with a sneer, "they'll fix your kids so you'll never see them again."

"Whose side are you on anyway?" Elson asked.

"Look, Professor, I've been a progressive since before you could fart. You stick to the books and let me handle the dirty work."

The resisters were paralyzed by Zimmer's mysterious bluster—which is not to say that nothing happened. Ovella Capps moved into her new home which Reed fixed on weekends and nights. And Blessings Winter discovered, after attending a series of seminars on self-expression and stress, that she was a gifted writer. Rather than continue to confront the members of various civic commissions and boards as well as the few friends she had left, Blessings began to leave written messages all over town. Most were short hastily penned notes impossible to understand. Others arrived as long letters which had little effect except upon the small band of resisters who tolerated somewhat awkwardly her mad dissemination of the truth.

Elson, depressed by the paralysis that had set in, withdrew even further to his study. Occasionally he would sleep there, which disturbed Linda. There was little she could do to draw him out of his shell. She encouraged him to jog with Wharfield, to visit him at the Daedalus, to accept invitations to travel to this or that scholarly meeting. She pushed him to see Dylan and Rachel on prescribed Sundays. He found the visits painful. It was as though his children were people he had known in some distant past but whom he could now hardly remember.

The professor began to feel listless, to lose his appetite, to sleep badly. Like his mother, his hair turned gray, almost white, before he was forty. All his adult life he had enjoyed nothing more than retreating to his bed, pulling down the shades, and reading by artificial light. The winter of his defeat was, then, nothing more than a slight exaggeration of the way he had always been, like a hibernating bear in a wallpapered cave.

After the beginning of the year Blessings heard that Tucker had been seen at Sisters Hospital. She rushed to tell Zimmer, who, temporarily mad with excitement over a recent upturn in the price of sugar, made what would prove a terrible mistake.

Every time Blessings called upon the community activist, he would try to seduce her. Zimmer took Blessings's unannounced appearances as provocation. She, in turn, considered his advances a sporting form of relation. As Shawn Luftman later said, she probably returned to see him as often as she did because his passes confirmed some unconscious wish to see men as domineering. In an odd way his sexual advances reassured her.

During this particular visit, Zimmer's insistence grew more intense until, intrigued by the rumor of Tucker's mysterious ailment, he seduced her with the only thing with which she might have been enticed—another secret. He promised to teach her how to read the social text if she would only sleep with him.

"The what?" she asked.

"The social text," Zimmer said, "is the truth about some important people around town. Nobody can read it except two or three in the know." Being party to something so discreet was more than even her deep distrust of men could bear. Blessings gave in, making a date for Zimmer to visit her at home where they made love once rather unsatisfactorily. As soon as Zimmer appeared to have completed the penultimate spasm of an only mild orgasm, Blessings withdrew and kneeled next to him on the bed.

"Okay, no more manipulation. We've had sex, now let's have whatever you call it—the social text."

"You call that sex?" Zimmer said. Then, taking long draws on a marijuana cigarette, he transformed the promise of a secret into a pernicious lie. Zimmer told Blessings that Tucker had AIDS and that it was only a matter of time until the others came down with it too.

"You mean Gloria?" she asked.

"I'm talking about Gloria and McPhail and his old lady." Zimmer withheld the story of child abuse in hopes of eliciting a second sexual favor.

"No, don't tell me she's sleeping with him too."

"You're sleeping with me, aren't you?"

No sooner had Blessings crawled out of bed than she began to scribble a flurry of notes telling of Tucker's illness. Despite a promise made to Zimmer not to reveal his confidence to a soul, she distributed her scrawls all over town. It was only a matter of days before the false news that Tucker had AIDS replaced the rumor that he had been seen at Sisters. No one, of course, was more concerned than Gloria Martinez, who rushed to see him in his new home.

"Is it true, Eric?" she asked, hardly inside the door.

Reed, who was chipping away at a large section of rot in a main beam just below the entrance, perked up and started the tape.

"Is what true?" Tucker replied.

"That you've got AIDS, and I'm the last to know."

"No, it's a lie. Who told you that?"

"The crazy woman, you know the one with the down parka, the one who's at all the meetings."

"Blessings Winter," Tucker said.

"For a plant waterer poor as old Job's turkey," Reed said to himself, "that woman sure gets around."

"The doctor says it's nothing more than fatigue," Tucker assured Gloria. Embarrassed, there was little she could say, and so she left.

Tucker was upset about even the possibility of such a rumor, and in the effort to track it down he placed one of the detectives belonging to the Beacon Special Forces on the trail. Within a matter of hours the detective confirmed what Gloria had said—the source was Blessings. Energized by the false rumor in which she took a proprietary interest, she would arrive at a public meeting, and, without waiting for it to begin, would stand up and announce simply, "Eric Tucker has AIDS. If you want to know more, read this note." Her scribblings were now mimeographed. "Got to run, bye." Such episodes caused a terrible disruption of the gathering, which would then spend the rest of its scheduled time discussing not what to do if Beacon's regime should change, but whether Blessings were mad.

Whether mad or sane, all of her gossip mongering would not have mattered as much as it did, finally, if she had not, in the fourth or fifth day after sleeping with Zimmer, compounded his lie with an indiscretion.

Driving home after a Broken Relationships Support Group, her sixth appearance of the night, Blessings passed the Traymor and impulsively decided to stop to see if Reed had heard the news. No one was at home, Reed having left earlier to tell Zimmer about Tucker's meeting with Gloria. The detective nonetheless reported the stop to Tucker, who recognized the name as that of the man who had been beneath his house for weeks. Suddenly suspicious, the aide decided to have a look for himself, and it was then, crawling in the dirt as Reed had done so many times, that Tucker discovered the recorder and a box of empty tapes. Pressing the *Rewind* and then the *Play* button, he heard, ". . . nothing more than fatigue . . ."

Tucker left things exactly as they were. The termite inspector was obviously finishing up the job. His tools and jacks were lying in orderly array by the crawl space trap. In fact, having purged the bugs from Tucker's rotten mudsill and frame, Reed, as fate would have it, had been hired to reinforce the foundation of the enormous Victorian Larry Newton and Pam Sidel had purchased at the top of Beacon's hill.

Tucker said nothing. Instead, he summoned Wasserman and Greer to El Pueblo, where he instructed them to put the fear of God into Moses Reed in a way he would not forget. "But be careful," he warned, "not to get caught."

"You want us to check it out with you first, boss?" Wasserman asked.

"No," Tucker replied, "the less I or anyone else knows the better. I look forward to seeing just how clever you can be."

As the two party flunkies left the El Pueblo, they were not entirely certain what he had meant by "put the fear of God into Moses Reed." Wasserman wondered if Tucker wanted them to brand him, while Greer, who had been drinking heavily all night, was convinced they had been instructed to kill.

"What else can the boss mean by 'mark him for life'?" the bleary-eyed Greer asked. They decided to compromise by arranging an accident that would prove who was right. Wasserman and Greer spent several days deep in what, in any other two individuals, might have passed for thought before discovering what they believed to be the perfect crime. They would drain the brake fluid out of Reed's pickup truck. If he survived, Wasserman could claim victory. If he died, Greer would win the dispute. The perfect crime was, then, a throw of the dice on the gaming table of Moses Reed's soul. Only trouble was they couldn't do it in front of the Newton-Sidels. The two henchmen began somewhat clumsily to trail their victim. It was, in fact, their calls on Reed's answering machine that made him nervous just before leaving for Luftman's the night of his death.

Greer had seen a TV show in which a criminal had been caught because the murder weapon, a particular kind of Italian designer ice pick, had been traced to the hardware store where it had been purchased. This made him especially careful, in preparing Reed's accident, not to shop anyplace where he might be noticed. He made several trips to supermarkets and kitchen supply stores, each time deciding at the last minute that buying a turkey baster just a week after Thanksgiving might appear suspicious. Then it dawned on him. Why had he not thought of it earlier? And so, knocking upon the door of his downstairs neighbors, who were none other than Sheila Singer and Tank Mountainfire, Greer asked if he might come in. In the back of the apartment an infant was crying.

Greer asked the two women if he could borrow a turkey baster. They giggled and began to hug each other. He thought they must not have heard and asked again. They only giggled harder.

"What's so funny?" he asked, "I know it's a little late for Thanksgiving, but things are a little tight this year, and I just thought . . ."

"No, it's not that," Tank rushed to explain. "You're welcome to borrow it. It's just, it's just that it's special to us. This is the baster with which Bette was conceived."

"Huh?" Greer grunted.

"Oh, nothing, go ahead and take it." Tank looked at Sheila. "Just be sure to bring it back."

Greer was convinced that the merriment of his downstairs neighbors meant they suspected something. He must be extra careful to follow the course he, however awkwardly, had set. This meant actually buying a turkey, which was roasting at the very moment Wasserman phoned to say that Reed had left the Traymor and was now parked at the top of the hill.

Without so much as stopping to wash the grease-filled long suction tube or turn off the oven, Greer left for the scene of the crime.

Reed died while Wasserman and Greer ate their belated Thanksgiving dinner. By the time news of a fiery accident on Campanella Street was broadcast over the radio they were drunk amid a pile of dirty dishes. It was only the next afternoon, after Blessings had alerted Sergeant Brainard and Tucker again summoned them to El Pueblo, that they realized something was wrong.

"Who screwed up?" Tucker said.

"What do you mean?" Wasserman asked.

"I told you to scare Reed, to put him on notice, not to kill him, and especially not to leave any marks."

"Marks?" Greer blinked several times.

"Yeah, marks, clues, like in cops and robbers, right on the pavement in front of that faggot shrink's."

"I told you we were supposed to brand him." Wasserman turned toward Greer.

"Come on guys, cut the shit, there could be trouble," said Tucker. "So let's level now and try to understand where we are. How'd you do it?"

"With a turkey baster," Wasserman volunteered. "Howie had the bird cooking while I was up the hill." Tucker looked puzzled as Terri Kantor arrived with beers.

"That's right," the red-faced Wasserman continued, "while Howie sucked the brake fluid, I sawed a little slit in the line. Only he got careless and some of the stuff squirted on me. We caught most of it in a pan, but you know how it can be, basting a turkey. I thought we got most of the drips."

"Jesus, I can't believe what a pair of fuck-ups you turned out to be." Tucker took a large bite of huevos rancheros on wholewheat taco.

"We're leveling with you, so you needn't become hostile. What do you want us to do?" Wasserman asked.

"All I know is that you didn't catch it all, and somebody's wise to your tricks." Tucker scowled. "What? What's this? You ask what I want you to do? I want you to get yourselves up that hill as fast as your incompetent little asses will carry you and take care of the mess. And do it this time without being seen." The two bunglers gulped their beer and were gone in less than a minute. It was late that night, after Greer had returned the turkey baster and borrowed a portable vacuum from Sheila and Tank, that they cleaned the oil and metal shavings from in front of Luftman's.

That same night Tucker was let into Reed's apartment by Sergeant Brainard. Alone inside, and after placing headphones over his ears, he began to listen to the tapes scattered throughout the disordered bookshelves. He would grab a cassette, listen for a few seconds, then insert another, each time placing those he had removed in a neat stack. "Goddammit," he muttered after hearing the beginning of at least a dozen tapes, "nothing but gospel and the Beatles." He replaced the tapes and left before the other residents might have become aware of his presence in the Traymor.

It was at Reed's funeral, huddled in the last row of the Necrobiotic Chapel of the Pines, that Zimmer said, "This is what I meant by total all-out war. You see, the fuckers know about timing too. They didn't pounce right away but waited for just the right moment. Then they got him."

"Isn't it ironic," said Wharfield, "that the progressives killed practically the only worker left in town?"

"A lot of good you and your timing did," Elson whispered as gospel music came out of speakers on either side of the room.

"Gentlemen, the news even at this sad hour is not all bad," said Zimmer. "Our time has come. If they're gonna play like this, then we can too."

Zimmer's duplicity in dealing with his comrades in struggle was only aggravated by his renewed sincerity, for the community activist might permanently have forgotten the original purpose for which they had placed money in his safekeeping, had it not been for the shock of Reed's death, coupled with such a steady climb in the price of bulk sugar over the last month that the original sum had almost doubled.

Elson, temporarily buoyed by the thought of carrying their plan to completion, again found himself in the headquarters of the PFL.

"I thought you had chickened out," Cinque X began. "This is pretty heavy stuff for middle-class folk."

"No. It's just a question of scraping together that much bread." Elson was sure he had cemented their bond by appearing to be in as great a need of cash as those in the vanguard of the revolution.

"I must tell you," Cinque X warned, "there's some risk involved. We'll go in with a helicopter and four men. They'll be armed. Something could always go wrong, but I don't see trouble."

"I know that," said Elson, impressed by the military air.

"Let's see, now, did you bring the pictures?"

Elson spread recent photos of Dylan and Rachel on the wicker table.

"Good, then let's get down to money. That's cash, of course, small bills, no series."

Elson pulled from his briefcase a stack of obviously used twenty-dollar bills and placed them beside the photographs. He noticed also lying on the table a marked-up plan of the inside of Dred Scott.

"Then it's like this. We'll pull them out and meet you here between twenty-two and twenty-three hours on Thursday, the sixth. You'll be watching right here." Cinque X pointed to a spot near Dred Scott. "As soon as you see the chopper come down, you will head in this direction and wait right under the bridge." Cinque X lifted yet another map and pointed to a large abandoned space near the edge of the freeway entrance to Canaan. "Here, take this." He held a copy toward Elson. "If I were you, I'd have tickets ready to take them wherever they are going. Now, is that a deal?"

The Elsons prepared everything. Norman's parents agreed reluctantly to take Rachel and Dylan until more permanent arrangements could be made. The plane tickets and boarding cards were ready, the bags with a modicum of fresh clothes all packed. Linda had even thought to buy a box of the children's favorite cookies and a couple of books they might enjoy on the flight. The parents had rehearsed over and over again what they would say in the hour or so between again gaining control of Rachel and Dylan and kissing them into exile. "It may not be long," Linda was reminded of something Luftman once had said. "But quality time is what counts."

On the evening of May sixth the Elsons, having left Alex with his favorite babysitter, drove to within a couple of blocks of Dred Scott. They turned off the headlights and waited for what seemed like a day, though the clock had measured only thirty-five minutes.

It was impossible to tell at first from what direction the deep roar came. Then they saw it, a large old personnel carrier left over from some ancient campaign, a great puffing bird that suddenly summoned Norman's fear of flying. "Too late now," he thought, "we're in the belly of the beast." Turning on the ignition and the lights, the Elsons, as instructed, headed toward the bridge and again waited for what seemed like an age.

"What can be keeping them now?" Norman asked in his habitual way that begged comfort.

"I'm sure nothing," Linda obliged. "These things take time."

Norman grew increasingly impatient as what Cinque X called their "lead time" dwindled from an hour and a half as planned, to an hour, then forty-five minutes.

"I'm sure everything's okay," Linda repeated every so often. "Why don't you turn on the radio? Maybe one of the networks has picked up the news."

"Are you crazy? What do you expect? Attention. Late news flash. Parents kidnap own children in daring escape from new-age educational experiment."

Every once in a while the loud diesel motor of a truck passing the last leg of the bridge seemed as if it were coming from the sky. The Elsons looked up, but the only helicopters to be seen carried late commuters back and forth between Canaan and Goshen. None came from the direction of Dred. They sat for the most part in silence, hypnotized by the distant twinkling lights of the city, and afraid. The Elsons, worried just a few minutes ago about whether their children would make the plane on time, slowly began to realize that they would settle simply for their safety. Norman began to regret having ever thought of taking Rachel and Dylan back or having become mixed up with urban guerrillas. He would have given anything just to know they had survived, wherever they were. "Even an unpleasant status quo," he would also have noted, had he had a 3×5 card and were his hand steady enough to write, "is always preferable to the unknown."

Suddenly, the big bird reappeared. Elson could feel his heart race at first, then the numbness which accompanies the end of anticipation. The machine set down, rocking, on the big grassy area between the bridge on-ramp and the railroad cars running along the water. A searchlight flooded the door which opened almost before it landed and out of which came two men carrying automatic weapons. Cinque X was the last to emerge. By the time the Elsons caught sight of the burly guerrilla in fatigues they had almost reached the great grinding machine which created a windstorm in the dusty field.

"There's been a hitch," the leader said solemnly.

"Is everybody all right?" Elson panicked.

"Everybody's fine. Only someone tipped them off."

Elson looked menacingly at Linda.

"It wasn't me," Linda said, trying hard to hold back tears. "Did you see Dylan and Rachel at least?"

"Never even got that far. The authorities were ready for us by the door," Cinque X muttered accusingly. "Surprise is the only way in operations like this. Somebody blew our cover."

"You sure everybody's all right?" Elson repeated.

"Now, if you would just step inside." Cinque X motioned with the tip of his rifle, and they started in the direction of the freedom fighters guarding the helicopter.

Once inside, Norman and Linda Elson found not Dylan and Rachel, but there, perched on the fold-down seat of the personnel carrier like a couple of lovebirds, sat arm-in-arm Eric Tucker and Gloria Martinez.

"We've been double-crossed." Terrified, Elson looked at Cinque X.

"No, man," the guerrilla said, his voice full of reproach. "You set us up. We could'a got killed walking into a trap like that."

"Well, now," Tucker greeted them, "so you thought you could pull a fast one. Let's have the tickets."

"I beg your pardon," Elson replied.

"You're not going anywhere, so let's have the airline tickets."

"I'm afraid I don't know what you're talking about."

"Get 'em," the aide ordered. One of Cinque X's guards ripped so violently at Elson's Gortex vest that the velcro came clean off the cloth. The guard handed the red and white envelope to Tucker. Winking at Gloria, he began to sing "New York City, here we come, right back where we started from|. . ."

At that very moment they took off in the direction of the bridge. "Good, now the trial can begin." Tucker paused. "For unprogressive thoughts and crimes against the regime, that is, bribery and attempted kidnapping, you are sentenced to die."

"Please," Elson said as the helicopter lurched higher, "I know we can explain." His mouth went dry, the tips of his fingers turned all cold.

"Explain nothing," Tucker said, "this is it. We've arranged your suicide. They'll find the abandoned car by the bridge. Old Cinque X and I have made a deal. He gets your things, and we get a little rest and recreation." Tucker kissed the plane ticket.

"You can't kill us," Linda pleaded, "we're parents, we have children. Remember Julius and Ethel Rosenberg."

"Nothing to worry about, they'll be taken care of just like everyone else. There are no more elites. Now, jump."

Norman and Linda Elson tried to embrace as the whirring bird seemed all at once to become stationary just over the pylon on the south side of the enormous suspension bridge. A gauzy cloud billowed through the open door. They abandoned each other and began to grasp for life at the opening wide enough for two parachutists at a time. Cinque X motioned with a tilt of his head, and the guards hammered at the clenched hands with their rifle butts.

Elson's students, upon arriving later that week at his never-to-be-completed seminar on the human condition, were greeted by a man dressed in white—white shirt, white pants, white jacket and shoes. "I'm from the University Attitudinal Healing Service, and I have some news that concerns us all," he announced. "Professor Elson won't be in class today. He has moved to another astral plane."

"Does that mean there won't be a final exam?" a muscular student in flowered bermuda shorts asked, lowering as if by reflex the mirrored sunglasses perched on his bleached-blond head.

"Not exactly," the man replied.

"What about our grades?" asked another student pointing to a stack of books on the seminar table. "Personally, I have put a lot of work into this course."

"I've discussed the matter with our grief work counselors," the man assured the expectant graduates, "and we agree that everyone enrolled in the Human Condition will receive an *A*."

"All right!" the muscular student exclaimed.

"There will, however, be a little asterisk next to the grade on your transcript, indicating that the professor underwent a significant life change which prevented his correcting the final. Now, I think we should conclude this course with a few little exercises to help us transcend ourselves. They might even put us in touch with Professor Elson. So, if you would just concentrate and close your eyes, you may be able to hear his spirit speaking through us. This is a really good class, I can see. Lots of good auras."

9

ORPHANS

■ A lean young man, bearded and clasping a shoe box under one arm, finally succeeded in forcing open the sprung door of a rusty old car against the pounding rain that came to Beacon two or three times a year. The unwilling hinge caused him to lunge into the street. Lightning lit the sky. With his heavy tweed hat and the earflaps which covered the collar of a threadbare parka, he looked like some prehistoric reptile emerging from a giant metal egg in the night of time.

So intent was he on escape that he failed to notice that the thrust which had succeeded in liberating one leg, now drenched, had also loosened his grip upon the box which fell at the very instant he cracked out. The lid drifted in the water that ran like a rivulet next to the curb. A clump of cards wrapped in a rubber band sat in the puddle that fed the gush of water. Had it been lighter it too would have been swept away. He lifted the box and stooped to pick up the bundle on which he could barely make out the letter *P*. A smear of ink spread across the top card, at first in little bare patches where raindrops hit, then more evenly, moving diaphanously across its printed lines. Still bent, he squeezed the dripping packet in with the others, carefully placing it at the front where the damage might be contained.

"Shit," he thought, racing now to the small clapboard house on Washington Street. "Father not only did himself in with all his quirks, but he did it in washable ink. Why couldn't he write in ballpoint like everyone else?"

He gained the shelter of the porch whose tiny slanted roof had begun to lose its shingles. He knocked, gently at first, then louder. There was no answer. He could tell by the lights in the window that someone was home. He put his ear to the door.

A strange vibrating rhythm throbbed against the sheets of rain that cascaded over clogged gutters all around. The noise seemed to be coming from the floor. He could feel it in his feet, a steady creaking back and forth. He knocked again, louder. Still there was no answer.

He set down the box between the door and the screen, then crawled toward the window. There, kneeling in the muddy soil of a flower box directly beneath what was by any standard a small waterfall, he saw the kid inside. But not like he expected. Attached by a wire to the stereo on the shelf, he was rocking back and forth, eyes closed, ears covered by large foam rubber cups, a burning cigarette in his mouth. He couldn't have been more than sixteen.

Drenched by the water pouring down his back between hat and coat, the lean young man moved back to the door. He held his hand on the knob until the metal grew warm from cold. He twisted slowly.

The door was unlocked. The half turn of the knob took longer than the trip from the car to the porch.

He slipped into the room where he stood unnoticed. After several long moments he walked toward the rocking figure and touched him gently on one shoulder. As soon as the stony eyes opened he knew he had made a mistake. From his crouch on the creaky old rocker, legs folded underneath, the thin, startled kid threw off the headphones, leapt from the chair, and ran to the back of the house. In his flight he made a little shriek, really more of a truncated stutter, which caused his cigarette to fly in the direction of the large bookcase standing against the back wall.

"Come back, come back, please. I didn't mean to scare you. You see, you don't know me. I mean, we've met. You may not remember. In Dred Scott." He followed the boy toward the kitchen, not daring actually to penetrate the space beyond the pantry.

"Come on. I'm not going to hurt you." He could hear breathing, short and uneven like that of a cornered animal. Still there was no response.

Now he could smell smoke coming from the other room. He hurried back to find a circle the size of a grapefruit glowing in the old ovular hook rug. He stomped on the dirty braided fibers that sputtered and then stank beneath his wet feet.

"Look, I'm awfully sorry," he said calmly back in the direction of the kitchen. "My name's Dylan, Dylan Elson. I've got some stuff you might be interested in."

The breathing in the kitchen was now punctuated every so often by a sob.

"I know you've been through a lot. I have too. But I think we might be able to figure out . . ." Dylan paused, wondering if the creature he had cornered was even listening. "I'm not going to hurt you," he said gliding down the length of the pantry. He could see nothing in the darkened room.

"Look, my father knew yours in the old days," said Dylan. "I'm holding right here in my hands his notes. It's a treasure for you too. Some are about your father's tapes. I thought we might work together to find out . . . oh, shit!" Dylan had almost reached the kitchen when the rear door burst open and Ocean Reed escaped into the downpouring night.

Dylan returned to the living room which was bare except for the rocking chair, a three-way floor lamp with only one bulb, and a large bookshelf filled with old newspapers, a few books, records, tapes, and assorted junk. He checked just to be sure no one was hiding in the darkened bedroom.

Under other circumstances Dylan might simply have left without a trace by the door through which he had entered. Yet he remembered seeing on a 3×5 card under the letter *D,* "The detective mind works according to the logic of three. It always allows for the hidden third term."

The kid had gone for help, Dylan thought. He looked at his watch. He picked up the headphones.

To his surprise, Ocean Reed had not been listening to music at all. Instead, muffled voices filled the noisy cassette, interrupted by what sounded like the distant sound of feet stamping, or fingers thumping against a mike.

Dylan removed the earphones from his head and again glanced at his watch. He figured there was time for one more look. Dylan's gaze fixed on the one object that stood out against the bareness of the floor, not more than a foot from the black hole in the rug—a fancy electronic telephone, alarm clock, and radio combined. It was a mass of buttons, *Alarm/Sleep, Hold, Flash, Auto, Pause, Memory, Mute.* He held it in his hand, hoping for some clue as to who might have talked through the sleek receiver. The room still smelled of burning rags.

Placing his finger on the mini-square marked *Redial,* he put the receiver to his ear. There was a dial tone, then a series of high-pitched bleeps. It rang. Once . . . twice . . . three times . . . a click, and then the hiss of another tape. Suddenly, the monotone of a deep male voice.

"Hello. You have reached the answering machine of Cinque X, Commanding Officer of the Popular Front for the Liberation of Beacon Land. I'm out right now returning power to the people, but if you'd care to leave a message, you may do so at the tone, and I'll return your call as soon as my mission is completed."

Dylan placed the receiver back in its cradle. He took from the cluttered bookshelf a ballpoint pen, chewed on at one end. He lifted the only visible piece of paper on which to write, the back of a discarded poster promising *Success Without Stress at Any Stage of Life* and scribbled:

> I've reason to believe that we might have
> things to say to each other. I leave to you all that's
> left of my father and take in exchange this tape.
>
> D. E. 843–1654.
>
> P.S. Sorry about the rug. Will replace in due time.

Dylan removed the cassette from the player and slipped it into his pocket. He placed the note carefully under the shoe box and left by the front door.

In the days that followed his mind turned in circles.

"Easy entry into the topic is often just a screen for the complexities that always seem simple in the beginning," he could recall seeing on a card under the letter *E.* He wondered if he would ever see the 3 × 5 cards again. Once they had been a fixation. He would sit and shuffle the multiple decks for hours, arranging them by subject. The little paper rectangles, mixed with assorted bits of wrapping paper, matchbooks, leader packets, the backs of envelopes and edges of newspapers, receipt slips, and at least one scrap of toilet tissue, were the only clues to what led up to the night his parents died. They represented a promise, a debt to the dead.

The contract was in the cards themselves. One day, as Dylan was thumbing through the packet marked *W,* he came upon a note entitled "Witnessing, subcategory Extermination." Norman Elson had copied, in letters so tiny and twisted that they might have been Hebrew, the story of a Pole being taken to the death camps. As the SS officers tugged at his coat he cried out to his own son, who could not have been any older than Dylan at the time of the writing, "My life doesn't matter, but someone must tell."

Dylan listened to the tape. He could tell it had been played many, maybe even a thousand, times. Its attraction was baffling. Mostly it contained old rock-and-roll songs interspersed with bits and pieces of dialogue like that he had first sampled. He could make sense of neither. The songs were a jumble. The selection was odd. An eerie feeling came over him to hear the Beatles sing, "When I find myself in times of trouble, Mother Mary comes to me, whispering words of wisdom, let it be, let it be." His heart stopped at the small extract from a song by the Police that his father used to play over and over again: "With every move you make, with every breath you take, I'll be watching you . . ."

He was no doubt reading too much into this or that fragment of a lyric. Yet he could also not read enough. And the occasional conversation offered nothing more concrete. The four or five brief exchanges seemed like some distantly recorded version of a play. The people involved spoke their lines with the unconvincing flatness of high school actors. Some of the exchanges were barely audible, and then there was the mysterious thumping, more silence, and another song. The only decipherable dialogue was still a mystery.

"We're pretty sure where it's coming from," a man's voice said.

"That little busybody's going to fuck everything up with all her meddling if we don't stop it," another gruffer voice muttered.

"Don't worry. She's one of Luftman's. There's a call into him already."

"That's not enough."

"Calm down. You know as well as I do we've got to wait for the right . . ."

There were creaks, thumps that sounded like walking, a long silence, then the second half of the Rolling Stones singing "Time, time, time, is on my side, yes it is . . ."

Dylan removed the little foam patches from his ears. He knew his parents had seen a marriage counselor named Luftman whom he had always suspected of knowing something about their disappearance. He found the Yellow Pages beneath a pile of papers strewn over one corner of his room. He opened it and thumbed furiously.

Dylan carefully checked out *Parapsychology*, then skipped by *Psychic Arts*. He turned to *Psychotherapy*, where, moving past the big ads for *Bioenergetics Growth Systems Associates* and *Empowerment Counseling*—he found it, a little notice inserted among the rest: *Shawn Luftman, Ph.D., trained and licensed by The Cathexis Institute of Beacon Land, Creator of Numistherapy, Individual and Transpersonal Growth, Problems of Age Regression Addressed in a Mature Manner, Reincarnation Hypnosis, Co-Dependency Intervention, Short-Term Sexual Disorders, Fee Negotiable.*

"Before we begin," Luftman explained as Dylan settled into the plush sofa opposite the therapist's sculpted leather chair, "I must tell you this first visit is free. After that we operate according to a sliding scale." The therapist pressed a lever at his side, and the lounger chair reclined. All Dylan could see of Luftman were the soles and elevated heels of a pair of alligator shoes.

"What does it slide between?" Dylan asked.

"We begin at thirty-five dollars an hour for those who can't afford more, and move right up to, well, you wouldn't want to know what the Institute charges some of its patients. These, of course, make it possible for us to serve the others. As you may know, I created an entire field of psychotherapy based on a concept that the proper use of money, combined with certain scientific breathing techniques, makes people happy. This corrects one of the fundamental mistakes of early psychotherapy where doctors in suits sat behind desks and assumed the patient had to suffer for therapy to work. I charge my patients only enough so that they have just the right amount money left over to have fun. You may have noticed, too, how casually I am dressed."

"I've noticed."

"It puts people at ease. You see, we have been talking already about things as personal as money and clothes. Some patients in a more traditional setting take weeks or even months before they can break through to these subjects."

"I don't feel uncomfortable with those topics."

"Feeling comfortable is half the battle," Luftman reassured him. "Now, what seems to be the problem? No, let me guess. You must be Norman and Linda Elson's son, and you're here today because it's time to come to terms with their death. There's nothing to be ashamed of. Perfectly natural. It's what we health professionals call our little Oedipal thing. Perhaps a bit late in your case, but that's understandable."

"Why, yes. I've often wondered . . ."

"You wondered whether it was really suicide?"

Dylan said nothing.

"I'm afraid the brutal truth is that it was. You know, of course, that the car was found abandoned near the bridge. But I don't think there's any indiscretion in my telling you, now that you're old enough, that I had firsthand knowledge of how psychologically despondent they were. You know they loved you very much."

"I'm not sure you would call the reason for my visit exactly psychological."

"Most problems are psychological at root," Luftman said, "even big international ones. If we just scratch hard enough, we usually find the cause in the personality of some world leader who makes events happen. So you should not be afraid of the word *psychological.* It's just a way of saying 'human.' "

"Then perhaps you might want to listen to this." Dylan removed the Walkman from his knapsack. Spreading the earphones with one hand, he proceeded toward Luftman who, caught unaware, grappled for the lever. Before Luftman could right himself, however, the more powerful younger man had placed the foam pads over the therapist's ears. Like a patient captive of some insistent dentist's drill, Luftman listened to the short dialogue which contained his name.

"Where on earth did you get that?" The therapist managed to sit up.

"Never mind where," Dylan said firmly. "I'm not sure we're dealing here with only a psychological problem. Can you tell me what this is all about?"

Luftman shook his head.

"Do you know who's talking about you?"

"No, I don't."

"Could it be that you are involved in a little dealing on the side. These have to be some pretty nasty customers, and they certainly know you."

"I have no idea who they are," said Luftman, "but I do have an idea what it's about, and I would advise you to let me have that tape."

"Why's that?" Dylan asked.

"Because what you're doing could cause great psychological harm."

"Harm who?"

"Professional discretion prevents me from saying any more, but I can assure you that you are threatening the well being of innocent people. I could see that you are richly rewarded."

"Whoa there, not so fast." Dylan placed the Walkman in his knapsack and walked toward the door. "There are certain things off the sliding scale. I think your secretary has my number. When you're ready to talk about what you know, give me a call."

Dylan slipped out the door more confidently than he had come in. This was the kind of moment he cherished, triumphant for having played a card. But the dizzying effects of the visit were short lived. For there, walking up the steps of The Cathexis Institute, was Ocean Reed. Dylan ducked below the ledge of the wheelchair access ramp as Ocean passed by.

Dylan remembered seeing on a card, "Life is a non-reversible narrative. Once written, certain gestures cannot be undone." Of course his father could have been wrong about that, and Dylan wasn't sure that a gesture—the entry was filed under *G*—was narrative, but in any case he felt the need to change course. Instead of heading home as he had intended, he turned in the direction of Washington Street. This time the kid would not be at home.

Dylan was again surprised as he drew close. There, descending the stairs of the house he had planned, with the best intentions, to enter for the second time in a week, was what could only be a plainclothes officer of the Beacon Police. Dylan swallowed hard when he saw that the man held in his outstretched arms a stack of cassette tapes piled high upon the shoe box that he had left the night of the big storm.

A bearded man in a maroon turban approached Dylan the instant he entered the Calcutta Copy Center. He had been talking to two women in saris behind the cash register, where there were also several small children whose heads barely reached the counter.

"May I help you, sir?" the man asked in a heavy Indian accent.

"Yes, I'd like to reproduce a cassette." Dylan removed the tape from his knapsack.

"I see, may I inquire whether you prefer oxide or metal?"

"I don't understand."

"Whether the tape you wish to copy is voice or music?"

"Actually," Dylan said, "it's a little of both."

"Very well, then. Sunita, would you assist the gentleman—one metal cassette." One of the women in a sari accompanied him to machine number six.

In all, it could not have taken more than a minute. The machine gave a click, and Sunita, who was amused by the intensity with which Dylan had watched her every move, handed him the two cassettes that she assumed must contain some extremely valuable history of the heart.

Dylan stuffed the change into his wallet and walked the block and a half to the Progressive Stationery Store where he purchased a tape mailer and wrote a note.

> If you think your goons got it all, have a
> listen. Tapes make copies just like fathers
> make children. Let's trade for the cards.
> No more break-ins. You'll hear from
> me when it's time.
>
> A Friend in Crime

Dylan inserted the cassette into the mailer, which he addressed in a purposefully infantile handwriting—To the Man in the Plainclothes Suit, Detective Division, Beacon Police. He dropped it ceremoniously into the postbox in front of the Urban Guerrilla Army and Navy Surplus. He checked his watch and raced to the he consigned the tape he had stolen from Ocean to the safe-deposit box whose existence he had learned of only long after his parents' death.

Dylan walked high into the Beacon hills. Looking at the sun which had begun to drop into the ocean, he had a sudden sense of fullness of the kind he had not experienced in some time. He stared at the lights of the city which started, first slowly and then in large clumps and long straight lines, to twinkle below. The bridge stretched like a pearl necklace across the watery throat of the bay. For years he had not been able to look in that direction without thinking of his parents' icy plunge. Now that he had decided to revive them, he sensed a welcome peace. The bridge was only part of a larger puzzle and not its design.

Dylan began his descent along the clay fire trails made redder by the diffuse dapplings of light which, even after sunset, still penetrated the thick pines. He had had nothing to eat since breakfast, and so he proceeded to the Chairman's Kitchen. He could remember having eaten there many times as a child, back in the days before all the changes. In fact, nothing had changed at the old Peking Garden except for the name. He ordered his regular fare—Three Traitor's Soup and a double portion of Sticky Buns for the Long March. It had been a good day's work, he reflected, caressing a fortune cookie. Ever since beginning therapy with Luftman he felt comfortable. Perhaps he was cured already.

He pulled the thin strip of paper like a tapeworm from the cookie's crimped edge. "A Strong Man Never Corrects Himself," it said. He left the uncracked biscuit on the table. They would put it back on the pile, he mused, and some poor slob would end up with no fortune at all.

"Come in, child, what is it?"

Cinque X, dressed in denim overalls, a red pajama top, and green beret, sat on his high cane chair while several men stood about the room in a sort of stoned, generic attention.

"He's come back," Ocean said.

"Who's come back?" the older man asked.

"The one who was there the other night."

"The one who robbed you?"

Ocean nodded.

"Did he break in again?"

"I wasn't there."

"How do you know, child?"

"He took the box of cards he left before and some tapes."

"No valuables? How about the stereo? No TV?"

"Nothing else."

Cinque X motioned to the young woman working at a desk in the far corner of the room. "Fetch the communiqué from last week." She immediately drew from the bank of file cabinets along the wall a thin manila folder and removed the note that Dylan had left the night he had scared Ocean sufficiently to send him running to his protector. Cinque X held it in one hand and pointed with the other to the mysterious initials and phone number, then gave it back to the woman.

"We'll need the reverse directory," Cinque X ordered. The young woman took her place in front of one of the computers lining the shelf under the front window. As she typed in the seven numbers, red lights flashed on a small plastic rectangle which also made little bleeps. The green screen rolled over convulsively in several waves until the little pulsating flasher darted to the left and quickly spat out its two-line highlighted message. Cinque X had neither said a word nor ceased staring straight ahead since she began to execute his command. She wrote the name and address on a slip of paper. Cinque X's two lieutenants took the slip and left by the back door. Ocean could hear the engine of a car as it passed beneath the porch.

Dylan was dead tired when, after stopping at the Aroma Café for a nightcap, he stumbled into the darkness of the furnished room in which he lived, or rather, in which he had squatted since he had been released from Dred. It took a moment for him to realize that he was not alone. Two black men sat on either end of the sofa. One had a sawed-off shotgun across his lap.

"Are you who it says on this paper?" the one with the gun asked.

"I don't know. What does it say? What if I am?"

"It says Dylan Elson."

"That means you're gonna take a little ride with us," the other one said. "Now if you'd show us your identity card."

"I can tell you right now I don't have much money," Dylan protested.

"We don't want your wallet," the other man assured him, fumbling for the little orange card that the citizens of Beacon were obliged to carry. "Yup, it's him all right. Let's go."

In all the two men had not been gone forty-five minutes before returning with their hostage.

Cinque X looked at Dylan but pointed at Ocean. "My young friend over there tells me you've harassed him in the privacy of his home."

"Well, actually, I didn't mean to. All I wanted was to talk to him. He got afraid and ran away. I never got the chance to explain."

"How are we to believe you?"

"Because I left a note with my number on it. How many thieves do you know leave their calling card? It was really more of an exchange."

"My friend tells me it's happened again."

"That's not true. It wasn't me."

"And you expect me to believe that?"

Dylan told the story of how he had driven by Ocean's and seen the plainclothesman taking the rest of the tapes and his shoe box. The freedom fighters looked at him as if his execution were imminent.

"How is it that you just happened to be passing by?"

"To be honest, I did go back planning to break in. When Ocean didn't call I wanted my box back. I meant no harm. Like I said, I only wanted to talk."

"Talk about what?"

"My father knew his father under the old regime. I thought we might . . ."

"It's better to forget those days and build for the future."

Cinque X said no more. As his secretary approached, he whispered something in her ear. She left for the back room. Dylan thought he could hear her speaking on the phone. He could not take his eyes off the oriental carpet that resembled the one he remembered in the living room of the home in which he grew up. A damp shiver ran up and down his spine.

The secretary returned and signaled for Cinque X to pick up the slim headphone set. He spoke so softly into the tiny microphone at the base of his chin that Dylan could make out none of the conversation.

"You're in luck." Cinque X looked at his prisoner. "The tapes have been taken into custody along with the box."

"Can we get them back?" Dylan asked, now that Cinque X believed him.

"I'm afraid that's impossible. It seems the box was full of degenerate thoughts. You're lucky to be let off so easy."

"What about the tapes?" Dylan looked at Ocean, who was staring at the floor.

"I can assure you that I will provide for my young friend. You must take care of yourself. Tonight is a warning. If I ever hear that you have bothered so much as a hair on his head or caused him to worry, I will make sure it's the last time. Do we understand each other?"

"Whatever you say."

"Now, if we have no further business, my men will escort you home." The guards approached Dylan, who rose from an overstuffed Moroccan cushion.

"This day just won't end," he said out loud in the back seat of his captors' car. Yet as soon as he was home and lay down on the bed that had not been made in weeks, he fell into a deep sleep.

Dylan dreamed that he was with his father camping. They had been fishing hard all day and had just returned to their tent when the waiter who had served his meal at the Chairman's Kitchen, dressed in tails and a white bow tie, announced that dinner was ready. He asked what they would be eating. "Catch of the day, sir," the man replied. But instead of the few small trout they had landed in the afternoon the man brought for display plate after plate of all kinds of odd-looking creatures. Some were eels, others like octopus, one resembled a prehistoric sea monster. "How would you like them prepared?" the waiter asked. When Dylan's father protested, the man pulled a revolver from his vest. "Very well, then, sir," he insisted, "our chef's specialty is boiled." He left and was back in no time with repulsive gelatinous urchins draped limply over the edge of a silver serving dish. The waiter called two assistants who force fed Dylan and his father while he stood there holding the gun. In the end they held a funnel in Dylan's mouth, the kind he remembered seeing his mother use for canning fruit in wide-mouthed jars. They shoved the slippery sea monster down his throat. He awoke in a cold sweat and with a sharp pain in one side.

Dylan hardly stirred all the next week. The following Monday he would again be at the university. He slept late, read in bed until way past noon, ate his favorite take-out foods in front of the TV. Occasionally he would sit at the desk and look through the scrapbooks his mother had put together. The pictures no longer made him sad because they no longer made sense. He had a hard time identifying at all with these early scenes of himself and his sister, and then their little brother, who now lived with relatives in the East. He had almost no memory of the perfectly standard happy vacations—in the mountains, next to a miniature steam train, on an Indian reservation, surrounded by cousins. He ceased making the connection between all the faces and the names, between the photos and the shadow moments of his own recollection.

It was curious to Dylan that the jumble of words on his father's cards should seem more real than pictures, but then he remembered the series of thoughts grouped under the letter *T*. His father had expounded at length some strange, exceedingly elusive theory about the three-dimensionality of texts as opposed to the flatness of a photographic image. "Words contain the power to infuse the world with time," Norman Elson had written, "whereas the photograph remains frozen in the instant. Cf. ref. Magic."

Dylan waited until the last possible moment on Monday to make the trip to the university to get registered for the spring semester, which would be his last. He dreaded the beginning of classes. It was not that he was a slow student. On the contrary, he had finished at the top of his high school class, though he still harbored bitter memories of graduation. Dylan had by strict calculation won the highly competitive Math and Science Prize. Yet the principal, under pressure from above, decided at the last minute to bestow the award upon the daughter of one of the local Party leaders. She was smart, Dylan knew that, but he also knew that he had beaten her fair and square on the exams. He demanded an explanation and was told simply that the Board did not think it appropriate for the son of unprogressive parents to be rewarded in quite so conspicuous a manner.

"But my parents are dead."

"I'm not personally responsible," the principal had said, "and I am truly sorry." Dylan lost interest in math by the time he entered Bountiful State University. Now he would graduate in a matter of months with a degree in Applied Literary Studies. Assuming the proper support from his department, he was eligible to begin teaching public school in the fall.

Out of breath from the steep climb up three flights of stairs in the Hall of Literary Theory, Dylan reached into the pigeonhole mailbox below his name. He separated the junk mail from the rest and began to sift through the computer cards in the thick registration packet. He might easily, without even looking, have thrown the rest into the trash had his eye not caught a bulge at the bottom of the papers. Beneath the notices of the semester's lectures and the announcements of various work study jobs and cheap flights was a thick mailer of the type he had sent to the Beacon Police. The handwriting on the outside, like the one he had mailed, was barely legible. Inside, he felt a cassette and nothing else.

Dylan gathered up the punch cards and stuffed them into his knapsack. Before the students standing in line across the hall had filed their study lists, he was sitting in the Café Aroma, a pair of earphones on his head.

The tape was poorly recorded, just like the one he had taken from Ocean's house. It began with lots of crackling noise, some thumps, and a couple of old rock-and-roll songs separated by long, silent gaps. Dylan's pulse raced. He was about to press the *Fast Forward* button when the silence was broken by a familiar voice.

"They call it a social text," a man said.

"A what?" another asked.

"I'm not exactly sure," the first replied. "It means something's up between the Winter woman and Zimmer. The telephone crew says she's bitching and moaning that he used fancy language to get her in the sack. I think it's some kind of mumbo jumbo code they use for getting in our face. Must have gotten it from the professor."

Dylan was shocked. The Winter woman was the kid's mother. Zimmer had to be the man who introduced himself as a family friend at the funeral. The professor was his father.

There was a click and then nothing for several seconds. Suddenly the hissing stopped. A disguised voice spoke directly to him. "For further information meet me on the fifth, 3:00 P.M., at the end of the Beacon pier. Any more police work and you will never know." The rest was blank.

Dylan missed the first day of class. Arriving early at the waterfront, he watched a group of teenagers pulling crabs from the water next to one of the pier's crusted posts. He walked halfway out, where the members of a gang in leather jackets were fixing their motorcycles. Joggers, pacing themselves with stop watches and portable heart monitors, tunneled on either side of the long wooden structure, turning before reaching the bikers. "Like ants trapped at the curved end of a test tube," Dylan thought. Every once in a while the roar of a motor could be heard in the distance as it bore its way between the huddles of old fishermen and strollers who had come to try their luck or simply to enjoy the sun.

Dylan wondered if it were a trap. "In every undecidable situation the pressure is always to one side," he remembered reading on one of the 3×5 cards. The further he walked toward the end of the pier, which seemed to disappear into the sea, the fewer people hung to the rail on either side. It struck Dylan as the perfect setup. Listening to the sound of the waves hit the last pylon, he waited.

At three o'clock sharp Dylan thought he saw the kid walking toward him. From that distance he appeared even slighter in frame and seemed to be limping. As he grew near, Dylan could see that he was carrying an old suitcase held together with a belt. He moved so slowly that the last hundred feet seemed to take a minute.

They exchanged cautious greetings. Ocean undid the leather strap from around the suitcase and removed an oversized sheaf of papers, themselves wrapped in cardboard and string. He extended toward Dylan photocopies of his father's 3×5 cards, laid neatly next to each other.

"I made these the next day."

Dylan began to thumb through the pages.

"Don't worry, they're all there," Ocean said. "I thought when you broke in, I mean came in, that they were out to get me."

"Who was out to get you?"

"The ones my mother said got my dad."

Dylan didn't know whether to believe him. He could remember his own father saying more than once that the kid's mother was certifiably insane.

"What about the tapes?"

"I had them copied too."

"The Calcutta?"

Ocean nodded. Dylan smiled.

"All of them?"

"All but the one you stole."

"Don't worry. It's safely tucked away."

"No flies on you." Ocean placed the photocopies back in the suitcase.

Dylan extended his hand, which held Ocean's beyond any normal shake. "We must be careful," he said.

"You know too?" Ocean asked.

"Know what?"

"How the tapes killed my mother."

Just as I feared, Dylan sighed to himself, the hysteria's hereditary. "Tell me about it," he said.

"After Moses's death, Bibi, that's what I called her, tried to find out who did it. She ran all over the place when the answer was right there at home sitting on the shelf. One weekend after they started letting us out of Dred she was home with a cold. Being sick was the only way she'd sit still. So she started listening to the tapes that were left to me in a trunk. That's when she got the idea."

"What idea?"

"That she killed Moses. Couldn't get it out of her head."

"And that's when she did it?"

Ocean, who couldn't say the words, nodded. Dylan had looked up the story in the *Tribunal* about how a desperate community activist dressed herself in the orange robes of a Buddhist monk, doused herself with gasoline, and lit a match in front of the fast-food counter on Truscott Plaza. The paper spoke of a long, in places illegible, and completely incomprehensible note detailing a plot against her by big business and the city elders. Dylan recalled too that a psychologist with a name like Luftman made a statement to the press to the effect that this tragedy was a classic case of paranoia.

"Maybe it's not a good idea for us to be seen together."

Ocean seemed to withdraw somewhat as they headed toward shore. "Come by when you get the chance. Only this time, knock first."

"I did last time. Look, can I ask you a question before you go?" Dylan said, but did not wait for an answer. "About the tape you sent. How is it your father never knew they were on his trail?"

"Best I can tell, he didn't listen," Ocean said. "Anyway, what could he do?"

"Listening is important to survival. What would you think about making his voice heard?"

"How?"

"By writing their story. It won't bring them back, but it's the next best thing."

Before the winter rains subsided, leaving behind the greenness that is the covenant of the promised land, the orphaned sons of the exterminator and the professor had pieced together enough of their fathers' eerily coincident lives to begin this chronicle for a new age.